THE ENI

DAVID MARTIN

Author's email address dmb08@hotmail.co.uk

CHAPTER 1

She sat still in the cellar. The house above had recently been destroyed by the ferocious weather and the only thing protecting her from the outside world was the cellar door at the top of the steps. It was pitch black and she couldn't see a thing, but the darkness gave her comfort, protected her from the horrors which lay behind the door above.

A storm was raging outside and the noise was deafening. Despite this she sat still, fearful that any noise she made would alert those outside to her whereabouts. Her life depended on remaining hidden.

The storm suddenly grew more intense and the cellar door started to rattle. She jumped up from her prone position and walked slowly towards the foot of the steps with her hands held out in front searching for any obstacles. Her shins suddenly hit the bottom step and she winced a little with the pain, but soon gathered herself and slowly crept up the steps. She had to stop the door from rattling. If she could hear it, then so could those outside.

The storm was reaching fever pitch. She reached up, grabbed both handles on the door and pulled down as hard as she could. The door fell quiet and she breathed a sigh of relief, hopeful that those outside were still unaware she was there. Experience had taught her that strong hinges and locks were the only way to stop storms ripping the hatch away from its mountings, but she suspected they would fail against marauding gangs' intent on reaching the spoils inside.

The winds slowly started to wane until quietness descended. They were in the eye of the storm and it wouldn't be long before the ferocious weather returned. She held her breath and continued to hold onto the door in the hope that she could stop those from outside coming in, should they find the camouflaged door.

She heard a creak from the door as it complained about the weight placed upon it. Someone was standing on it. She heard muffled words being exchanged, then another creak as the foot was removed. She exhaled slightly as relief swept through her, but continued to hold onto the door. They weren't out of the woods yet. The darkness deprived her of sight, meaning all her senses were focused on her hearing. Her primal desire to survive had given her powers she didn't know she had.

She heard a noise from behind and instinctively spun her head around, only to be met by the same inky darkness. Her desire to shout out was over powering, but she resisted knowing that those above would hear. She returned her attention to the door, hoping she had done a good job of camouflaging it. Hoping that those above would soon tire of their search and look for pastures new.

'Someone's been living here,' said a man's voice.

There was no response and she suspected the person he was talking to was simply giving a nod of the head. She released one hand from the door and felt around to confirm the padlock was doing its job. Big mistake. In her desperation to return her hand to the door, she brushed against the padlock and it tapped lightly against the door. She cursed herself. How could she be so stupid? Why did she need to confirm what she already knew?

She stopped breathing. Listening, hoping, praying that they hadn't heard. They had. She heard a scurry of feet, then a hollow sound as someone banged their foot against the door.

'Here. There's something here,' said a man.

Another scurrying of feet, then a brushing sound as hands busily ripped away the camouflage that she'd carefully attached to the door. Would the lock hold? Would the hinges hold? She was confident they would, but now their hiding place had been found there was no way they would give up their prey, even if it meant starving them out.

The door rattled manically as though they were desperate for the prize, but soon went quiet as they realised something more forceful was needed. The quiet was broken by a huge bang as something heavy was smashed against the door. Further attempts were made and dents formed in the metal door but it held firm. They needed more than that, she thought.

She heard a distant roar. It wouldn't be long before the winds returned. Would the weather be her saviour this time, rather than her nemesis? All she could do was hope.

The banging stopped. Had they given up? She doubted it. She heard a screeching noise of metal against metal as a crowbar appeared underneath the door. Her first thought was to wonder where they'd got it from, but soon dismissed it. Knowing the answer wouldn't save them. She tightened her grip on the door in a vain attempt to thwart them, knowing she had to do something, even though it was only a token gesture. The end of the crowbar lifted and the door began to creak. The padlock held firm but the latch it was holding down eventually gave way and the door was free. She continued to hold onto the door, but there was nothing between her and her attackers.

The door started to lift and she valiantly held on. They were going to have to work for their prize and there was no way she was going to give up without a fight. She felt the door shudder as the wind got hold of it. The winds had suddenly returned with a vengeance and the door flung open. She instinctively continued to hold on and her hips smashed against the sides as she was lifted outside into the daylight by the force of the wind. She winced as her eyes adjusted to the brightness, but she soon focused on her attackers who had been flung in all directions.

The wind was stronger than before and the men were obviously struggling to get up. She lowered herself back into the cellar. Her head was the only thing above ground now and her neck muscles were struggling to cope with the buffeting. The door was flapping around and threatening to smash her skull so she ducked lower and waited. Eventually the other hinges gave way and she saw the door fly away. She quickly went back in the cellar, returning soon after with two hammers. There was only one way in and she was going to defend herself to the end. She waited for the shadows to appear above, gripping the hammers so tightly that her knuckles hurt. If they went in head first, they were dead. If they came in feat first she would break their legs. Eventually she would be over powered, but she would go to her grave with a sense of satisfaction.

The wind grew louder and the shadows didn't appear. The not knowing was eating away at her. She was desperate to find out what was happening and she slowly walked back up the steps, bracing herself before raising her head so she could see outside. Debris and dust was flying around everywhere and she could hardly see anything. The visibility temporarily improved and she saw five men crouched down against a wall and holding onto each other. The wind was battering them and it looked as though waves were dancing slowly across their faces. She caught the eye of one of them and a sickly grin came across his face. The look filled her with horror and she quickly went back into the cellar. Their fate had been delayed, but was inevitable. As soon as the wind died down they would come again. She looked back into the cellar at their anxious faces. Her community. Her responsibility. She couldn't lose anymore. She had to keep the numbers up if they were to survive.

CHAPTER 2 (2 YEARS EARLIER)

Presentations had been made and the facts were clear, but it wasn't that straight forward. History had proved that party policies having a detrimental impact on the electorate's standard of living or made them change their habits, never got elected. Quality of life and the future of their children just wasn't worth the hardships parents would have to suffer in the short term. It was either that or they didn't believe the overwhelming scientific evidence and this was their justification for doing nothing. It was like a smoker who refused to believe that cigarettes caused cancer because they didn't want to, or couldn't, give up. Of course if they did get cancer, there was always plenty of remorse and regret, but it was usually too late.

This was the case with the environment. The warnings had been clear for decades, but successive governments across the world had done very little, tinkering with carbon emissions simply wasn't enough. Humanity was now on the brink and something had to be done, but opinion polls suggested that the electorate was still not prepared to make the necessary changes, declaring that it was too late now to do anything

China and Russia had joined the world community, together with India, and they were now the G10. Democracy had spread across China and that had released the pent up greed that was always held in check by successive dictatorships. The people had demanded a better standard of living and governments had delivered without any consideration for the environment. Speed and short termism are an essential element for any democracy and materialism had spread quickly across China, resulting in un-paralleled pollution.

India was already a democracy, but governments had realised that mass industrialisation and pandering to the electorate's desire for more, that is greed, was a guarantee of re-election. So they went along the same lines as China.

Both countries now represented over a third of the world population so the impact was profound. Other developed countries had also done little to reduce their impact on the environment so it was little surprise that the world was where it was.

The year 2100 had arrived and, like cancer ravaging a smoker's body, the climate was changing everything. Temperatures had risen by over four degrees and heatwaves, droughts and flooding had become common place. The artic was free from ice every summer and sea levels had risen by over one metre. Over 40% of the world's population lived 60 miles from the sea so the impact was huge. Cities were under water and many areas were experiencing regular flooding, including the Nile Delta, Rhine Valley, Nigeria and Mississippi. Ocean acidification had all but destroyed marine life and half of the land previously devoted to food production was now un-usable. Food security had become a major issue.

People were moving from the tropics and sub-tropics into more temperate zones. There was mass migration from Central America and Mexico to the USA and from

Africa and the Middle East, to Europe. Those receiving the refugees were tolerant at the moment, but their patience wouldn't last. They had to look after their own.

Governments were losing control and society was breaking down. Despite this, the G10 were still squabbling on what needed to be done and finally agreed a new set of targets and lots of positive rhetoric, rather than specific and co-ordinated action. It was basically a continuation of what had failed before and Harvey Burton knew it as he looked at the news coming out of the summit.

He was the chief scientist leading the scientific clamour for real action by governments, as he had done for many years. And for many years he had failed. 80 years ago it would have only taken 1% of the World's GDP to prevent environmental catastrophe. Now, no amount of money could save humanity as we know it. He knew it, but governments and people were still in denial, so desperate were they to maintain their standard of living.

Harvey looked at his family over the other side of the room. He was a late thirties, highly intelligent and, surprisingly for a brainy man, an emotionally stable person. He and his wife had married in their early thirties and he had resisted having a family knowing what a future world would look like. His wife had eventually worn him down and he had convinced himself that, maybe, the world would actually be a better place when they grew up. It was bollocks of course.

His job had given him some wealth and their rather nice house was neatly situated in the posh London suburbs. Luckily for him, the UK government had invested heavily in flood defences to protect the capital, other world cities weren't so lucky.

He felt so bad about his hypocrisy. Big carbon eating house. Big car, although it was electric, and the biggest polluter of all. Kids. Populations needed to reduce and he wasn't helping. Like everybody else though, his desire to live on through his kids far outweighed his principles.

His six month old baby girl happily wriggled around on the floor, oblivious to what was going on around her, and his three year old son was stood at a low table playing with something. The downstairs was completely open plan, apart from the toilet, as was the trend, and he was looking at his wife busying herself with something in the kitchen area. The low ceilings gave it a cosy feel and there was plenty of light streaming through the windows to cheer it up. A large dining table and chairs sat in the corner and a huge sofa looked into an open space where 3D images were projected of whatever took their fancy. He had given into his wife's desire for trendy open plan living but, particularly at this moment, he yearned for a separate downstairs room so he could think in peace.

He turned his attention to the empty area opposite to where he was sitting and said, 'news'

Perfect 3D images of a desk and news reader appeared before him, reporting the conclusions of the G10 summit. Of course he knew it already and immediately regretted his instinct at this time of day to watch the news. TVs had long disappeared, replaced by 3D images transported into the room which didn't look that different from the real thing.

'Scientific debate,' he said instantly wanting something more stimulating and less depressing.

It didn't work, scientists were discussing the pros and cons of the G10 summit. A definite con, he thought. 99% of scientists were convinced about climate change, yet some of the 1% were in front of him placing doubt on the evidence presented by the 99%. There was no one to challenge their ridiculous logic and Harvey immediately turned it off in frustration. They weren't part of any scientific community and he suspected, no he knew, that they were bankrolled by big companies trying to protect their profit margins.

'It's ready,' said Thea walking towards the dining table with two plates of food.

Harvey instinctively got up, suddenly realising his stomach was complaining. The UK and all other European countries had agreed quotas for accepting refugees fleeing the middle east and Africa. Europe was coping for now, but food had become scarce so many households had grown food in their gardens. This meant there was enough food for those not able to grow their own. People had become vegetarian through necessity as animals grown for meat was an inefficient method of food production and there was scarce room for crops, let alone animals. Pets were a thing of the past, one of the few unpopular government laws that got through parliament.

'Don't waste any,' she continued. 'There's not much in the garden at this time of year.

Harvey nodded at the daily instruction and tucked in, along with his wife and son who had his own plate loaded with bits from his mum and dad's plates. Their daughter continued to wriggle around on the floor.

'You ok?' she said inquisitively.

'No,' he said with uncharacteristic honesty.

He was deliberately terse in the hope that she wouldn't ask any more questions. It didn't work.

'Same thing as normal is it? You shouldn't watch the news. You know it frustrates you. Can't you do anything about it Harvey? You're famous. You can influence people.'

Thea didn't nag him much about his job, but she was also frustrated by the whole thing. She used to be a scientist, pretty low down in the pecking order, but very intelligent all the same. She had sacrificed her career for the kids and was quite happy to do so. Her career could easily be put on hold, her biological clock couldn't. Technical advances meant that infertility was no longer a problem, but the NHS had far higher priorities and private health care was no longer an option. All available medical resource had to be directed towards the fallout from climate change.

Harvey thought about ignoring her, but quickly dismissed the idea. Mentioning his name meant she wanted a response

'I've tried everything. You know that. The politicians just won't listen. You know that' he said hoping that would be the end of it.

'Speak to the people then. Use social media. People'll listen to you. They don't trust politicians. They trust scientists.'

'We've been through this before. You know the government can block any messages they want. It won't even get on there.'

'Don't lie Harvey,' she said dismissively.

There it is again, he thought. Saying my name.

He put his knife and fork down before sitting back and saying, 'they've got sophisticated tracking equipment now. Anything they don't like is blocked.'

'Unless you're a scientist. I spoke to Josh and he told me there's a way around it.'

'When did you speak to him?'

Harvey's only friends were scientists and Josh was his best friend. They met at university and, although their fields of expertise differed, they remained friends.

'I have a life outside you and the kids you know. I saw him in the park this morning and we went for a coffee.'

'Can you still get that stuff?'

'Just. And stop changing the subject. You know Josh knows about these sorts of things and I can't believe you haven't spoken to him about it.'

Despite his intelligence, it took him a couple of seconds to understand the double negative comment.

'Ok. So I do know how to get around it. Josh gave me some software.'

'So you've been talking about it then?'

'Yes.'

'And?'

'There're risks Thea,' said Harvey.

'And there're certainties if you do nothing. Nothing will be done by the politicians. You at least need to try.'

'They'll take the message down within a few minutes.'

'A few minutes is all that's needed. It'll go viral in seconds. People need to know.'

'They already know. They can see it with their own eyes,' said Harvey sounding frustrated.

'They can only see what's happening now. You can tell them the future, based on facts. All they hear is what the politicians tell them. They need to know there's still hope if we change the way we live.'

Harvey picked his fork up and started playing around with his food as though lost in thought.

'They'll come for me,' he said.

'Damned if you do,. We'll all be damned if you don't.'

After noticing the look of upset on his face, she quickly continued, 'I'll be with you all the way. We'll be with you,' she said looking at the kids.

'No way.'

'We'll have to be. D'you think they'll be happy with just getting to you. They'll be after us as well. We're all in it together.'

He thought about continuing the argument, but re-iterating the risks was pointless. She was right. He had to at least try, but the world hadn't been prompted into action in the past, so why should they do anything now.

Because now they could see what was actually happening, rather than being told by some scientist using a data model.

He looked up defiantly from his plate and said, 'ok then. But we'll need to go into hiding. I know someone who can disable the tracking devises in us.'

She looked at him confused and said, 'you've been thinking about this for a long time haven't you? You don't usually make quick decisions like that.'

'Of course, it's obvious. Climate change will speed up in the next few months and the world will fall into chaos.'

'Where will we go?'

He looked at her as though wondering whether to tell her a secret or not.

'I've bought a place in Scotland. An old bothy in the middle of nowhere. I've built a cellar. Somewhere for us all to hide out.'

She looked confused and unable to say anything so he continued, 'it's got provisions for at least two years and the climate's a lot cooler up there now so we can grow crops.'

'What? Leave all this behind?' she said looking around.

'It won't be long before we have to leave it anyway Thea. It won't be long before mother nature starts talking louder.'

'But you've always said there was hope?'

'Yes in the long term. But the damage has already been done and this life won't last much longer. If I'm successful, then humanity will rise from the ashes, but there'll be a lot of pain and suffering before that happens.'

'But you said there were solutions,' she said hopefully. 'You said there was a way out of it.'

He looked at her with a resigned look on his face and said, 'it's too late for that. The climate has changed and nothing will stop it. The only solution is to get people prepared for it, but the politicians are scared of the panic it would create.'

She let out a gasp of air and her head dropped. He said nothing, hoping that what he'd said would sink in.

Eventually she said, 'then you have to tell the world. We have nothing to lose.'

He nodded his agreement and said, 'I love you Thea. You're right. I just needed you to convince me.'

'Tomorrow then?'

He nodded and said, 'the sooner the better. Thinking about it, they may already think I'm a threat that needs to be dealt with. I'll show you where the Bothy is just in case something goes wrong.'

He got a paper map out and showed her where it was. Sending electronic directions was a risk.

CHAPTER 3

Social media platforms had become obsolete. Governments around the world had reacted to public demands for more controls over the content, following endless controversial comments by users. All such messages were now blocked and users prosecuted. It had worked, but governments had taken it a stage further and used it for their own ends, so now the platforms only included pointless small talk and government propaganda. But Harvey had the technology to get around the controls and he was going to use it.

His family were at home with him, waiting by the door with one suitcase. They had to leave most of their possessions behind, but that was of no concern. The bothy they were fleeing to had everything they needed to survive, including weapons in case of attack. He knew it wouldn't be long before chaos descended over the world and humanity needed to prepare for it. Unfortunately people were still in denial and he doubted whether his warnings would be heeded, but he had to try. Was the G10 right? Would his message cause chaos? That chaos was going to happen anyway, he concluded. And it wouldn't be long. Temperatures were rising every month.

He had written down the message he was about to send. Pens and paper were no longer needed or readily available, but Harvey had managed to find some and treasured them like a special toy that gave him fond memories. It was a symbolic act and not something a logical scientist should resort to, but his feelings got the better of him and he felt a hand written draft was appropriate.

He was not well practiced and was having trouble reading his writing. He decided to go online first.

'Derek. Open social media accounts.'

The head of a bespectacled man with huge eyes, a neat side parting and a long pointy face appear in the space in front of the sofa. The image and name Harvey had created amused him and reminded him of a stereotypical scientist from the olden days. No one wore glasses anymore.

Derek said in a monotone voice, which also amused Harvey, 'your account has been closed.'

Harvey didn't question Derek. He was never wrong. He turned to Thea and said, 'go. Run. Don't take the car. Meet in our special place.'

She obeyed without question and they were gone within a few minutes. He returned his attention to Derek and tried other personal accounts. Derek said the same thing. Then Derek disappeared. He was completely off line. They'd found out what he was trying to do. But how? There were no listening devices in the house. Someone must have told them. Josh? Yes, it must have been Josh. He cursed his friend. If he couldn't rely on him, who could he trust?

He sprung up from his chair and ran to the door, but his whole body recoiled when the armed soldiers swarmed through the door, pushing him to the floor. He lay on the floor, slightly dazed and looked at the soldiers that surrounded him.

'Where's your family?' said one of them whilst looking around hurriedly.

'Safe,' said Harvey triumphantly and hoping that his demeanour would indicate they would have no chance of finding them.

The soldier said, 'rip this place apart.' He then turned to Harvey and continued, 'how'd you remove your tracking devices?'

Harvey didn't answer. The soldier didn't pursue it.

'No one here,' said another soldier breathing heavily.

'Search the surrounding area.'

'They're long gone,' said Harvey. 'You won't find them.'

'Bring him.'

Harvey was lifted from his prone position by two soldiers and manhandled to a waiting vehicle before being thrown in. The door slammed shut behind him. He tried the door in the vane hope it would open. It didn't. He soon gave up, sat down on a bench against the side of the vehicle and stared out of the barred window opposite. His only concern was for his family. His future was in the past.

....

Thea walked as fast as she could. She carried the only suitcase with one hand, her 6 month old daughter, Nicola, was under the other arm. Her three year old son, Lance, was trotting alongside without complaining, as though he realised they were in a dangerous situation and he needed to obey without question.

She saw the government vehicles arrive at their house and uniformed men and women stream out. She slowed down and thought about returning, before deciding it was a terrible idea and continued her journey away from the house. Tears started to stream down her face, something that hadn't happened since she was a teenager and would certainly be frowned upon in the modern world, especially in the science community.

She quickly got herself together, realising that thinking clearly was more important than pointless emotions. Had they taken Harvey? Was there any point going to the meeting place? She carried on in hope rather than expectation and eventually arrived at the meeting place.

'I'm proud of you Lance'

Lance looked up with a tired and confused look on his face before saying, 'where's daddy?'

'He'll be here soon,' she said losing eye contact with him and looking to where they'd come from in the hope that Harvey would miraculously appear. The area they lived in was heavily concreted, although small manicured park areas tried to give a feeling of the countryside. The familiar heat was something no one had got used to, so most people moved around in their airconditioned cars. It made them stand out and they got inquisitive looks from people in passing vehicles.

She guided her son towards a bench in a park which was surrounded by tall dense vegetation with access through a small arched cutaway, meaning she was well hidden from prying eyes and particularly the soldiers, should they come looking for them.

This was where Harvey had proposed to her and where they often came to chill out and talk. It had become more difficult in recent years due to the intense heat spells and ferocious storms that had become common place and today was one of those hot and humid days. The tears on her face had been replaced by sweat and she could tell both kids were suffering, but the shade from the vegetation provided some relief.

'Daddy'll be here soon,' she repeated unconvincingly.

Lance didn't answer, preferring to look for something to play with. Neither child seemed to suffer from the heat as much as she and Harvey did, probably because they had been born into it and knew no different.

An hour went by and there was no sign of Harvey. He should have only been 10 minutes behind, if that, but it was of no surprise that he hadn't turned up. She tried to hide the panic and turmoil inside her, knowing that it would only upset Lance. She reached inside her dress pocket and pulled out a piece of paper with a map and clear instructions on how to get to the Bothy.

....

The vehicle accelerated quickly and Harvey leant to one side before correcting himself. Images danced quickly across the barred window and he stood up to try and find out where they were going. It was a government vehicle and therefore authorised to fly at low level, above the other traffic. Traffic jams and speed limits were avoided, a definite perk for the privileged few who owned such vehicles. The blurry images suddenly disappeared and darkness descended as a screen came across and blocked out any light coming from the window. A bright internal light came on after a few minutes and he initially squinted before his eyes adjusted.

Where were they taking him? All government institutions were in London and, judging by the time and speed of this flight, they were far away from the capital. It wasn't long before he gave up guessing. He was a man who based his judgement on facts and there were no facts to be had at the moment.

The vehicle suddenly decelerated and he corrected the tilt of his body again. It came to a stop and he looked at the locked door with nervous anticipation, expecting the worst, but hoping for the best. Hoping that his family would be stood on the other side, safe and well. Hoping that someone was there to say that everything was fine.

The door opened and his hopes were dashed.

CHAPTER 4

Thea had to think. Her children were now the priority. It gave her some comfort that Harvey would agree and that fact relieved her conscience. Traffic in the south was terrible, but it thinned the further north you went so the trip to Scotland wouldn't be too bad. The problem was the car was still at home and there was no other means of getting there. The poor weather meant that flights were no longer possible.

She looked up into the sky. The heat and humidity would soon give way to ferocious thunderstorms, meaning the streets would be deserted. She could easily seek cover in some café, but would the weather represent an opportunity?

Dark clouds appeared in the distance and she knew it wouldn't be long. The few people in the parks that had braved the heat were heading towards the exits. She had to take a risk. She picked Nicola up with one arm and the suitcase with the other, then ushered Lance to follow her. He immediately discarded what he was playing with and trudged along behind.

They were soon walking back to the house. She stopped when it came into view and looked around nervously. The streets were almost empty now and those still walking around were looking at her suspiciously, probably thinking she was an irresponsible mother for still being outside just before the storms and wondering why she was carrying a suitcase. She ignored them and continued her journey to the house. Still no sign of anyone. The car was still there. Why hadn't they taken it? She decided not to waste time searching for answers and hurriedly walked towards it.

'Open all' she said.

All the doors opened and Lance instinctively jumped in, whilst she put Nicola in the child seat. Seat belts were no longer needed, self-drive cars simply didn't have accidents. She got into the driver's seat and read out the address of the town closest to the bothy. The car immediately pulled away.

Within 15 minutes the skies darkened significantly and there was, suddenly, no one walking around on the streets. The intensity of the storms and the size of the hail stones put people at risk, but vehicles had been designed to cope with the weather. Vehicles were restricted to roads which had the drainage to cope with the deluge, so the resulting traffic jams made progress almost impossible. The weather forecast said the storms would be particularly bad that day, but the unpredictability of the weather made forecasting unreliable. History suggested that people would stay off the roads with such a bad forecast and Thea was hoping it was wrong. If she was lucky, she would have a clear run.

A few minutes later and the rain started to slap the wind screen. The car diverted from the road she was using and headed towards the roads that could cope with the rain. She arrived and, as expected, the roads were quite clear.

Something crashed against the windscreen. The hail had started. She looked back to see the kids happily asleep. They had grown up with the extreme weather conditions and knew no different.

She returned her attention to the front windscreen, although the rain and hail meant she could see nothing. She eventually decided to put the windscreen wipers on to see how threatening the skies were. They quickly flicked from side to side and she managed quick glances of the clouds. They weren't growing darker. Everything was now automatic and the car would stop when conditions got to bad and she would be unable to over-ride it. Human intervention was minimised in a lot of things, technology was considered safer and more reliable. Thea smiled to herself. Health and safety now ruled everybody's lives, yet society was happy to ignore climate change which scientist warned would eventually claim billions of lives. Greed was indeed a more powerful driver than survival.

The car sped up, a sure sign that the road ahead was clear. She leant back in her seat and closed her eyes, hoping to get some sleep before they arrived. There was no road to the bothy, only a rough track that was never used. Would the car get through? She doubted it because the rough track was a deterrent to those looking to get to the bothy, although off road vehicles stood a better chance. However, Harvey had given her instructions on how to get there.

The winds started to buffer the car, but she ignored it. The car could easily cope with these conditions.

An hour later and the buildings started to thin out, but not disappear completely. Increasing populations and the influx of refugees from Africa meant that most of the countryside and farm land in this part of the country had been replaced by houses. Farming had moved north where the climate was more receptive to agriculture.

Thea was lucky, the weather hadn't worsened and they had made good progress. It wouldn't be long before the roads filled with traffic again, but she was confident they would have reached the farming areas by then, where the traffic would be a lot lighter.

The rain stopped and she could clearly see the drainage channels alongside the road. The car suddenly veered off onto a side road, a sure sign that the weather was getting better. 30 minutes later and they had reached their destination. The whole journey had taken three hours, only because she had been lucky with the weather and the clear roads. She had often wondered why they built cars that could go so fast, when the volume of traffic meant they rarely reached their potential.

The car stopped in the centre of the village where people were milling around the streets, oblivious to the strange car that had just arrived. Agriculture had not yet reached these parts and the village had a very rustic nature to it. Conditions were a lot more pleasant and extreme weather was not as common, but governments had resisted house building, knowing that the land would eventually be used for agriculture. For now it was mostly wild countryside and Thea was hopeful that the bothy was in the wilderness where she would be anonymous.

She should have continued to the bothy, but she was inquisitive. She got out of the car and looked around. Still no one took any notice of her and she suspected they were either tourists or locals that were familiar with tourists.

The village only consisted of houses and there were no shops or any other sign of a materialistic world. The houses were different., Old and a little weathered, like she had seen on internet history sites. Of course there were old looking houses in London, but a quick look inside showed a modern, technology driven way of life. From what she could see through these windows, the modern world had by-passed this village.

There was one main road going through the village with houses on either side. The road spilt into two and branched out and the houses followed. A village green filled the gap in between, before the roads merged again. There was the odd side road with no houses on, she suspected they gave residents vehicle access to the rear.

'Self-drive' said Thea.

A hologram of a steering wheel appeared in front of her and a foot pedal on the floor. They were only images, but had the feel of something solid. She pressed the pedal and headed to one of the side streets, stopping at the end and looking around. The rear gardens were huge and stretched into the distance. Some had plants growing, others had grazing animals. Her inquisitive instincts got the better of her and she got out to look around, staying close to the car. She looked hesitantly in the car, initially fearful of leaving the kids, then walked quickly towards the first garden. She took a picture and returned to the car. A quick internet search gave the identity of the plants and animals. Vegetables and livestock. She hadn't seen anything like it before. Most food came delivered to her house pre-prepared and she hadn't even thought about what they looked like.

Were these residents self-sufficient? Was this how future life would be? She decided to ignore such big questions for the moment and got back into the car. She looked back, Nicola was slowly waking up and it wouldn't be long before the hungry cry would start. Lance was also starting to look a bit agitated, hunger was probably crossing his mind as well.

'Boot open' she said before getting out of the car.

She rummaged around in the suitcase before, triumphantly, holding up refreshments for Lance and a bottle of formula milk for Nicola. She got back in and handed the food to Lance and the bottle to Nicola who eagerly grabbed it and started sucking. It was convenience food and they could easily feed themselves, leaving her to think about her next move in peace. She turned the car around and drove back onto the main road, stopping soon after.

The Bothy was five miles away down a track and, in hindsight, walking there with two small children and a suitcase just wasn't an option. Hopefully, Harvey's plans would mean they wouldn't have to do this.

Thoughts of Harvey and the future suddenly invaded her mind. Was she doing the right thing? Should she look for her husband? Should she return to the life of comfort and privilege she once had? She soon discarded such thoughts. She was a wanted woman and that life was not going to return. Her husband would fully support what she was doing. The kids were her priority. The world had beaten many things in the past, killer viruses, nuclear holocaust and rogue states hell bent on world domination, but not this time. This time the damage had been done and there was no turning back. Harvey wasn't one for exaggerated and emotional responses to problems, so if he had built a shelter to protect his family, then the situation was serious, real and imminent.

A knock on the window catapulted her back to reality and her head spun around to see an old, weathered looking man mouthing something. She should have just driven off, such social interactions just didn't happen in London, but she was so taken aback by the unfamiliar situation that she instinctively opened the window, but not far enough so that he could reach in.

'Are you alright?' said the man in a broad Scottish accent.

Yet another shock for her. Regional accents had disappeared down south and it was strange to hear them.

'Yes. Yes thanks.'

'Travelled far?' he said ignoring Thea's obvious reluctance to talk.

'No. I mean yes. London. We've come here for a few days holiday.'

The man looked into the rear of the car and said, 'not much of a holiday with those two though.'

He looked at the passenger side and said nothing, Thea suspected he wasn't brave enough to ask where her husband was.

She smiled and said, 'no, but it's good to get away from the heat and the concrete. It's lovely around hear,' she said looking around.

'Aye, but don't tell anyone. You staying local?'

She hesitated a bit then said, 'no just driving through.'

'Oh aye. Where to?

She didn't know any towns in the area and her initial hesitation to respond turned into a lengthy silence.

She eventually said rather awkwardly, 'I can't remember. The car knows though.'

He looked at her suspiciously then said, 'come in for something to eat. We've got far too much food and it looks like those little ones could do with a rest.'

Thea was stunned into silence, such friendliness and generosity was alien to her and she instinctively questioned his motives.

'No. Please don't trouble yourself.'

'Oh it's no problem. I insist. Anyway, it'll be nightfall soon.'

An old woman appeared by the man's side and her welcoming smile put Thea at ease immediately.

'You accosting strangers again Ian?' she said extending her welcoming smile into a broad grin.

'Just being friendly dear.'

The woman moved her head closer to the window and said, 'he's right, we've got plenty of food and you'd be doing us a favour. We'd love the company.'

Thea looked beyond them to the setting sun, darkness would soon reign and there was no chance of reaching the bothy before sunset. They looked harmless and, if she was lucky, she would get a room for the night. Suddenly she realised her options were limited and their kind offer was a blessing.

'Ok. Thanks very much.'

CHAPTER 5

The rear doors to the vehicle were open and Harvey was sat down in the back looking at two casually dressed and stern looking men. There were no signs of weapons, suggesting he was in a secure place and there was no chance of escape. Behind them there was a white wall with a narrow corridor with no distinguishing features stretching into the distance. There was that all too familiar smell of something new, he thought.

'Please come with us Mr Burton,' said one of them.

They parted to let him out of the vehicle and he complied after initially hesitating. The square room and white washed walls looked very clinical. There was a huge door at one end, probably to accept other larger vehicles, and doorways of various sizes were along the side, suggesting it was some sort of delivery area There was no one else around. A few vehicles were dotted around and the temperature was cool and in stark contrast to that outside.

'Where are you taking me? What am I doing here?'

'Follow us.'

Harvey decided not to pursue the questions and complied. He followed one of them, the other was behind and Harvey felt a little intimidated, nervously glancing to the side so his peripheral vision could see what the man behind was doing. They passed several doors and eventually veered off and headed towards one of them. It was no different to the rest of the doors and there was no placard to indicate what was behind it. The door automatically opened when the man in front got closer and they all went straight in without slowing down.

The room was again white and clinical and full of holograms with people stood in front of them, either working on something or talking to an image of someone. He tried to stop and take it all in, but the man behind nudged him in the back and they continued their journey. The room was huge and Harvey couldn't see where it ended. They eventually reach another door with a glass window beside it. He couldn't see in, but suspected those inside could see out.

Again the door opened automatically and Harvey was ushered in. It closed behind and silence descended. The room had antique soft furnishings with a sofa and two armchairs. Paintings adorned the walls, some were classics, and sideboards displayed rather nice crockery. A bookshelf housed numerous books, something Harvey hadn't seen in years. There were various doors, possibly bedrooms, and an open archway led to a kitchen and dining area where he saw a man busying himself with something. The man seemed engrossed to start with, but suddenly looked around, a wide grin coming across his face. As he walked towards Harvey, the two men accompanying him left.

'Mr Burton. Please sit down,' said the man pointing towards the sofa.

Harvey didn't move or say anything. He'd been abducted and didn't know where his family was, so wasn't about to obey the potential perpetrator.

'Please, let's not get off on the wrong foot,' said the man getting closer.

'Prime Minister,' said Harvey sounding confused and shocked. 'I hardly recognised you.'

Harvey immediately did as he was told and sat down, an automatic reaction to someone in power.

The prime minister sat next to him and said, 'don't call me Prime Minister Harvey. It won't be long before that job ends.'

Harvey looked at him confused and didn't know what to say.

The prime minister continued, 'Bill. Call me Bill.'

Bill Marshall was the tory member of parliament for one of the poorer southern constituencies. Like many constituencies, it was a traditional Labour stronghold for many years, but went Tory when living standards rose. This was a common trend across the country and reflected the electorate's desire to keep hold of their new found wealth, no matter how small it was. The Tory party was the epitome of materialism and always delivered.

Harvey leant forward, his elbows resting on his legs and said, 'why've you brought me here and where's my family?'

'I don't know where your family is and they're of no interest to me.'

Harvey continued his posture, looked into Bill's eyes and said, 'And why am I here?'

He was seething at how callous Bill was, but decided not to pursue it for the moment. He was a scientist and needed all the facts first.

Bill leant forward as well to show he was sincere about what he was about to say.

'The planet's finished Harvey. You know that.'

'No it's not. The planet's had to put up with more than this.'

'Ok then. Humanity won't survive as we know it.'

'I fucking know that. That's what I've been telling you and you've ignored me. You've ignored the whole scientific community.'

'No we haven't.'

'You've hardly done anything to reduce ecological catastrophe. No government has.'

'You know we wouldn't have got elected if we'd done something about it. You can't just blame governments. Everyone's to blame.'

Harvey sat back as though accepting Bill was right and said, 'someone should've been statesman like and agreed cross party policies.'

'If we'd done that, another party would've risen. Democracy always wins in the end.'

'You should've tried.'

'I'm not here to justify what we've done or not done Harvey. We are where we are.'

Harvey held his stare for a few seconds knowing that Bill was right.

'Yes we are where we are. So what now? What's this all about?' said Harvey looking around the room.

'Things aren't going well. Extreme weather conditions are getting worse.'

'Tell me something I don't know. You know that things will accelerate in the next few years and then who knows what'll happen.'

'Yes. Yes. I know all this,' said Bill dismissively before silence descended. Harvey decided to let it run and said nothing. 'There's a new virus.' Again, silence. 'An African virus. Refugees have brought it to Europe and it won't be long before it surges through populations across the world.' A calmness spread over Harvey. The time for emotion had passed and logic and information gathering was now the order of the day. 'We only found out about it in the past week. The current thinking is the body can't produce anti bodies to fight it. Scientists will no doubt find a vaccine in time, but time is one thing we don't have.'

'What d'you mean?'

'There's civil unrest across the world, caused by mass migration. In other words there're too many people and not enough space. The result is inevitable Harvey. This virus is only going to make people panic. Make things worse. Speed things up.'

'So why haven't I heard anything about it?'

'All media is under government control now.'

Harvey nodded, looked around and said, 'so what's all this?'

'A contingency. We've got similar establishments across the country. Other governments across the world have done the same. If things go as expected, then this and other places will give people a safe place to live. Humanity will continue one way or another.'

Harvey was dumbstruck, which didn't happen often. Bill was describing something that he knew would happen, but not for a few years at least. The virus was the unexpected and unknown development.

'So why am I here?'

'Someone needs to lead the development of the vaccine.'

'But why me? I've no experience of immunology.'

'But you know the science community. You can co-ordinate the effort.'

Harvey lost eye contact with Bill and stared out of the window at the multitude of holograms and people busying themselves.

'Why didn't you just ask me rather than kidnap me,' he said returning his attention to Bill..

'We had to act quickly. We're not stupid Harvey. We knew what you were going to do.'

Harvey looked out of the window again. How did they know, he thought before deciding it was pointless trying to find out.

'How long have I got?'

'All I can say is ASAP.'

'How long have I got?' repeated Harvey more assertively.

'Six months.'

'What? There's no chance. The trials alone will take longer than that.'

'There won't be any trials,' said Bill knowing there was no need for further explanation.

Harvey didn't challenge him, but sat back as though resigned to the reality of what Bill was saying.

'I'll do it obviously, but the chances of making a vaccine and getting it out there are slim to say the least.'

'I know, but we have to try.'

Harvey thought about having a rant about the ineptitude of government, but decided it was pointless.

'This place isn't a contingency is it? It was built for environmental catastrophe which isn't a risk because it's definitely going to happen. The virus just speeds things up a bit.'

'Yes,' said Bill as though relieved he didn't have to waffle like he normally did when justifying decisions.

'And what about my family?'

'We'll find them and bring them here. They'll be safe. D'you know where they are?'

Harvey remained silent for a few seconds, thinking about the remoteness of where his family was then said, 'no.'

CHAPTER 6

Thea woke up early. The kids were on the floor, wrapped in sleeping bags and sleeping soundly. Calan Macnally and Belinda Lennox had been married for 20 years and were devotedly religious, like the vast majority of the population. A surprising thing to happen in these times of materialism and science, but people needed a greater and un-explained power in their lives and religion gave them that. It gave them hope of something better than what they had. It gave them a sense of community.

In these days of equality, the woman no longer took the man's name but thanks to religion, monogamy was paramount and most couples complied, whether in heterosexual or same sex relationships.

Calan and Belinda willingly took them in and said they could stay as long as they wanted. They didn't ask about Thea's predicament, all they knew was that she was in trouble and needed sanctuary.

This was the second night and Thea was grateful for the space and time they'd given her. The stone cottage was very traditional with wooden beams and wooden furniture. A wood burner downstairs wasn't needed nowadays, but Thea suspected it was good enough to warm the whole house. The slightly damp smell somehow added to the homeliness of the place. The low ceilings and small rooms made it feel a little claustrophobic, but Thea concluded that this was because she wasn't used to it.

She felt comfortable and safe and the thought of staying was tempting, but she didn't want to impose on her hosts, although she suspected Calan and Belinda were grateful for the company and probably found it all a little exciting. There were also her husbands' instructions, and they were instructions, to seek refuge in the Bothy

Her thoughts returned to her husband. What'd happened to him? The government was clearly responsible, but why would they take him? Did they really know what he was about to do? Feared surged through her body at the thought of what they might do to a traitor and tears sprung to her eyes. She quickly got herself together, concluding that she couldn't do anything about it apart from do what Harvey wanted and get the family to safety.

She rose from the bed and looked at her watch. 6:30am. The kids were still sleeping soundly, as they would be normally at this time. They were obviously oblivious to what was going on, and she was grateful for that.

She went into the en-suite shower, something every household had, whether they needed it or not, and returned soon after feeling refreshed and invigorated. The kids were still sleeping so she slipped the clothes on she'd left by the bedside and exited the bedroom into the hallway.

She heard muffled talking from downstairs and immediately descended the staircase. Calan and Belinda had made her feel so welcome that she didn't feel awkward in their presence.

She stopped in her tracks when she got to the bottom. What were they talking about? she wondered. They were the nicest people on earth to her face, but she needed to confirm it and listening into their private conversation was a sure way to find out what they really thought. What she was about to do made her feel guilty, but her need to know soon took precedence.

She crept towards the kitchen door, stopping outside and holding her breath so she could listen. Luckily the solid stone floors meant she could sneak up without making noises that would give the game away. The door was open half way and she could hear what they were saying.

'They're a lovely family. It'd be lovely if they stayed a while,' said Belinda.

Calan didn't say anything so Belinda continued, 'Lance loves playing with you. I forgot how much you loved kids.'

And I forgot how much I loved playing. But it can't go on. Where's the husband? What're they doing here?'

'Oh come on Calan. That's no business of ours. Let's make the most of it whilst they're here. I'm sure they'll move on when they're ready.'

'I'm not sure. I don't want us to get in trouble.'

'What could they've done that's illegal? They're a young family.'

Calan said nothing, obviously understanding Belinda's logic, but still unsure.

Eventually he said, 'you're right. Anyway, it's not the Christian way. We should welcome all God's people, no matter what their past is.'

Thea immediately felt at ease. They'd been far too nice and accommodating and she was beginning to doubt their motives. Calan's admission of his concerns and their obvious Christian values gave her some re-assurance that they were human and trustworthy.

She started to move back to the stairs intending to make some sort of noise to warn them of her imminent arrival, but stopped when she heard a familiar ping from the kitchen. It was one of the frequent government messages that went to everyone and usually gave out some sort of instruction. In normal circumstances she would've treated it with disdain and had put such messages on mute. Her current circumstances made her take notice though. She looked at her watch. The message hadn't been sent to her. Her confusion led her to delay her grand entrance and she returned to the slightly open door, looking through the crack to see what was happening.

'Look at this,' said Calan bringing the message up as a hologram.

Thea was about two metres from the door, but clearly saw images of her and the kids. She couldn't decipher the words underneath, but she made a good guess on what they said. Her whole body tensed. 'What would they do?'

Calan quickly looked towards the door. She recoiled. Had he seen her? Nothing. She slowly retuned to looking through the crack in the door to see Belinda continuing to read the text. Calan was looking intently at his wife for a reaction as though willing her to come to the same conclusion as him.

Belinda lowered her voice and said, 'it is them isn't it?'

'Yes. And it's a lot of money.'

'But it doesn't say why they want them.'

'Does it matter?' said Calan as though wondering why she even wanted to know.

'I suppose not. D'you think we should contact the authorities?'

'It's our duty,' he said sitting more upright as though showing her he meant what he said.

'What about our duty to God? This isn't the Christian way.'

Calan looked a little flustered as though searching for a reason for what he wanted to do.

Eventually he said, 'we have to trust the government has Christian motives Belinda. There's a right way and a wrong way and this is the right way for us. The money for God's sake Belinda. Think about the money. It'll see us for life. We'll never have to worry again.'

Belinda looked indecisive, her eyes darting around as though looking for an answer. Eventually she said, 'you're right. Yes you're right. I trust the government.

This was a view held by most people which showed the power to influence the electorate through propaganda.

What now?' she said.

Thea quickly went back to the stairs, stopping half way up and making a slight coughing noise to warn them of her presence. Silence descended and all she could hear were her footsteps on the stone floor as she tried to make as much noise as possible. She decided to hum a tune as she walked through the kitchen door as though she was relaxed and unaware of what they were trying to do. A quick look at Calan's watch indicated he hadn't had time to send a message to the authorities.

'You sound cheerful. Had a good sleep?' said Belinda rather nervously.

'Yes thanks,' said Thea.

She was rather surprised at her external calmness. Inside her mind was racing, searching for a solution to the unexpected problem. She walked towards one of the kitchen units, hoping to avoid further communication. It didn't work.

'Kids still asleep?' said Belinda.

'Yeh.'

'What're your plans for today?' said Calan immediately regretting any suggestion that they wanted them to leave.

Belinda immediately picked up on it and said, 'you're more than welcome to stay as long as you want. We love having you around. The kids make us feel young again,' she said smiling.

Thea returned the smile and said, 'you're so kind. Living down south in London, I didn't think such kindness still existed. I was hoping to stay a little longer if that's ok. Thought we'd stay in all day. Promise not to get in the way.'

Calan and Belinda needed them to stay in the house for the authorities and Thea's commitment to this meant they didn't have to make a hasty decision.

Belinda said with obvious relief, 'oh that's lovely. We don't get out that much. To hot for us. It'd be lovely to have some company.'

'Oh I thought there'd be a lot of community things going on around here.'

'There are, but we don't partake. Not our thing really,' said Belinda giving a knowing nod.

'Does anyone even know we're here?' said Thea.

'Well, we haven't told anyone,' said Belinda.

'Thought you might want to keep it quiet,' said Calan. 'Word gets around and people get nosy. Want to know your business and I guess you don't want to tell them.'

'Thanks,' said Thea.

She was incensed. They were probably sincere, but the temptation of money had obviously meant they'd dumped all their principles. She had to think fast. Leaving the kitchen gave them an opportunity to send a message. She had to stay close to them.

Thea continued, 'is it ok to grab some breakfast?'

'Of course. Help yourself,' said Belinda.

The sound of crying from upstairs was the last thing Thea needed. She couldn't let them out of her sight. Think, she thought. Both looked at her, confused by her inaction, and she started to panic.

'Sometimes they go back to sleep,' she said.

She instinctively looked at Calan's watch. Why'd she done that? Did he notice? The look on his face suggested he had.

Belinda hadn't noticed and said, 'we did the same with our kids. Sometimes it worked. Sometimes it didn't.'

The crying got louder and Thea heard movement upstairs. Lance was obviously getting out of bed in response to his sister's need for attention.

'I'll feed her upstairs.'

'Have you got some milk?' said Belinda.

'I breast feed. Science hasn't yet produced anything that's better,' said Thea proudly before coming back to the reality of her predicament.

Calan suddenly sprung to his feet and stood motionless as though working out his next move. Thea moved hastily towards the kitchen door, only to see Calan move to block her exit. She decided to stop before he got there and returned to the kitchen cupboards as though she hadn't noticed his threatening move.

'D'you have some tissues? She's a messy drinker,' said Thea.

Belinda said nothing, noticing her husband's intentions and waiting for him to make the next move.

Thea saw the tissues, but she was really looking for anything that'd give her an edge. The only sure thing was that they wouldn't harm her or the kids, that would put the reward at risk and they were no different to anyone else with their need for money.

Then she saw it. Food grown in the gardens meant it didn't come ready packed and had to be prepared. An array of knives for that very purpose hung invitingly against the wall. The largest blade showed her fuzzy reflection, but she was more interested in the dark shadow moving menacingly up behind her. Her instincts to protect her family made her move quickly. She grabbed the largest knife and spun around to see Calan almost upon her. She was sure his only intention was to apprehend her and then keep them all locked up until the authorities came. She didn't want that. Her husband wanted her and the kids to escape from the authorities and she trusted him more than anyone else.

Calan suddenly stopped inches from her and stood motionless. The bewildered look in his eyes suggested he was trying to process what'd just happened to him. He looked down as Thea withdrew the knife and slumped to the floor. Like any mother protecting their young, fear was replaced by anger and weakness was replaced by overwhelming strength.

Belinda looked on horrified, before looking in Thea's eyes and realising her fate. She got up and darted for the door, Thea instantly moved to stop her. She didn't have time to digest what she'd just done, there was still more to do. This time though she was the hunter, not the hunted. This time the motive to kill was less strong. This time her conscience raised its ugly head, telling her it wasn't right.

Thea reached the door to block Belinda's escape and their eyes fixed on each other.

'Please Thea. I'm so sorry. It was a mistake. I won…'

Calan's look was replicated by Belinda and she fell to the floor.

....

The afternoon storm had died away, leaving a slightly cooler, but still warm evening. Thea had been upstairs all day waiting for darkness to descend. She could no longer trust anyone. She was on her own. The thought sent shivers down her spine and she momentarily considered giving herself up, but concluded the risks to her children were too great.

The bodies lay where they'd fallen, there was no point moving them. Anyway the strength she had during the kill had deserted her. She'd fed the kids in the bedroom and packed the few belongings they had.

The almost moonless dark skies had eaten the daylight and Thea prepared to make her escape. It was well past midnight and the lack of light coming from neighbouring houses suggested everyone was asleep. She'd turned the lights out at bedtime, not wanting to draw any attention, and sat motionless whilst her kids slept. Sleep for her wasn't an option.

She suddenly got up and opened the bedroom curtains, using the light from the quarter moon to see what she was doing. Her kids didn't stir, they were in deep sleep. She carefully picked up Nicola and carried her downstairs. Opening the front door, she looked around nervously and breathed in the warm humidity that always came after the storms. Anyone seeing her would've been instantly suspicious of her behaviour, but at 3 o'clock in the morning, no one was around.

Her attention switched to the vehicles parked on the side of the road. It was a small community, but like the rest of the population, everyone had a car so there was very little kerbside space available. The cars also looked the same and no longer had registration plates so her car wouldn't have been noticed by anyone.

'Open,' she said.

Small lights flickered in her car and she walked quickly towards it, whilst looking around. She put Nicola in the rear seat and the safety belts instantly clamped her in, causing her to stir a bit. Thea stood still, praying she'd go back to sleep. She did.

She went back to the house, returning soon after with a sleeping Lance who didn't stir at all when put in the car. She returned to the house for the final time to collect the suitcase, stopping at the kitchen door when she caught sight of Belinda's lifeless body. She shuddered at the thought of what she'd done and suddenly felt sick and dirty. It was a new experience that didn't sit well with her and she questioned whether it was necessary, considering her and the kid's lives weren't at risk at that point. It was the thought of what would happen when the authorities got hold of them that scared her. They obviously considered her a threat, otherwise why send a message to the whole population. No, she was right to do it. No one else in the village had seen them so they were anonymous again.

She continued her journey upstairs and purposely avoided looking through the kitchen door as she struggled past with the suitcase. Conscience was something she couldn't afford to have.

She got in the car and said, 'Bothy Glendhu.'

The car instantly drove off, but she knew it wouldn't get there.

45 minutes later and the car stopped automatically after travelling gingerly up a mountain track. It wasn't the end of the track and they still had a long way to go, but it was the end of the road for the car which could no longer cope with a surface it wasn't designed for.

Daylight was starting to poke through, which was the only good news. The Bothy was still a long way off and walking was the only option, unless Harvey's plans worked.

She looked at the kids who were still sleeping soundly and decided to wait until they'd had their full ten hours of sleep. The last thing she needed were grumpy, tired kids for the challenge they were about to face.

She got out of the car and decided to walk on ahead to see if she could see what was around the next bend. The kids would be perfectly safe as they were strapped in and it was highly unlikely that people would venture out here.

She walked a few hundred yards to the bend, frequently looking behind as any mother would do when leaving their offspring. She took one last look before going around the corner.

There was an empty run down stone barn with no roof on. She was looking at the side of it, but could just tell there was an opening around the front with no door on. She remembered Harvey's instructions and relief swept through her.

Trusting her instincts, she went close to the rock face by the side of the track and crept along towards the barn. Her confidence grew as she got closer and she stepped back into the centre of the track to get a closer look at the open doorway. Nothing. She carried on tentatively. They were in the middle of nowhere so why were her senses on edge for no reason?

Her fears got the better of her when she got closer and she dived back into the, supposed, safety of the rock face and stood still. Should she go back to her kids? No. They had to go past the barn anyway, so she had to find out if this was the place her husband was talking about.

She continued walking along the rock face until she reached the side of the barn, then slowly crept to the open front entrance. She put her head around the corner. There was nothing inside. The bare rock walls inside were complemented by the rough soiled floor which was interspersed with vegetation, obviously encouraged by the light coming from above.

She breathed a sigh of relief and hope before going inside and casually looking around to see if there was anything she could use.

A beam of light flashed across her face, followed by a voice.

'Hello Thea. This is Harvey. Don't worry. If I'm speaking to you, then I guess I'm not here. I need you to stick to the plan. The drone will take you and the kids the rest of the way where you'll be safe. I'm probably dead or in custody so I'm relying on you Thea. Do this for me Thea. Do it for the kids. Trust me. I love you so much.'

The words were typical Harvey. Straight to the point with little flannel and they tore her apart. There was no time for emotion though. The floor ahead of her moved up a little before sliding to one side. A drone then slowly rose up, using the electrically powered engine underneath to hover quietly in front of her. Two large cylindrical engines were on the rear for forward propulsion and a large circular capsule was attached by struts to the engines.

'The drone is voice driven. Put the car in the barn. It'll be taken care of.'

It was as though Harvey was there. Protecting her. Looking after her. But he wasn't and she'd probably never see him again, she concluded.

She immediately returned to the car and drove it to the barn entrance. The kids were still sound asleep.

She got out of the car and said, 'drone, forward slowly.'

The drone did as instructed and, when outside, she said, 'stop. Open hatch'.

The roof opened. She got the sleepy kids out of the car and put them in the drone. She then instructed the car to go inside the barn where the floor slowly sunk, taking the car with it. A hatch then slid across to leave the same soiled and vegetated floor. There was no sign at all of anything untoward.

She got into the drone and said, 'Bothy Glendhu.'

It immediately rose up and did as instructed.

....

They arrived soon after. The track to the Bothy below had eventually disappeared, probably through lack of use, and there was no way she could've walked it with the kids. She suspected Harvey had managed to acquire the drone through his scientific contacts. It wasn't something that was readily available to the general public and flying it around down south would've resulted in instant imprisonment. Up here though there was no one to apprehend them.

The bothy looked run down from the outside and didn't look any better on the inside. It was dark and uninviting, but it had the basic amenities, with beds, toilets, cooking facilities and various electrical appliances, all run from solar and wind power. There was no other technology. Thea guessed that anything connecting them to the outside world would result in them being found.

The kids had woken and it was only then that she realised they had no food. She could easily cope and Nicola would be happy on breast milk. Lance wouldn't be so tolerant and the moaning and uncontrolled crying would soon start, but Thea was prepared for it and had decided to ignore it.

Harvey had put written instructions on laminated paper in the drone. She read them carefully and was impressed at the detail. Surely they'd be safe here.

CHAPTER 7 (HARVEY ONE YEAR LATER)

Harvey had successfully managed the production of the vaccine. Scientists had been used from around the world and he guessed they were in the same predicament as he was. He'd been effectively imprisoned in the underground shelter, having no contact with the outside world and only speaking to scientists in the lab or via communication channels, if they were in another location. His thoughts often turned to his family, but he was confident that they were safe and that one day he would join them. They should be well away from civilisation, if Thea had followed his instructions, therefore delaying their infection. His plan was to get to them and deliver the vaccine before it happened.

Limited testing had been carried out on those within the bunker and no initial concerns had been raised. That was enough for governments from around the world to give the go ahead and mass production was about to begin in the UK. Other countries didn't yet have the facilities or, more importantly, the main ingredient for the vaccine. but they soon would have. Or so Harvey thought.

Harvey was sat staring at the hologram detailing the design of the production facilities. It'd been hasty and he was concerned about the poor testing, both at the vaccine design phase and planned testing after batches had been produced. Of course he'd expressed his concerns, but they were brushed under the carpet. Risks had to be taken, he'd been told.

‘That’s it then?’ said Dave.

Dave Walker was a gifted scientist, preferring facts and information to people and feelings. He knew his social skills were limited and had no interest in improving them as he found small talk and emotions annoying and confusing. Without Dave, the vaccine would’ve taken a lot longer and Harvey had been told on numerous occasions that time was of the essence.

Yep,’ said Harvey sitting back in his chair. ‘It’s over to the production people now.’

‘I’m not happy about the testing. Will we oversee the production?’ said Dave sounding unsure.

This was the first sign of emotion Harvey had seen from Dave and it unnerved him a little.

‘They still need us Dave.’

Dave looked confused and said, ‘but they won’t at some point.’

He was now sounding like a worried child about to have something taken away from him. Harvey said nothing for a short while as though thinking of a response, but he was more shocked at Dave’s demeanour.

He eventually said, ‘they’re not animals Dave. They don’t just kill people when they don’t need them anymore.’

Harvey knew that straight talking was the only way. Dave would only get confused if the message was mixed up with waffle. He was pretty thick in that respect. Dave was sat forward in his chair and didn’t move as though he needed further assurances.

Harvey continued, 'I'll be straight with the PM and ask him what happens to us now.'

Dave sat back as though happy with the response and said, 'thanks.'

Harvey turned off the holograph and got up to signify the conversation was over. As anticipated, Dave didn't get the hint and remained seated.

'Go Dave. We've finished talking.'

He immediately got up and hurried out of the room, leaving Harvey alone. He sat down again, pondering his thoughts. He was cocooned in this bubble of scientists, not knowing what was happening in the outside world or other parts of the bunker. Apart from scientists, he only spoke to the PM and that was strictly business. Any questions raised by him about his predicament were brushed aside, saying that the focus had to be on the vaccine. He'd not pushed the point, knowing that the PM was right. A lot depended on him and his team but, now they'd delivered, he needed to know what was going to happen next.

....

Harvey and the PM were in Harvey's room. It was a small and purely functional space with bright white walls, a small kitchen area, a single bed, a beige sofa and a small desk with two chairs, which they were sat at. One door led into the toilet and shower and one to the rest of the bunker..

Pleasantries had been exchanged and yet another sign of appreciation from Bill Marshall was accepted by

Harvey with a simple nod. Harvey had arranged the meeting in his room on the pretence that he needed to show the PM something. It was a ruse. He wanted the meeting to be on his terms and in his domain, rather than the comfortable and serene surroundings of the PMs office, home, room, whatever you want to call it. It was going to be a tense meeting and it needed tense surroundings.

'Is there a problem Harvey?'

'Yes,' said Harvey wanting to raise Bill's stress levels.

'What? With the vaccine?'

Harvey stared at Bill for a few seconds then said, 'no. There's been no change, but you know I'm not happy with it. The testing's been shit.'

Bill waved his hand as though dismissing Harvey's concerns and said, 'we've been through this before Harvey. We need to take a chance and get the vaccine out there. The virus is causing a lot of problems.'

Harvey winced at Bill's political waffle and said, 'you mean a lot of people are dying?'

'Yes Harvey, but the vaccine will save billions of people. It'll save humanity and it's all down to you and your team.'

Harvey leant forward, resting his weight on his elbows and said, 'so you're done with us lot now. What's going to happen to us?'

'It's all about the vaccine and getting it out there. Not about you and me.'

'What's going to happen to us?' said Harvey assertively repeating himself.

They stared at each other for a second until Bill said, 'you'll stay here with the rest of us until things have calmed down a bit.'

'How long will that be?'

Bill shrugged his shoulders and said, 'a while.'

'Don't fuck with me Bill. What's happening out there? You've finished with us now and I need to find my family. You can't keep me here as a prisoner any longer. I've not complained because I've known the importance of the vaccine. Now it's finished.'

'You can't leave Harvey.'

'Why? My work's done. There's nothing I can do.'

'New strains may develop. You know that.'

'That doesn't mean I have to be a prisoner in here. I can come back. Put a tracer on me. You can get me back here anytime you want.'

'It's not that simple.'

Harvey looked confused and then worried.

'What aren't you telling me?'

'I'll be straight with you Harvey. The mass migrations have caused problems. Too many people and to little land to live on. Wars have been springing up everywhere and many millions have died. Millions Harvey,' said Bill trying to emphasise the point. He continued, 'those that've survived are crammed together and the virus thrives on close contact. It's sweeping through humanity. Climate change has accelerated, adding to the problems. Bodies are piling up causing widespread disease. Transport and communication links are breaking down.

We're totally reliant on satellite navigation systems, but they won't last forever.'

'What're you trying to say? If you release us, we'll die.'

'That's right Harvey. We can't afford to lose you.'

'What about the vaccine? How will that be rolled out?'

'It won't be.'

Both men sat in silence. Bill was looking for a response, but Harvey was too busy trying to rationalise everything that Bill had told him.

Harvey eventually said, 'so you lied. Is this the end?'

Bill instinctively looked to the side without saying anything.

Harvey continued, 'this isn't a contingency is it? We'll have to stay in this god forsaken place?'

'It was to start off with, but we've known for years what was going to happen, and so have you.'

'Yes, but not this quickly.'

'You're a scientist Harvey, but you don't know about people. We do. It's a basic human, actually animal, instinct to want land to live on. Wars were inevitable, but the virus has sped things up a lot.'

'But this has all been caused by inaction on the environment. We could've easily coped with the virus under normal circumstances.'

'Don't preach to me again Harvey. We've been here before and we are where we are.'

Harvey sat back in his chair and stared at the ceiling, before looking out of the window at the throng of scientists working away.

'So this is a prison?'

'Yes, but things'll calm down out there.'

'And the vaccine is only for people in here? There's going to be no high volume production?'

Bill nodded and said, 'the main ingredient is here and we can't get it out there. Only we can produce the vaccine and we can only give it to those in this bunker.'

'So this is the future of humanity. An underground cell. Everyone out there will die,' said Harvey looking around.

'Yes,' said Bill realising the need for direct talking. 'We'll go back into the outside world again when the virus no longer has anything to feed on and dies.'

Harvey said, 'And bring back a free democratic world again, so it all happens again. How big is this place? How many people live here?'

'It's big enough. We have the key people and their families. The people who can get civilisation going again. Possibly not in their life time, but we have a breeding programme and their genes and skills will be passed on. There'll be no room for anyone who can't contribute.'

'So anyone who doesn't fit the template will be killed. The disabled, for example.'

'Politics doesn't exist anymore Harvey so my one word answer is yes.'

Harvey was impressed by his honesty and shocked by his brutality, but this wasn't the time for emotions and he understood Bill's logic.

'And who will lead them?'

'Ah, now that's a good question. Structures have been put in place for governing now and when we return to the outside world.'

'You didn't answer my question.'

'Well for now, I'm in charge here and so are the respective leaders in the other major countries who have the bunkers, but the virus will get them in the end.'

'And they know that?'

'They do now. I've told them and they're resigned to their fate. Some have taken matters into their own hands and destroyed their bunkers. The virus is ruthless and painful.'

'And after that? Who takes charge after you?'

'Democracy won't work so a leader will be chosen. A ruthless person who needs to assert their authority. They'll be backed by a small army who'll have weapons not available to anyone else. Between them, they'll rule supreme.'

Bill paused waiting for a question, it didn't come so he continued, 'anyway that's for the future Harvey. Let me show you around.'

Both rose from their chairs as though thinking the same and headed for the door. Reaching the exit, Harvey's eyes were scanned and they both walked through into the huge corridor which went in a straight line in both directions for as far as the eye could see. Smooth bright white walls were only broken by doorways and the odd person wandering around made it all look somehow real, rather than a computer image.

One of the doorways nearby was guarded by two heavily armed guards, who had recently been posted.

'This is the future of humanity Harvey. Right here, and you're part of it. The place is secure and the only risk to the people down here is the virus, but you've solved that problem. We've kept it out so far, but only just. The vaccine is the final part of the jigsaw puzzle and you'll be the first to be vaccinated, apart from the test cases.'

'And what about my team?'

'They're next. Do you want to be the first Harvey?'

'What about those who don't want the vaccine?'

'Refusing isn't an option. We can't risk someone in here catching the virus.'

Harvey hesitated for a short while, then nodded.

Bill guided him down the corridor and they soon reached the guarded door.

'No one can get in here. It can only be opened from the inside. We can't risk people getting overly enthusiastic about the vaccine.'

The door eventually opened and they strode in. It closed immediately behind them and they were met by another two heavily armed guards. The guards parted and both went further into the room. The walls were adorned with pictures, mainly of highly colourful, non-definable images.

'We thought long and hard about décor. Something to keep the spirits up, but not remind people of the outside world they're missing,' said Bill sounding proud.

'It works,' said Harvey nodding his head with approval whilst looking around.

'Please. Sit down,' said Bill guiding Harvey to an empty chair.

Apart from the bright paintings, the room was quite bland with a wooden table and chair and a large cupboard in the corner, probably containing the vaccine, thought Harvey. Two women in white coats and masks stood waiting with needles at the ready. Harvey's sleeve was lifted and within a few seconds the needle pierced his skin and the contents entered his blood stream. He was in some sort of dream and was having trouble rationalising everything he'd been told, making him unable to resist what was happening to him.

Bill said, 'of course we don't know how long it'll last, but we have plenty of supplies to protect everyone in here over a long period.'

Harvey still didn't respond, he was only capable of staring at the pinhole in his arm.

Bill continued, 'are you ok Harvey?'

Harvey immediately came out of his trance and said, 'yes, yes of course I am. It's just a lot to take in that's all.'

'And let me be the second.'

Bill sat down and within no time the needle also entered his arm.

Bill said, 'everyone's in the same position Harvey. They don't know what's been happening and have been in bubbles of their own, similar to yours. It's a form of social distancing to prevent spread of the virus. People are starting to get anxious about the virus and they need something positive. If we can show them that the scientists know the situation and have willingly received the vaccine, then we're confident that other bubbles will follow. We can all then return to as normal a life as possible. Will you do this Harvey?'

'Of course I will. You should've trusted me Bill. Kept me in the loop. I'm not distracted by emotion when a logical solution is required and what you're doing is logical.'

The look in Bill's eyes suggested relief and excitement at the same time. This was yet another hurdle overcome in his quest to save humanity.

'So you think you can convince them? The scientists that is?'

'Yes.'

CHAPTER 8 (THEA ONE YEAR LATER)

There was still plenty of the food left by Harvey, but the successful harvest had meant there was less reliance on it. Life had changed for Thea and the kids from survival to comfortable.

They lived high up in a secluded valley close to the Scottish north coast and Thea had absolutely no contact with the outside world. The internet and mobile phones weren't needed for survival and significantly increased the risk of them being found. Abstention from such so called luxuries hadn't presented a problem for Thea, but she longed to know what'd happened to her husband and yearned for social interaction.

The weather had been getting worse and more extreme, particularly the strong northerly winds which got funnelled up the valley. The bothy was holding for now, but frequent repairs were required. Thea was surprised at how quickly she'd developed her practical skills.

The children didn't seem to be suffering, indeed they were flourishing, and she had done her best to educate Lance who was now four years old. Nicola was walking, but talking was taking a little longer, hindered by the lack people to stimulate her.

The life she'd carved out was so much better than the one they'd had in London. Stress free, few responsibilities and no materialistic niceties that make your life complicated. It was indeed a natural way of life that humans had evolved to feel comfortable with, apart from the lack of company. She was desperate for it. She was desperate for her husband. She was desperate for friends and conversation. Her own happiness was dependent on it, but getting it would put her family at risk. Her and Harvey's family at risk. What would he do? Would he want her to live like this? Had he considered it would be a problem? She doubted it.

She stared out of the window. The reinforced glass Harvey had put in was easily dealing with the ferocity of the weather, but would it hold long term? Would the building hold out? she thought looking back into the bothy. It was very basic, but sturdy. The roof was the big risk, being more open to the elements and flimsier than the sturdy walls. She doubted that even Harvey would've anticipated the drastic worsening of the weather in such a short time.

She returned her attention to the window and looked across at the barn opposite. The drone was still in there and she'd charged the batteries the previous day for no particular reason at the time. It was only now she understood why. Her sub-conscious had told her to do it. The drone was her freedom and she needed to be sure it was ok, just in case she needed to get away. She now realised that she had to escape. It was a risk versus reward scenario. The risk to her family versus the reward of company.

She looked back into the bothy again. The kids were playing happily, their contentment was obvious and she felt guilty about wanting something more than this. Was she being selfish? The kids were happy now, but would they grow up to be happy without other children around. Was she finding reasons for something she was going to do anyway. The risk was worth it.

'Can I go out mummy?' said Lance.

Thea continued looking out of the window, lost in her thoughts before turning around and saying, 'Yes. Take Nicola with you.'

Lance immediately got up, encouraging his sister to do the same, and sauntered outside. Thea looked at them happily playing and doubts crept in. How could she want more than this? Letting your kids just go out and play in London simply wasn't an option.

She continued staring out of the window then sat back. But they were playing alone. She'd made her mind up. She had to do something.

CHAPTER 9 (HARVEY)

All the scientists had been vaccinated, apart from Dave. He'd refused outright and Bill Marshall couldn't persuade him otherwise. Dave simply didn't trust the vaccine and was prepared to take his chances with the virus. If it'd been anyone else then Bill would've simply thrown him out into the outside world, but Dave was an important member of the scientific community and his reluctance would be noted by others.

'Can't you persuade him Harvey?' said Bill with a pained expression on his face suggesting he was desperate.

Bill had been a regular visitor to the lab during the vaccination of the scientists, reflecting his desire to get this part of the job done. After that, Harvey doubted he would see him again, which was fair enough as far as he was concerned.

'I have,' said Harvey triumphantly.

Bill looked at him perplexed and said, 'How? He was so reticent.'

'He wants me to go in with him when he gets the vaccine. For support.'

'Fine. Sounds a bit childlike though.'

'He is a child. I want you in there as well. A figure of authority is always a good thing.'

'I'll get things ready,' said Bill as though wanting to take the opportunity before it was too late.

Bill immediately got up and left, returning 30 minutes later with a slight grin on his face.

'It's ready.'

'Let's get him then,' said Harvey

Dave was in solitary confinement as a safety precaution. A decision had been made to separate vaccinated people from the rest and Bill had decided that Dave couldn't join another group as there was a risk he could cause panic.

Both men got up and went out of the main exit door into the long corridor, the second time for Harvey in just a few weeks. Dave was stood there with two burly security men, one on either side. Harvey and Bill instinctively walked towards them, the fear on Dave's face was plain to see.

'Don't worry Dave,' said Harvey with a reassuring smile on his face.

It didn't work and Dave's fearful expression remained. No more words were said and the security men gently guided Dave around and towards the vaccination room. He didn't resist, as though accepting his fate. They reached the door and within a few seconds it opened.

The three of them trouped in, leaving the security guards outside. It was the same set up as before with two technicians and two security guards inside.

'Let's get this done,' said Dave sounding impatient.

One technician guided him towards the chair, he instantly complied but didn't sit down.

'Sit down' said one of the technicians.

Harvey injected the nearest security guard in the neck, whilst Dave darted across the room and did the same to the other. They instantly fell to the floor. The biggest threat was out of the way. One of the masked female technicians leapt to one side, intent on raising the alarm, but Dave intercepted before she had chance. He took a syringe out of his pocket and injected her. She fell instantly to the floor.

In the meantime, Harvey had got hold of Bill and pinned him to the floor. He was no match for Harvey physically, being scrawny and thin which exaggerated his oversized head. The remaining technician had nowhere to go and held her hands up whilst cowering to confirm she'd surrendered. It didn't help and Dave inserted a needle into her arm.

They didn't have much time, it wouldn't be long before the guards outside suspected something. It didn't take that long to stick a needle in someone's arm.

'How'd we get out of here?' said Harvey.

'How'd you get hold of that?' said Bill nodding towards the needle.

'We're scientists. Now, how'd we get out of here?'

'There's no way out.'

'Fuckin liar.'

Bill held his arm up as though expecting an attack. He wasn't disappointed. Dave stepped over and planted a knee in his ribs. Bill doubled over in pain and sounded as though he was choking.

He eventually regained his composure and said, 'we're still having deliveries from outside. Building up provisions. It's the only way in and out.'

Bill was a strong and ruthless politician, but he lacked gumption when it came to a physical fight. Harvey was a little disappointed that he didn't resist a little longer. It would've given him great satisfaction to inflict pain on a man he despised as a person and for his ideology.

'Where is it?' said Harvey.

Harvey was trying to remember a year earlier when he was captured and brought here. It was a large car park with delivery points around the edge, but the place was so bland and characterless that there were no focal points that could show him how to get there.

Bill hesitated as though he was desperately looking for an answer that would prevent further pain. I can't tell you, but I have something that can show you. Harvey instantly searched inside his jacket pocket.

'Is it this?'

'Yes.'

'Is it a tracking device as well?'

'No. It's just to make my life a bit easier. Everything looks the same in here and there're no direction signs.'

Harvey threw it to Dave and a few moments later he said, 'got it.'

The needle went into Bill and he was out cold.

'Let's get into their uniforms. Quickly.'

They undressed and climbed into the uniforms, grateful that the helmets would give them some anonymity. They dragged the limp bodies to the back of the room, there was nowhere to hide them completely. Harvey then went to the cupboard, pulled out a package and slipped it into an inside pocket.

‘Shit. How’d we get out of here?’ said Harvey sounding desperate.

Dave immediately spun around and started looking.

‘It’s got to be something straight forward,’ said Dave.

Harvey saw a touch pad by the door and said, ‘it’s got to be a fingerprint. Grab one of them.’

They picked up one of the technicians and dragged them towards the door.

‘Wait,’ said Harvey. ‘They’ll know something’s wrong straight away. Get the syringe at the ready

Dave did as he was told and stood at the ready with the syringe. Harvey held the technician as vertical as possible before placing her finger on the pad. The pad was to the left of the door and the door opened from left to right so Dave was hoping the guard on the left would be the first to look around. He was right so went for him first. He instantly collapsed, leaving the other guard staring at his partner on the ground. He then joined his partner as Harvey let go of the technician and thrust the syringe into his side. They dragged them both into the room and stood outside until the door closed.

‘They’ll be out for a couple of hours at least,’ said Dave.

‘But we don’t know at what point they’ll be missed, especially Bill.’

Dave gave him a momentary look then said, ‘let’s get going then.’

Dave looked at the tracking device and said, ‘up there, first left.’

‘Take it steady, we don’t want to draw attention,’ said Harvey.

Dave didn’t respond and slowly walked down the corridor. Harvey soon caught up and they both walked slowly, side by side. There was no one around, probably reflecting the social distancing rules currently in place. Things would probably look a lot different after the vaccination programme had been completed, thought Harvey.

‘Have you got the vaccine?’ said Dave.

Harvey nodded.

On reaching the junction they turned left to see another endless corridor. After several more turns they reached a corridor that had a door at the end.

‘That’s it,’ said Dave.

A rush of excitement swept through Harvey, but he soon tempered his enthusiasm. The door was closed and there was no clue on how to open it.

‘There must be something on these uniforms to open it,’ said Dave hurriedly looking down at his uniform.

Harvey ignored him and said, ‘it’s a goods delivery place. There must be other entrance points. Not everything comes out through this door.’

‘Of course. The lab had a hatch where stuff got delivered. These other rooms must have the same.’

‘But there’s no way we could escape through there. They’re bound to have some sort of security.’

Both pondered for a while, but soon got distracted when a message came through on their helmets.

‘Everyone to the delivery area. This is not a drill’

‘Shit, they’ve found us,’ said Dave. ‘There’s nowhere to hide.’

‘We need to get behind one of these doors.’

Dave spun on his heels and started to run, but Harvey soon caught him and held him back.

‘There’s no point running,’ said Harvey.

‘At least let’s get away from here. It’ll give us a bit more time to think.’

The sound of running attracted their attention.

‘Quick,’ said Harvey. ‘Run to the other corridor up there.’

Dave didn’t ask for an explanation and they both sprinted, stopping when they arrived at the junction.

It’s coming from up there. The footsteps,’ said Harvey looking up the corridor they were about to go into.

‘Hide around the corner and let them run past,’ said Dave.

They pressed themselves flat against the wall and within a few seconds a swathe of uniformed guards came down and turned left toward the delivery area. Their relief was short lived when Dave looked back and saw a black mass moving towards them.

‘There’s more. They must’ve seen us,’ said Dave.

Harvey looked around the corner at the other corridor. More were on the way and there was no escape. Why would they need this many, thought Harvey?

‘Follow me,’ said Harvey.

They ran towards the group, who'd just past them, tagging on the end until they reached the delivery door. It opened immediately and they all went it.

Gone was the sense of organised calm he'd experienced when last here. Gone were the neatly parked vehicles. Gone were men and machine working in harmony to move stuff around. Mayhem ensued.

The first thing to hit Harvey was the noise. Wild shouting filled the room and men and women ran around, seemingly with no purpose. Some noticed the door they'd entered was open and made a beeline for it, pushing past the guards in their desperation to escape. The guards didn't stop them. Harvey breathed a sigh of relief, grateful that they hadn't yet found out about the vaccination room and almost elated that they were in the delivery area. A message came through the helmet intercom.

'Spread out and secure the threat.'

The guards immediately spread out evenly in all directions as though they knew exactly which way to go, leaving Harvey and Dave stranded by themselves. Harvey knocked Dave's arm and nodded his head towards the only guard that remained. He was dressed in a grey, rather than black uniform, suggesting he was the leader. The guard looked around and glared at them, prompting Harvey and Dave to join the others.

The message had somehow got around that there was an escape route and all those not in uniform were heading towards the door from which the guards had entered. Within no time only the guards remained.

Harvey and Dave were still together, hurriedly looking around for an exit out of the underground shelter.

'Look,' said Dave pointing in the direction where all the guards were now heading.

Cars seemed to be jumping in the air and crashing down, but the guards were partially blocking Harvey's sightline and he couldn't see what was causing it. He tried to ignore the disturbance, hurriedly looking around for a way out. There was none. He returned his attention to the mayhem. Bodies were now being hurled into the air.

'Hold your fire,' said a voice in the headset.

Whatever it was, they were desperate to keep it alive, thought Harvey. Both were grabbed by the arm and catapulted towards the danger, a not so gentle reminder from a passing guard about their responsibilities. Both complied, not wishing to draw attention to themselves, but they hung back a bit, hoping that their involvement would be minimal.

A pulsating sound filled the room, making Harvey slightly woozy. Some form of stun gun, he concluded. The mayhem died down a little, but not completely. Another shot from the stun gun slowed them both down again.

'The threat is subdued,' said a voice in their headsets.

Harvey looked at Dave and said, 'stay with the crowd until we find an exit.'

Dave nodded his agreement then both returned their attention to what was happening. It was grotesque. The sprawling body on the floor had arms, legs, a body and a head, but that's as close to resembling a human as it got.

A tough, dark scaly like skin covered its body and the muscles were bulging as though trying to escape. Harvey assumed it was naked, although its skin was so un-natural that he first thought it may have been some sort of coat. It had no genitals and the head was a huge with two small lumps on the top. The eyes were a dull orange and the long nose pointed downwards towards the closed mouth which had spittle running out from either side. Harvey guessed it was about seven feet tall, although it was difficult to tell in its prone position. Despite its size and obvious strength, it looked almost childlike and not yet fully formed.

The man in the grey uniform was now kneeling beside it, injecting it with something, but its eyes remained open. He ushered towards a guard next to him holding a bag, and another syringe was given to him. This time the orange eyes slowly closed and its twitching limbs calmed down leaving an eerie post battle tension where the victors thought they'd won, but weren't sure.

Eventually the man in the grey uniform stood up and shouted to the men closest to him, 'get it to the secure area outside.'

Harvey suddenly looked over at Dave who was obviously thinking the same. Outside meant freedom. They moved forward as though eager to volunteer, others didn't have the same enthusiasm and visibly shuffled back a few centimetres. Harvey heard the electric whine of a vehicle and turned around to see a forklift truck inch its way forward through the guards who parted to ease its way.

Harvey and Dave stood over the lifeless body just as the forklift arrived and then tried to hoist it on, but it was too heavy. Other guards realised their predicament and moved to help them. They eventually heaved the body onto the forklift and it was slowly lifted. The truck then slowly moved forward and Harvey and Dave followed it, others didn't.

'You, you, you, you,' said the leader pointing at random guards. 'Go with them. Now,' he shouted.

They'd been conditioned to obey orders and did exactly as they were told, taking a few steps to catch up to Harvey and Dave.

The truck and its entourage slowly moved towards a giant door, the exit door to freedom, thought Harvey. As they got close, it opened rather quickly, but they weren't greeted by sunlight, it was an empty chamber. They all moved in and the door closed behind them. Harvey looked over at Dave who looked confused.

The other guards raised their arms in unison and pressed a button on the sleeve of their uniforms, Harvey and Dave immediately did the same, hoping that their slight hesitation hadn't raised suspicion. A cold sensation covered their entire bodies just as the door ahead of them opened.

Harvey hadn't seen sunlight for over a year and he raised his arm to protect his eyes, Dave and the other guards did the same. A minute or two later and everyone's eyes had adjusted, arms were lowered and the convoy moved out into what looked like the abyss. Despite the cooling suit, Harvey could still feel the intense heat from the midday sun burning into him. There was no one around, but then again he suspected security was strict and wouldn't allow anyone to get close to the site.

The creature started to stir a little which prompted the guards to hurry up. The forklift picked up its pace towards a huge animal like cage that stood on a concrete plinth. The cage door opened when they got close and the forklift went inside, dropping its cargo unceremoniously on the floor before hurriedly exiting. The door then closed.

'That fucker's getting bigger every day,' said one of the guards to Harvey. 'Genetically engineered so I heard.'

The guard sounded like a normal human which surprised Harvey who was expecting all the guards to be robots.

'What's it for?' said Harvey.

'Dunno. We just follow orders. Gets taken in there sometimes and comes out bigger, that's all I know,' said the guard nodding towards the door they'd just exited.

'Why'd they keep it out here?'

'Think it loves this shitty weather. Don't want the fucker in there anyway,' said the guard nodding towards the open door again.

Harvey looked around. There was even less greenery than when he first arrived here a year ago, suggesting the periods of drought were getting longer. There seemed to be no sign of life.

The guard continued, 'come on, let's get back in before that virus gets us as well.'

The guards walked quickly back to the open door, leaving the forklift where it was. Harvey and Dave hesitated before following them.

Harvey was in turmoil. They couldn't go back in. They had to escape. They had to act quickly. On reaching the door, they all went inside and turned to look outside as though it was their last look at freedom.

'The forklift.' shouted Harvey looking at Dave.

They both instinctively ran towards the daylight.

'Shit. Bring it back boys,' said a guard before the doors closed.

On reaching the forklift, Harvey looked at Dave and said, 'they'll be expecting us back soon with the forklift. We have to get out of here.'

Dave looked at him blankly as though unable to provide a solution to their predicament.

Harvey looked around. 10 minutes is all they had. It would be shorter if there was CCTV. A road stretched out in front, probably for the delivery vehicles. Was it the only way out?

A noise distracted him. Made him jump. He looked around just as a solid structure around the cage slowly rose out of the ground. It crept its way up the sides, making the creature sit up. It seemed to be fully awake now and the stare it gave Harvey before the structure engulfed it sent a shiver down his spine. He'd never seen such evil. Never seen such purpose. But the thing that concerned him most. He'd never seen such intelligence and cunning. It was almost smiling as though its time in captivity would soon end, leaving it free to do whatever it wanted.

Harvey wanted to know more, but he'd more pressing problems.

He looked into the skies and said, 'somethings coming in. Get to the forklift. Look as though we're using it.'

Dave sat on the forklift and pressed the foot pedal gently making it move forward very slowly whilst Harvey pretended to look busy. The drone gently landed and one of its passengers got out. It was a woman and her tall, slim figure together with the grey suit, gave her a sense of authority. She looked unflustered and Harvey suspected she also had some form of body cooling device. A very burly looking and well-dressed bodyguard soon followed, suggesting the woman was someone of importance.

'Who's that?' said Dave.

Harvey looked without making it too obvious and said, 'can't see, but that things our ticket out of here.'

He jumped on the forklift and said, 'drive towards it.'

Dave put his foot down and was surprised at the speed it went towards the waiting drone. The bodyguard saw the approaching vehicle out of the corner of his eye and immediately reached for his weapon.

Harvey stopped, put both hands up and said, 'sorry. We're waiting for a delivery. Guess it's not you.'

The bodyguard looked at the uniforms and relaxed a little, although not completely, and said, 'no its not.'

'This drone going back or is it staying here,' said Harvey trying to sound officious. 'We just need to know.'

'It's going back.'

'Come on Sid. We need to get going,' said the woman.

Harvey started to panic. Time was running short and he had to do something. Taking a risk was something a scientist wasn't familiar with, but he had to. The bodyguard turned around and reached inside the drone for what was probably an overnight bag.

'Here, let me take that,' said Harvey getting off the forklift and moving towards him.

'No. That's ok.'

Those were his last words as Harvey got close enough to plunge a needle into his leg. He heard a slight hiss as the guard's cooling system punctured and he instantly fell to the floor.

Harvey looked over at Dave and said, 'get her and put her in the drone.'

Dave grabbed the woman and threw her in, luckily without screaming. She landed on the rear seat and bumped her head leaving her a little dizzy.

'Get him on the forklift and put him behind the cage,' said Harvey.

They both heaved the body on and then Dave dumped him out of sight behind the creature's cage, whilst Harvey stayed with the woman who was still dazed. The drone's rotors started to whirr.

'Hurry,' shouted Harvey.

Dave was still at the creature's cage and looked around to see Harvey frantically waving his arms. He jumped off the truck and ran towards the drone, reaching it just before it rose from the ground. He could've probably easily walked on, but the adrenalin pumping through him made him jump through the open door and he landed un-ceremoniously on his face.

The drone rose up and Harvey looked down to see the parched landscape engulfing the structure. There was no sign of them being found out, but it wouldn't be long.

CHAPTER 10 (THEA)

The drone rose up and Thea looked down to see the lush green landscape engulfing the bothy. North Scotland was becoming more fertile, suggesting the opposite was happening further south.

The drone rose higher, eventually going above the highest peak. Her eyes were darting around trying desperately to see any threats. She could see the odd bothy, but nothing else. She hovered for a while before going higher. The village she'd escaped from came into view in the distance. She quickly lowered the drone in the unlikely event that someone may see her.

'Where're we going mummy?' said Lance.

She ignored him and continued to look around. The new lush vegetation stretched as far as the eye could see. Amongst it, young trees were finding their feet and it all seemed a bit surreal. This wasn't the wild moorland that Thea knew from her youth when visiting Scotland. Then the doubts surfaced. The climate was good for food production. Why hadn't people migrated here?

She put her doubts to one side and the drone descended to the supposed safety of the valley. When she felt safe, she took in a deep breath and moved the drone slowly forward following the river that'd been responsible for carving out the valley.

The hills on either side eventually got lower and she turned her attention to a barely distinguishable track in the distance. She made a beeline for it and it wasn't long before she saw the barn she'd been looking for. It was already in a rundown state when she was last here and it didn't look that much different.

'We're going to land,' said Thea continuing to look ahead.

Lance decided to say nothing, trusting his mother implicitly, like any four year old would.

The drone descended, easily coping with the strong winds which regularly came along in the afternoons. It soon touched down, but Thea didn't move, looking anxiously around and ready to take off again should there be any sign of danger. Silence. Even the wind had waned in the valley floor, protected by the hills on either side. It wasn't a northerly wind today, concluded Thea.

She got out of the drone and looked at the kids sat in the back who were looking hopefully at their mother for an imminent release from their seat belts.

'Stay here,' she said. 'I'll be back soon.'

The disappointment in their faces was obvious, but her tone suggested her instruction wasn't up for debate.

Thea knew that the drone only recognised her voice and she could easily instruct it to take off should any danger present itself, taking her kids to safety. Her kids! They weren't her kids. They were their kids. Her thoughts went to Harvey again. He was still alive, she was sure of it. She suddenly hesitated. She'd no plan. Was she so naive to think she'd be welcomed with open arms? Would Harvey do the same? Was her need for human company worth it? Then the realisation set in. She desperately missed her husband and the children needed their dad. That was her main motivation and she needed other people to help her find him. It was worth the risk.

She walked apprehensively towards the barn and a beam of light flashed across her face. She jumped a little before remembering the same thing happened when last here.

The ground inside the barn immediately drew back and the car rose up looking the same as it did the last time she saw it. When at ground level, it moved slowly forward until it was a few feet away. She looked around at the drone to see Lance straining his head to see what was going on. She immediately walked back, released their shackles and got them out of the drone.

She squatted down enough so that she was at eye level and said, 'we're going on a journey. An adventure,' she said smiling.

'Are we coming back?' said Lance looking worried.

'Of course we are, but we need help and you need children to play with.'

Lance looked confused before saying, 'I like playing with Nicola.'

Lance had obviously adapted to his circumstances and got used to not having other kids around.

'Come on we'll have fun. Promise,' said Thea turning towards the car and deciding that there was no time for an in depth conversation. Would the car be charged after being left for a year?

Her kids dutifully followed, knowing there was no alternative. She instructed the drone to enter the barn and it sunk into the ground, leaving no sign.

CHAPTER 11 (HARVEY)

Harvey turned around to the woman sat in the rear seat. She was nearly fully conscious so he climbed into the back to make sure she didn't do something stupid and attack them. This was the first time he'd had a good look at her and his mouth opened slightly.

'Home Secretary. I.? I didn't realise it was you.'

Dave spun around and was stunned into silence, preferring Harvey to take the lead.

She squinted at him as though trying to focus and said. 'who're you?'

Harvey fumbled at his helmet, eventually taking it off so she could recognise him.

'No,' said Dave. 'There's no point telling her who we are.'

'They'll soon know who we are,' said Harvey.

'Harvey,' said Louise sounding dumbfounded. 'What're you doing? Let me out of here.'

Louise Gardner was an ambitious politician who'd reached high office, but she'd always wanted more. She was confident, ruthless, an excellent communicator and her stunning looks certainly helped her get what she wanted. Even in these modern times, the electorate were still very shallow in that respect and a deep mistrust of politicians meant they voted on how they looked and spoke, rather than their policies.

Harvey decided to ignore her question and said, 'where's the drone going?'

‘It’s. It’s going back to my home.’

‘Why’re you going to that bunker?’

‘I’m not saying anything until you tell me what you’re doing?’

Harvey looked out of the window. They’d soon reached a coastline which looked like it had defensive structures and warships were patrolling the waters. The bunker was on an island, probably the Isle of Wight, concluded Harvey.

‘You’re not in a position to make demands Louise. We’re desperate men.’

Louise looked into his eyes and immediately saw his intent.

‘I’m getting my vaccination.’

‘You don’t need to go there for that.’

She hesitated a bit before saying, ‘the government’s consolidating.’

‘Don’t waffle with me. You mean everything’s gone tits up and key government officials are saving their arses.’

‘There’s got to be some semblance of rule and order in this chaos.’

Harvey decided not to pursue it. He’d more pressing concerns. He looked down again as they passed the short stretch of water and reached another coastline. It’d now been 15 minutes since they’d left the other guards in the chamber and went back to, supposedly, collect he forklift. The drone wouldn’t have raised any concerns as they would’ve been expecting a return journey. Harvey was thankful for their luck.

He said to Dave, 'can you fly this thing?'

'Yes, I think so.'

'Get us down. It won't be long before they find out what's happening and we don't stand a chance in the air.'

'We've got her though, said Dave.'

'They don't care about her and we're not important anymore now they've got the vaccine.'

Dave decided not to discuss it anymore and immediately started to fiddle with buttons on the control panel, soon gaining control of the drone. They descended and landed. Harvey ushered Louise out and Dave followed. The drone stood motionless for a few seconds before rotors un-expectantly started to rotate and it took off again.

'They've found out and got control of the drone,' said Dave.

'They must know where we are. We've got to get out of here.'

'What about her.? She'll slow us down.'

Louise said, 'you can't leave me here. I don't stand a chance with these marauding gangs and what about the virus?'

Harvey looked around. The landscape still looked desolate, although he could see trees in the distance, probably the new forest, and houses were dotted around, but no signs of life. A year ago, people were moving from the far south of England for the more agreeable climate further north. That migration seemed to have continued, thought Harvey

Harvey looked at Louise and said, 'we'll take her.'

'But Harvey.......,' said Dave.

'We're not barbarians. She'll die here. Take her,' shouted Harvey.

Dave withdrew into his shell, accepting Harvey's words to be final.

Harvey grabbed her by the arm and continued, 'we'll head towards those trees. It'll give us some cover.'

They soon found a tarmacked road heading in the right direction and walked purposely towards the trees, grateful that their cooling suits gave them respite from the heat. They soon reached cover and stopped in the supposed safety of the trees. A calmness spread through them, but it was short lived.

'What's that?' said Dave instinctively crouching a little.

Harvey focused his attention on the distant talking, trying to make out what they were saying, but all he could workout was that they were a group of men.

Dave whispered, 'maybe they can help us.'

'No,' said Harvey. He turned to Louise and continued, 'what's this about marauding gangs?'

'It's only in the far south. Most have migrated further north, but some've stayed behind. There's no law and order around here and gangs are fighting each other. Many have died.'

Harvey was impressed by how calm she was, suggesting she was used to high pressure situations. He returned his attention to the voices again. They were getting closer. Maybe they'd seen the drone land and were coming to investigate, he thought before concluding that seeking an explanation wasn't a priority. He noticed a thick clump of vegetation amongst the trees that'd survived the drought so far.

'Follow me,' he said, walking off before the other two had a chance to respond. They quickly caught up to him.

Reaching the bushes they nestled in the undergrowth, trying not to make a sound.

'We could've made a run for it,' said Dave sounding slightly annoyed.

'They were too close. They would've heard us.'

Dave decided that he'd made his point and further discussion was pointless. He returned his attention to the approaching gang who were now in sight and looking around either nervously or expectantly, it was difficult to work out. There were about eight men, all dressed similarly in khaki shorts and white t shirts as though it were some sort of uniform. All had beards, there skin was dark brown and gleaming with sweat. Despite the heat and no means of cooling themselves, they didn't seem distressed, suggesting they'd got used to their environment.

'Someone must've got off that thing,' said one of them. 'Let's look around. Spread out.'

'What's the point?' said another coughing out the words.

The first one who spoke looked at him without saying anything, then raised his hand to his mouth and said, 'get rid of him.'

The others immediately raised their hands as well before one of them kicked the man in the stomach. He doubled over in pain, then a rock crashed against the back of his head. He fell to the floor and was probably dead before he hit the ground.

'Leave him. Don't touch him. It's the virus. Has to be.'

Harvey looked on in horror. Coughing wasn't a symptom of the disease and he suspected these men knew that. Were they so worried about the virus that any sign of illness was met with a fatal response?

The remaining men immediately moved away from the body, showing no concern at all for the man they'd just killed.

'Fan out,' said the man reminding them of his original order.

Harvey suspected he was the leader. They immediately parted and went in all directions.

'They'll find us,' said Dave sounding petrified.

'Not if we stay still,' said Harvey.

Dave remained crouched, ignoring his desire to run. He was a scientist and wasn't used to these situations. All he could think of was the worst possible outcome. A torturous death. He looked over at Louise. Her face suggested she was a woman without fear and in total control of herself, which was in total contrast to what he was feeling. He despised himself for being so weak. Even in these days of equality he still felt he should be better than a woman in these situations. He cursed himself. He cursed her for being better than him. He cursed Harvey for taking control. And what was he? A nobody. Well he had a solution to their problem. The only solution. A solution that had no time for agreement by the others.

He looked out of the bush towards the approaching man about 100 yards away. How stupid was Harvey. It was a good place to hide and therefore the first place anyone would look.

He glanced at Harvey, the annoying confident expression was gone, replaced by a fear of what was going to happen next. Well Dave had a solution. He turned around, Louise was also looking worried. He had to act. He grabbed her by the arm and catapulted her out of the bush with the strength only a man about to die would have. She landed on her front and quickly looked up to see the man stop and look at her. She sprung to her feet and ran. The man was so focused on her that he didn't even consider looking in the bush.

'Over here,' he shouted as he ran.

Within a few seconds, others came running.

'What're you doing?' whispered Harvey whilst trying to sound assertive.

Dave decided not to answer and said, 'come on. Let's get out of here.'

All the men had, by now, run past them in pursuit of their prey. When the coast was clear Dave tentatively rose from his hiding place and looked around, suddenly sprinting away when he was sure there was no one around. Harvey remained routed to the spot, unsure what to do. Should he run? Should he try and save Louise? Should he stay put? The answer was obvious. His family should have been the priority which meant he had to save himself, but his feeling of guilt took priority. He'd kidnapped Louise and could hardly just leave her to a fate worse than death.

He leapt from the bush and ran towards the danger, not knowing what to do when he got there. He wasn't equipped for this type of thing, but he had a good brain. He had to outsmart them.

The noise of the chase got closer suggesting they'd caught up to her and stopped, no doubt basking in the glory of the prize they'd captured. Harvey slowed down, eventually stopping when he saw movement ahead and hiding behind a tree. The man who'd been giving the orders was circling her. Even from this distance Harvey could see the lecherous look on his face as his hands caressed every part of her body. The others were looking on, equally excited about what they'd get when their leader had taken his fill.

'I'm the home secretary,' said Louise sounding defiant. 'You can't treat me like this. There will be consequences.'

The leader ignored her baseless threats, stopped in front of her and saying, 'who was with you?'

'There were 13 men with me. They went to get help,' she said telling the lie with confidence like a good politician.

'Liar,' he said slapping her across the face. '13 men couldn't have got in that poxy drone.'

She said nothing and tried to stare him down. The guilt washed over Harvey. Even after kidnapping her and throwing her to the lions, she wasn't going to give them up.

The leader turned around to his men and said, 'go back. Find the others. I'm staying,' he said returning his attention to Louise again and smiling.

She smiled back at him. She was good, thought Harvey. Using her most potent weapon, her body.

The men disappeared without question, suggesting his rule over them was strong and not to be questioned, but that was of no concern to Harvey. He moved around the tree as they came past to prevent being seen, before returning to his original place when the coast was clear. The odds were now even. One on one and he had the element of surprise, but he had to be quick, the gang would soon return.

He peaked around the tree and his eyes were met by Louise's desperate stare. He quickly retracted, suspecting she would give him up. Nothing. He looked around again. The leader had his back to him and his face was buried in her neck. His right hand held a knife to thwart any unlikely resistance. She was stood rigid and still looking in his direction as though pleading for help. He had to act. He came out from behind the tree and crept towards the target, careful not to make any noise.

He was soon halfway there and she was now on her back with the leader kneeling over her and ripping off her top and cooling suit. She wasn't putting up any resistance and it wasn't long before he was lying on top, her head was off to the side and the grimace on her face suggested she was in hell. He was resting all his weight on his hands. This was his chance. The leader was completely distracted and unlikely to respond quickly to a sudden threat.

Harvey sprinted the last few yards, crashing his boot down on the leader's right hand. The snapping sounds suggested Harvey had successfully broken a bone. He rolled off her onto his back, the look of agony was soon replaced by confusion and surprise as he looked up. Harvey picked up the knife and held it threatening in front of him. The urge to kill was overpowering and the look on Louise's face only encouraged him, but he resisted.

He grabbed her by the arm and hoisted her up, whilst continuing to stare at the leader.

'You won't get away. My men'll get you. We need women to breed.'

'You disgust me,' said Harvey unable to resist responding even though he was wasting precious time.

Had society really regressed into this primitive state in such a short period, he thought.

'Join us. We need more like you.'

The approaching rustling sound and of a man struggling made Harvey look up. They'd caught Dave.

The leader looked towards the sound, then Harvey and said, 'my offer still stands. Otherwise you don't stand a chance.'

'I'd rather die,' said Harvey before grabbing Louise by the arm and running in the opposite direction.

He looked around to see the marauding gang in hot pursuit. Louise was running bare foot, but the pain wasn't slowing her down. Despite this the gang was catching them, a year in the bunker hadn't done Harvey's fitness any good and Louise obviously couldn't run fast enough. They'd eventually be caught. What'd he done? What about his family? What about the future?

They were almost upon them. Tiredness was making them both stumble, their legs no longer having the strength to lift over obstacles. Harvey was now looking back more than in front, relying on Louise to show him which way to go.

She suddenly stopped, the terrifying sight making her ignore the exhaustion she was feeling. Harvey carried on a few more yards before stopping and turning around to look at her. Her eyes were huge and her mouth wide open as she stared ahead, oblivious to everything else around her. Harvey was about to say something, but changed his mind and looked in the same direction.

A wall of bodies stood motionless. The sun was behind them, making their features un-recognisable. There was nowhere else to run.

CHAPTER 12 (THEA)

It was night time as Thea stopped the car on the brow of a hill and looked down at the village below. It was in total darkness, but light from the half-moon gave her some perspective. It was springtime and a little muggy, unusual for this time of year, even with climate change.

She looked back at the kids happily sleeping in the back of the car, the insecurities and fear of the unknown suffered by adults had not yet infiltrated their minds. She returned her attention to the village below. Not a single light was on. Were there no night owls? she thought.

Driven on by the need to find out what had happened to Harvey, she instructed the car to move forward. It crept off the brow and slowly made its way down the track, soon reaching the outskirts of the village. Still no sign of life, but why would there be at this time of night, she concluded. Going back to the village where she'd killed two of its occupants wasn't a good idea, but it was the only road out and flying a drone made them a sitting target.

She got out of the car and looked around tentatively, before walking a few yards further towards the village. The depth of night was the best time to make their escape, but she had to be sure that the coast was clear first.

She stopped and looked back at the kids and the doubts re-surfaced. Was she doing the right thing? Was it worth taking the risk on the slim chance that Harvey was still alive? Surely he would've contacted her by now if he was. If he was being held captive, then what chance would she have of saving him? None.

She dismissed her concerns, her overwhelming desire to know one way or the other took precedence and she returned her attention to the street in front of her. She breathed in slightly and held her breath, desperate to blank out any noise that would prevent her hearing anything. Nothing.

She returned to the car and got in, looking at the kids again for confirmation they were still ok. She looked forwards and thought about blasting through. She could easily get to the other side before anyone realised what was happening. The thought was appealing, but not ideal. Yes, she would get through, but there was a significant risk that someone would notice and inform the police. She had to creep through quietly, if possible, only making a run for it should someone see her.

She instructed the car to proceed and the seatbelt automatically locked her in before the car moved forward. Thea was continually looking from side to side for any signs of movement and was a bit surprised by how the village had become so run down. Litter was flying around and some of the window shutters many had erected for sun protection, were hanging off.

She decided to ignore her concerns and steadily continued. A very dim light shone through a crack on one of the downstairs window shutters. She slowed down and stopped, staring intensely at the house. A shadow blocked the light for a second and an instant film of cool sweat swept across her forehead. The desire to make a run for it was overwhelming, but she resisted. That was her last resort. She continued staring, ignoring everything else around her.

She felt the car rock a bit as a fist smashed against the outside at the same time as a muffled man's voice said, 'who the fuck are you?'

Thea spun around and looked panic stricken at the mask staring back at her. It was like a gas mask that she had only seen in old films. Others were stood behind, similarly wearing masks and looking equally menacing, the dark boiler suits they all wore enhanced her feeling of dread.

She focused on the man who spoke. His piercing eyes behind the mask looked as though they were searching for an answer, but also looked equally terrified. What was he scared of?

'Don't let her out,' said the man looking around at those behind before returning his attention to Thea and shouting, 'Go. Get out of here. We don't want you here.'

Thea wasn't about to argue and said, 'self-drive.'

A tiny steering wheel came out of the dashboard and two pedals from the floor. She pressed down hard on one of the pedals and the car surged forward. She looked in her rear view mirrors to see bodies recoiling backwards and she felt a slight tinge of power and satisfaction.

She continued at speed, feeling uncomfortable and out of control. Like most, she rarely drove, relying on the car to do it for her, but these were extenuating circumstances that the car wasn't programmed to deal with.

She reached the end of the high street and took a sharp right, knowing that it was the only road out of the village. A few seconds later and she passed the last house where she took a sharp left to the open road which followed the valley back to civilisation.

That's where she thought she was going. That would be the next part in the journey to find her husband. All she needed was to get hold of some communication device and find out what was happening. She was sure technology would give her the answer. The thing that they'd been weaned off over the past 18 months had suddenly become an essential part of her ever evolving plan.

The thoughts had distracted her for a few seconds at most and she failed to see the blocked road ahead. She had plenty of time to apply the brakes, but panic and a lack of driving experience meant she froze.

'Drive,' she shouted.

The car immediately recognised the danger and applied the brakes whilst swerving to the right. There was no way of avoiding a collision, but the car knew that a right turn would save the driver from some of the impact.

The impact was enough to crack Thea's head sideways, but the harness held the rest of her. She immediately looked around at the kids who were also securely fastened in, the look of horror on their faces soon turning into un-controlled sobbing. Thea didn't have time to placate them, turning around again to assess the situation.

Masked people had already surrounded the car, they must've already been there, she concluded. A tall barricade was flush up against the passenger side and the car had hardly made an impact on the structure, suggesting it was permanent and well built.

'Self-drive,' she said.

The steering wheel and pedals came out again, but she didn't attempt to drive off this time. The only other road out was back to the bothy, then they'd know where she was.

She couldn't see their faces but she could feel the fear. Their bodies made slight defensive movement when she made any movements. Why were they scared of her?

She reached for the door handle, preferring to open it manually, and slowly opened it. They suddenly stepped back.

'Stop. Get back in the car,' shouted one of them.

Thea didn't respond and continued to get out of the car. They all started shuffling around and looking at each other as though not knowing what to do.

'This is your last warning,' said another trying to take the initiative.

'Not until you tell me what's going on. Why're you scared of me?'

A gust of wind swept through and dust got into her mouth, making her cough a little. The last thing she felt was an object hitting the side of her head. The last thing she heard was the sound of her screaming children as she slumped back into the car unconscious.

....

Her eyes slowly opened. There was no headache or feeling of dread. It was that stress free feeling when you first wake up and reality hasn't yet taken hold. She stared at the bright white ceiling for a second, then her eyes widened and she suddenly sat up, hurriedly looking around to make sense of where she was.

The walls were equally bright, making her squint a little, but she soon adjusted. The room was square and the white walls made it look bigger than it probably was. There was a cut out in one wall which she suspected was the exit door. Her initial reaction was to make a beeline for it, but she resisted, knowing that any rash decisions could be fatal. She had to assess the situation first.

There was nothing in the room in front of her or to the sides. She looked down. She was laid on a bed with crimson sheets and nothing covering her. It was then that she realised she was naked and her instant reaction was to scan the room for camera devices. Nothing.

She got up and pulled the sheets off the bed to cover her. It was then that she saw the matt black wardrobe behind her standing tall and looking imposing. She instinctively stepped back, continuing until her progress was stopped by the wall. Her head started to pound, brought on by her head injury and the sudden surge of adrenalin, but she ignored it.

The wardrobe must have been six foot square and the two front doors each had a handle. The surface was perfectly smooth, suggesting it was made out of plastic. It looked bland and functional, like the room, but what was its function?

It was the only object in the room and the only thing worth investigating. She scanned the room again for any other clues, but there were none.

'What d'you want?' she shouted out in the vain hope that someone would answer.

A faint laughing noise surrounded the room and she pressed her back into the wall before darting towards the exit door. She pushed it, then tried to dig her fingers into the crack, but it refused to move. She realised the sheet covering her had slipped to the floor and she quickly picked it up and turned around again to look at the wardrobe.

'That's your future Thea,' said a voice which was faint, but seemed to surround the room.

Was the voice in her head? Was she imagining it? She closed her eyes and slapped her face, hoping it was all a dream. A nightmare. Slowly opening her eyes, she was faced by the same horror. The horror of not knowing. It was then that she realised she'd no choice. The wardrobe was the only focal point in the room, the only thing that would give her answers, good or bad.

She tied a knot in the sheet so it stayed up by itself and stared at the wardrobe doors before walking towards it and stopping. She grabbed the handles. Slow or quick, she thought. She had to make a decision. Quick. It gave her the element of surprise.

She stepped back and flung the doors open, holding onto them in case she had to close them again. Lance and Nicola were stood there in the same clothes she'd dressed them in. Their tanned faces looked slightly paler, probably because of the bright white walls shining onto them, she concluded. They looked content and were asleep. The relief swept through Thea, knowing her kids were safe. Why were they asleep? They can't be asleep. They're standing up.

Her confusion made her reluctant to reach forward and grab them. To hold them and make them feel safe. Her eyes looked around the rest of the wardrobe for answers and then she saw it. A pair of legs stood behind. She hadn't noticed them because the trousers were the same mat black colour as the wardrobe. She looked up to see the masked face holding both children upright. They weren't sleeping. Her children were dead and this thing was responsible, she concluded. She was very much a glass half empty person.

Her grief took a back seat as she reached out for her kids, but the masked thing let go, giving them a slight push so they soon reached the floor, their limp bodies bounced slightly as they rebounded.

Thea instinctively reached out for them, hoping all was not lost. Hoping that she could save them. Hoping they were still alive. But the masked thing had other ideas and pushed her back.

‘It’s inevitable Thea,’ it said in a muffled voice. There’s no point suffering. I’ve done them a favour.’

She wasn’t up for a discussion and flew at the thing, revenge was now top priority and she had no concerns for herself. She bounced off it and recoiled as in slow motion. The door was coming towards her. Slowly. Purposefully. It opened and she was back at her house in London. The last safe place she remembered. But it wasn’t safe now. A line of masked people stood before her. One was holding a gun and she could feel it smiling behind the mask before it pulled the trigger.

Time slowed until nothing was moving apart from the bullet, slowly making its way towards her. She used every muscle in her body to get out of the way, but no response. She stood watching the bullet come closer and closer until it reached her forehead and slowly started pressing against her skull. The pressure grew until the headache added to the pain. The bullet eventually pierced her skin.

The sweat rolled off her forehead and down the side of her face, making her eyes open suddenly. The pain in her head had gone and she was staring at a different ceiling. It was a grey roof high which came to an apex. She rolled her eyes around as much as possible without moving her head, trying to assess the situation before she made any significant movement.

She saw people milling around, busying themselves. They looked ragged and their movements were laboured, but the masks were gone. It’d been a long time since she’d seen another face and, in some ways it gave her comfort. Then relief swept over her at the realisation that it was only a nightmare, although she felt that real life wasn't that much better.

She slowly raised her head, desperate to find her kids. They were standing about 10 feet from the bottom of the bed she was lying on and someone seemed to be giving them food.

'Lance. Nicola,' she shouted in delight.

They looked around and shouted back, 'mummy,' before racing towards her and throwing themselves on her chest.

She winced slightly as the pressure of the impact made her head throb, then she remembered being hit and falling backwards into the car. Despite the pain, she wrapped her arms around them and held them tightly. This was a moment she thought she'd never have again and making the most of it was her priority at the moment.

Her grip on them eventually weakened, but the kids remained clamped to her chest.

'Let mummy get up,' said a woman's voice

They did as they were told and Thea slowly sat up from her prone position. She was confronted by a wall of people staring at her and she immediately tensed.

'Don't worry. We're not going to hurt you,' said a woman stepping forward.

She was middle aged, had long straggly hair. Her clothes hung limply on her, suggesting she'd lost weight. Her face had a couple of small weeping spots, which added to the sense of poverty. Thea looked around and saw other men and women looking similar.

'Where are we? What're we doing here? Let us go,' said Thea sounding desperate.

The woman looked around at the others and said, 'I'll sort this out.'

Everyone instantly dispersed, understanding the implied instruction, and the woman sat down next to Thea.

She continued, 'I'm afraid we're captives here and there's no chance of escape.'

Thea sat up and scanned the building, which looked like an old military hanger. The sides were made of metal and the large doors at one end seemed impregnable. There were other smaller doors dotted around which looked just as secure and the meagre light was coming from windows very high up on the very tall walls. The concrete floor looked cold and rather tatty looking beds were dotted around. A section of the hanger had a group of toilets, but there were no walls and some people were using them, seemingly having got used to the lack of privacy. Another section of the hanger looked like it was a kitchen.

The woman noticed Thea looking at the windows and said, 'we've tried it. Probably re-enforced glass. It's an old army place where they used to keep artillery and stuff like that. It's secure as hell.'

'Why're you here? Why're we here?'

The woman looked at her confused and said, 'where've you been? Don't you know about the virus?'

Thea said hesitantly, 'no. I've been out of circulation for a while.'

'Wait a minute. Aren't you the woman who stayed with Calan and Belinda.'

Thea immediately looked nervous and stood up before shuffled back without saying anything.

The woman smiled and continued, 'oh don't worry. We've got far more important things to worry about. My name's Morag. Morag Russell'

'Uh, Thea, she said looking down quickly to confirm with relief that she still had her clothes on.'

'And your children?'

'Oh, sorry. Lance and Nicola.'

'They're lovely. We've quite a few kids living here.'

'What's this all about,' said Thea realising she was safe.

'We've all got the virus dear. Most are resigned to it, but some are hopeful. Some think there's a way out.'

'But you said it was a fortress.'

'No. They think there's a cure. There's no chance of getting out of here.'

So it's highly contagious and we're in isolation are we. But this seems very make shift. Hasn't the government managed it all? Aren't there isolation centres?'

'I don't think government exists anymore, although we're not sure. There's no internet or anything in here.'

'But this is inhumane. They can't just lock people up. What about the law?'

Morag looked at Thea as though trying to weigh her up then said, 'there is no government. There is no law. The virus is deadly and we're in here to die.'

Thea took a deep breath, swallowed, then said, 'but we've not got the virus.'

'You have now. It's highly contagious and you would've been infected as soon as you came in here.'

'But we didn't have it before, so why would they put us in here.'

'Everyone's so nervous. People I've known for years have been ruthless. Anyone with any sign of the virus is put in here straight away. Coughing is the first sign.'

Thea immediately thought back to the crash and her slight cough after breathing in dust.

'But that's not fair,' said Thea regretting leaving the sanctuary of the bothy.

'It's a painless death Thea, but it takes a while I'm afraid. Some've taken their own lives, but most want to make the most of what time they've got left.'

'How can you be so blasé about it? Don't you want to fight? Be free? Where did the virus come from? How far has it spread? Sorry I need to get my head around this.'

Thea walked away whilst looking around. Her kids played happily, oblivious to their fate. People were in groups talking. The hanger exaggerated the noise, making it sound like a loud hum. There must've been about 100 people at least and the village wasn't that big. How many were left out there? How many had died already?

She heard a bang and three or four people immediately went towards the noise, the others only looked up. Thea followed to discover a pile of food, mostly vegetables that had probably grown locally, she thought. She stared as they gathered the food.

A woman looked up and said, 'my name's Judy. Judy Dunsford. You're new. Haven't seen you in the village before.'

'Um, Thea Burton. No. I came here to get away for a few days.'

Judy looked at her suspiciously, knowing it was a lie, but deciding it was pointless challenging her. She was skinny and had more spots on her face than Morag, suggesting the virus was more advanced.

Expect it'll be more than a few days now,' she said looking resigned.

'Are you cooking that?'

'Yeh. We've got a kitchen area over there,' she said nodding towards a small area with some basic kitchen appliances.

Thea looked across briefly, then returned her attention to Judy and saying, 'have you tried to get out of here?'

'No. There's no point. We're going to die anyway so we may as well stay here where we'll be looked after.'

Thea had calmed down a bit, although she was still trying to comprehend the dramatic events. One day a go she and the kids were safe inside the bothy. Now she was locked up in a virus ravaged community with death as their only escape. Her regrets were immeasurable and she felt like a failure, eventually placating herself with the realisation that she couldn't have anticipated any of this.

'So you cook it over there and dish it all out?'

'Yeh. There's enough food for everyone.'

Thea glimpsed at Judy's body. She noticed and said, 'you lose your appetite after a while, but I feel ok. I'll join my husband soon. I can't wait.'

Thea's eyes immediately filled with tears, partly for the wretched people and partly for her children who were oblivious to everything. She walked away, unable to say anything, and found her kids. Sitting down, her head slumped and she looked at the floor as though resigned to her fate.

The door slammed again. This time it wasn't food. Someone was laid on the floor coughing. Another victim, thought Thea. Another one thrown into this hell hole to die. In such a short time she'd acclimatised to the hopelessness of her surroundings and she didn't like it. She didn't want to be like them. She didn't want to give in and she certainly didn't want to die here.

The man who'd just been thrown in was laid on the floor. He raised his head and shouted, 'they're going to burn it down.'

Morag was, by now, fairly close, having made her way over when realising there was a new occupant. She was the leader and was responsible for greeting new arrivals. Having heard the man speak, she quickened her pace and arrived a few seconds later.

'What d'you mean?' she said sounding concerned.

By now the man was lying face down on the floor again. He slowly raised his head again, straining as though it required all his strength and said, 'someone's decided there're too many new cases and more needs to be done. They think the virus is escaping from here. They're going to burn it down.'

'What're they going to do with us? We're their friends,' said Morag.

The man looked at her as though she was stupid and said, 'you won't get out alive.'

CHAPTER 13 (BILL)

Bill Marshall was a compassionate man, but also a realist. The escape of Harvey and Dave and the disappearance of Louise was unfortunate, but not worth devoting resources to. The scientists had delivered what he wanted and Louise was dispensable. He had other more pressing concerns.

Reports coming back from the outside world were sketchy, but suggested the spread of the virus was accelerating way beyond what was anticipated. Communication links had collapsed and the bunker was now on its own. Bill concluded bunkers in other locations around the world were in the same predicament, although he had no way of knowing.

All occupants had been vaccinated and the side effects were minimal. A slight sniffle at most. The vaccine hadn't been rigorously tested and he thanked his lucky starts that he'd got away with it.

Transportation had disintegrated, so it hadn't been possible to deliver the vaccine to other parts of the world. Meaning everyone would eventually succumb to the virus, leaving the occupants of Bill's bunker the only human survivors. One day when the virus had run out of humans to feed off, it would disappear, leaving humanity to be re-born. At this rate Bill didn't think it would be that long.

He sat in his very homely apartment looking through the one way window at the throng of people busying themselves. Post vaccination, people were mingling freely. The scientists had been disbanded and communities within the bunker were springing up everywhere. Bill was happy to let this develop organically, rather than for him to issue dictates. And it was working. But he knew this was a temporary existence and sooner or later everyone would be released back into the world, when the threats of a dying civilisation had evaporated.

He knew that people couldn't be locked up for long. Tensions would rise. People would get greedy and want more than they've got. Some would rise to the top and try to dominate. It was his responsibility to quash these behaviours and he'd initiated preventative measures to keep a lid on things. His main solution was to keep people busy, giving them less time to mull over their situation. If that failed, he had an army of dedicated and loyal soldiers to quell any up-rising and he wouldn't hesitate to use them.

He rose from his very plush armchair and stood by the window so he could get a better look at what was going on. Everyone did indeed look content, or was it relief that they were still alive. The lucky ones maybe.

He was distracted by a door opening on one of the bland white walls and a number a people exiting. This was the control room which housed screens showing snap shots of what was happening around the world and the few remaining news channels, although all this would eventually disappear when humanity died out and the infrastructure broke down.

His cabinet had been discussing the food situation in the bunker, not that there were any problems. Temperature controlled greenhouses outside meant that food production wasn't subject to the erratic weather, so productivity was guaranteed. Almost.

He walked to the door in his apartment and opened it into a narrow corridor, grateful that he didn't have to exit through the control room. The corridor soon opened out into a larger walkway which gave him access to the whole bunker. Flowers had been strategically arranged around the bunker since people were allowed to interact, to provide a more pleasant and homely atmosphere. Similar niceties had also been put in other areas of the bunker, another measure put in place by Bill to alleviate tension.

People were purposely walking around as though busy, some diverted through doorways which were now permanently open to reflect the more open lifestyle Bill was trying to promote. A few uniformed soldiers moved amongst them to show the rule of law should anything get out of hand.

He continued his journey, nodding and smiling at people as he walked along, a necessary chore that he hated. He eventually reached a closed door, scanned his eyes and hands, then said, 'open.'

The door opened and he walked in, it closed instantly behind him. The caged creature stared at him. The product of human interference. The product of human curiosity, with no purpose but to see if they could do it. Someone decided they wanted to play around and the

British government agreed to support it, thinking it could be some form of weapon they could use, but secretly thinking it would be cool to have something no other country had.

The thing had started off as a gorilla, one of the few that were held in captivity. There was no way it could survive in the human created climate and experimenting on it was a good way of making use of the creature. It had to earn their keep.

The gorilla had been genetically modified, using the genes from animals that had been roaming Earth for millions of years. They'd survived in the wild despite human activity and, surprisingly, were thriving in the climate.

It was in its infancy and still growing many years after it was originally created. The original blue print for the creature had continually evolved and through genetic engineering, surgical procedures and drugs, the thing had developed immeasurable strength and intelligence. How far this would develop as it grew was very much an unknown, but in the normal world there was no way it would be a threat. The bunker was a different proposition. There was a significant risk that the creature could escape and wreak havoc, with no substantial defence mechanisms available to Bill. He had decided it needed to be destroyed, but a blood test revealed it was completely resistant to the virus.

The creature would be the saviour of humanity and Bill got a small team of scientists together to use its blood to create the vaccine. They were the only ones who knew of the source for the vaccine, even Harvey didn't know. The scientists were sworn to secrecy and all were eliminated when the vaccine was finally made. Bill was the only one who knew the truth.

The creature was known to security staff, but they only saw it as an experiment and nothing else. Some had grown wary of it, more so as it grew older and bigger. And so they should've been. Things were happening inside it that no one understood. An energy source that wasn't expected. What was it for? How had it developed? No one understood its purpose and that lack of understanding made Bill nervous. Now was the time for it to be destroyed. It'd done its job.

The creature continued staring at him as though reading his mind. Bill was mesmerised. The creature was getting into his head, reading his mind, making him hesitate. Why had he come in the first place? There was no need for him to be here, he could simply send out instruction and someone else could've destroyed it. Had the creature summoned him?

The creature had no facial expressions, but Bill could tell it was feeding off his fear and indecision. Laughing at his pain. Relishing the hold it had over him. He broke eye contact with the creature and turned to leave.

'I can help you,' said the creature in a deep gravelly voice. The words were not well formed, but the message was clear.

Bill spun around again, his eyes betraying his shock and surprise. The creature had never spoken before and its words suggested it knew what Bill was thinking. It was making an offer in the hope of saving itself. He stared speechless for a while, resisting his initial reaction to flee.

He said in a slightly shaky voice, 'no one said you could speak.'

'They do not know me. I am growing.'

Bill tensed even more. The not knowing was the big risk. First the energy growing within it, now the talking. None of the scientists had anticipated this. What would come next? The unknown was why this thing had to be destroyed, he concluded. Nevertheless!

'What can you do for me?' Bill asked.

The creature moved a little as though seeing an opportunity then said, 'I can protect you.'

'We don't need looking after.'

'Yes you do. I have been outside. Seen your security. Seen the weather getting worse. None of your weapons will work in the storms. There's a whole nation on your doorstep and it will not be long before they find out that you are here.'

Bill was astounded by its knowledge and vocabulary, although the gravelly voice made it hard to understand

'They can't get in this place. We'll just close the doors,' said Bill looking around

'You grow your food outside. They will starve you out before the virus gets them.'

None of what the creature was saying was a surprise. His security people had warned him of the risks, but how did the creature know? Was it reading people's minds? Again, the fear of the unknown hit him hard.

'What's your offer?' said Bill as though interested.

'Put me on the mainland. There is only one way to get here and I can thwart any attack. If I cannot, I can at least warn you.'

Was the thing stupid? How could it hold back a nation? thought Bill. But the look in the creature's eyes suggested confidence.

'And how will you do that?'

'I can do more than you think,' said the creature, its dark red eyes squinting a little.

The unknown hit Bill hard again. What can it do? Was it a threat to the bunker? He had to destroy it, but something inside him was fighting. Stopping him from doing what was necessary.

For the first time in his life he was stuck for words. He knew what to do, but couldn't do it. The creatures offer started eating into his head, its piercing eyes encouraging him to accept.

Eventually he said in a shaky voice, 'what can you do? How do I know you won't just run off?'

Oh how he hated showing his fear, it'd never happened before.

The creature was about 2 metres high, so not that much taller than Bill. Its scaly limbs did not look particularly powerful, although its chest was bulbous and its large stooping shoulders resembled a gorilla. Its head followed the downward direction of its shoulders and only came upright when it spoke.

The creature grabbed two of the 20 centimetre iron cage bars, its head filling the gap in between and tore them apart, whilst staring blankly at Bill as though it required little effort. Bill spun on his heels and darted towards the door, but the door didn't open. He suddenly remembered the security needed to get in was also needed to get out.

He placed his eyes on the retina scan, then looked around to see the creature almost upon him. He didn't have time. The creature grabbed him and Bill closed his eyes and held his breath, expecting the worst.

'I could crush you.'

Bill made a vain attempt to escape, but the creature easily held on.

It continued, 'you do not have to kill me. Trust me. You have nothing to lose.'

Bill stopped struggling, realising the imminent threat of death had gone. He turned to look at the creature, its breath smelt sweet and the eyes! Those piercing eyes. They were pleading with him, as though desperate to survive. He suddenly felt empathy. Felt as though he needed to care for it. Killing it was no longer an option.

The creature released its grip and Bill slumped to the floor, he quickly looked up to see the mangled bars, then the creature standing over him. He suddenly felt akin with the creature. Maybe it could be of some use.

'Ok,' he said hurriedly before gathering himself and standing up. The creature made no attempt to stop him.

Bill continued, 'I'll let you go.'

The creature stepped back to give reassurance that it was no longer a threat. They looked at each other, but it was Bill who held the stare, keen to show he was true to his word. The creature relaxed and looked away. It was telling the truth. Marauding gangs were a threat to the bunker and it was in its interest to protect it. Releasing the creature also meant it would no longer be a threat to the bunker. There was no way Bill was going to let it back in.

CHAPTER 14 (HARVEY)

Harvey and Louise stared at the wall of silhouetted figures before them, unable to make out their features, only knowing that they were human and probably male. A few seconds passed before they both turned around, expecting their pursuers to be almost upon them. They were also stood motionless, the sun shining brightly on them making them squint and their features clear. They were in stark contrast to the silhouetted figures.

They backed away slightly, knowing they were outnumbered, but also thinking about having a go. Was the prize worth it? The leader looked at them and quickly decided it wasn't. He moved back further, whilst maintaining his stare on the figures before spinning around and running. The others did the same.

Harvey looked back at the motionless figures again. If their pursuers had fled, then were they a greater threat? Should they also run? He looked across at Louise, who looked equally unsure and seemed to be expecting him to make the decision. They couldn't keep running. He needed help.

'Can you help us please?' said Harvey quickly deciding that a threatening manner would only cause problems. Best to appear helpless.

A man stepped forward so they could see his features more clearly. Harvey and Louise instinctively moved back a little.

'My name's Spencer. Spencer Jacks,' said Spencer in a rather normal and none confrontational voice.

His beard was thick and his hair long. He wore cream trousers, although the ingrained dirt gave them many different shades. His top covered his whole torso and arms and looked like some sort of animal skin. An old baseball hat was perched on his head. Harvey was stunned by how quickly civilised society had fallen.

Louise said with a slight smile and conciliatory voice, 'Louise Gardner.'

She was good, thought Harvey. A true politician using all her skills to defuse a volatile situation.

Spencer looked at her and the slight widening of his eyes suggested he recognised her.

'Harvey Burton,' said Harvey quickly after noticing Spencer's reaction to Louise.

He did the same to Harvey before saying, 'have you got the virus?'

'No,' said Harvey and Louise together.

Any hesitation would've indicated they were lying and they'd both seen what happened when there was even the slightest sign of the virus.

Spencer nodded his approval, happy to accept their word and said, 'come with us. We'll give you shelter.'

Spencer immediately turned, expecting them to follow, but they stared at each other, unsure on what to do.

Spencer stopped and looked back before saying, 'don't worry. We're not like them. I'll explain when we get back.'

Harvey shrugged at Louise as though they had no other choice.

....

The gang were all men and dressed differently, the only consistency was that their clothes covered their bodies and they all wore hats and adorned beards. One had a small dead animal over his shoulder, Harvey thought it was a baby screx, the only animal to have thrived in the new environment.

They reached their destination after about an hour's walk. A tightly grouped set of about one hundred houses looked quite new and appeared to have been built to withstand the inhospitable weather conditions. Grouping them together so tightly also meant they protected each other from the ferocious weather.

All had solar panels and, as was normal with modern houses, they were built on stilts to avoid the frequent flooding. Flood defences were no longer capable of dealing with the deluges, although there were some channels to re-direct the worst of the rainfall. But flooding was the least of their problems. In this part of the country the arid dryness was the biggest problem and infrequent rainfall only encourage limited growth before the heat killed it off.

Spencer showed them into the communal courtyard in the centre of the estate. A well was situated in the centre and Harvey suspected houses relied on it for their water needs. It was a growing trend for arid regions before he went into the bunker.

Spencer saw Harvey looking at the well and said, 'we get all our water from there. It's used for the crops as well.'

Harvey continued looking before saying, 'have the houses got compost toilets?'

'Yeh. We use it as a fertiliser for the crops.'

Harvey nodded and said, 'I saw a lot of these estates being built before I went into the bunker.'

He instantly realised his mistake and chose not to elaborate, hoping that Spencer wouldn't pursue it. He was lucky for now.

'Yeh. But there aren't many people around now to live in them. Probably why we've not had much trouble from other groups. There's plenty for everyone if you can put up with the heat.'

'What about that group who were chasing us?' said Louise. 'They looked like trouble.'

'They're one of the few rogue ones. Live by the laws of the jungle I'm afraid, but they're not much trouble. Their numbers are small and they're too disorganised to be much of a threat.'

'And the virus?' continued Louise.

'That's another reason why there aren't many around. People're dying. We're all shit scared of it.'

Louise noticed the fear in his voice and decided to change the subject.

'What're you going to do with us?' she said sounding wary.

Spencer looked confused before saying, 'of course. I'm so sorry. We pick up strays sometimes,' he said smiling. 'You're more than welcome to stay here. Count this as your home. We've plenty of space and we need people like you,' he said glancing at Louise for longer than was comfortable. Eventually he continued. 'Come, we've some spare rooms over here.'

Harvey hesitated for a while. His plan wasn't to stay anywhere. He needed to find his family. Despite his concerns, he followed Spencer along with Louise who still didn't look comfortable. They soon reached a house and walked through the front door to an empty hallway.

Spencer said, 'you'll be staying here with Grant and Teresa and Jack and Maggie. They're out in the fields at the moment. I'll tell them you're here. Come, I'll show you your room. Expect you'll want to rest a bit,' he said walking up the stairs.

'But we're not…….. Well we haven't got any other clothes,' said Harvey deciding not to say what was originally on his mind.

Louise knew what he was referring to, but decided not to say anything. Her mind was still in a quandary. How had she got into this situation? Not that long ago she was heading towards the bunker for a life of safety and security whilst the world around slipped into death and decease. She was now in that world and Harvey was to blame.

Spencer said, 'no one has. We've only got what we're wearing. It's not important, just wash them every now and again,' he said continuing up the stairs as though he was only addressing a minor concern.

Spencer showed them into the room and said his goodbyes, saying he'd come back in a couple of hours.

They both looked around the room. The heat was unbearable for Louise, her cooling suit wasn't working anymore and she simply wasn't used to it. Harvey suit was still working and his less harassed demeanour was evident.

The room was big and dimly lit, thanks to the window shutters which cut out most of the light and the hot sun, although the white walls made an attempt to brighten it up. There was an abundance of soft furnishings and a large bed dominated the centre of the room.

'We're not a couple,' said Louise with a dour look on her face just in case Harvey had any ideas.

'I'm over there,' he said nodding towards a plush sofa and with an equally dour look on his face.

He walked towards a door, opened it and said, 'bathroom looks ok.'

Louise immediately went towards it, almost pushing Harvey aside before stopping and looking around. There was no light switch, but the light from the bedroom gave her just enough to confirm it was ok.

She returned to the bedroom to see Harvey stood looking at her. This was the first time the pace had dropped since their escape from the bunker, giving each a chance to assess the situation. Louise spoke first.

What's going on Harvey?' Why'd you escape from the bunker and why take me? The bunker's the only safe place.'

'I need to find my family.'

'Why aren't they in the bunker? Everyone else's family is? D'you even know where they are?'

Harvey felt a little aggrieved. Why did he have to justify his actions to this woman? It had nothing to do with her. Then the guilt washed over him, realising that he'd got her into this situation. He needed to placate her.

'I don't want to live in that place. I don't want them to live in that place. And yes, I do know where they are.'

'And what about that other guy?'

'Dave… He's in the same situation. Wants to find his family.'

'Well he won't stand a chance now will he.' said Louise looking at Harvey as though he was to blame for whatever had happened to Dave.

'He deserved it. He gave you up to those barbarians to save his own skin.'

'And why take me,' said Louise repeating her earlier question.

'I wasn't thinking at the time. Thought I could use you as a hostage in case anything goes wrong.'

'But you don't need me now.'

'Look. It was a mistake taking you, but we're here now and we need to stay together.'

'Why should I be interested in finding your family? Maybe I should just make my way back to the bunker. I'm no use to you now.'

Harvey turned and looked towards the window as though thinking. She was right. He felt responsible for her and that meant letting her go. He turned to face her again.

'You're right. I need to put things right and get you back there.'

Harvey noticed a slight relief on her face, suggesting she needed his approval, which of course she didn't.

She moved towards him and said, 'you're a good man Harvey, but scientists can be stupid. I'll be blunt. The virus is going to wipe everybody out, including your family. They don't stand a chance. Go and get them. Bring them back to the bunker. I'll make it good with Bill. Deep down he's a forgiving man.'

Harvey looked down. In her own mind she was right, but she didn't know about the vaccine he was carrying. The lifesaving vaccine which meant his family could live free outside the bunker and away from what will become a fascist dictatorship. History proved that this always happened and he didn't want to be part of it.

He stared at the floor, but was suddenly distracted by the small spot on his hand. A unique looking spot that indicated the first signs of the virus. He turned his hand over so Louise couldn't see.

CHAPTER 15 (THEA)

The man stood up to face Morag and shouted, 'I'm telling you they're going to burn this place down.'

There was an audible gasp from the crowd quickly gathering around the man.

'They can't burn us alive. That's inhumane,' said Morag.

'They're desperate,' said the man sounding shocked that no one believed him. 'They don't know what to do.'

Someone in the crowd said, 'can't they just give us guns. We can shoot ourselves, then they can burn us. I don't want to be burnt alive.'

Morag was taken aback. Assisted suicide had become an option for many in the civilised world who had a terminal illness and wanted to choose the way they wanted to die, but few took the option. This however, was not a civilised world.

'No,' said Morag, 'They're wrong. We're miles from the village and there's no way the virus can spread that far without being carried by the wind and we're inside. There must be some other source. Maybe the virus is being carried by the wind from another community far away.'

'They're not thinking logically,' said the man. 'I don't have the virus. I'm only here because I disagreed with them.'

'They're barbarians,' said Morag.

'They couldn't even kill me. They'd rather I burnt to death in here than see the whites of my eyes,' said the man with disdain.

'What're we going to do?' said Morag looking around at the crowd which by now consisted of everyone in the building.

She was the leader only because of her compassion and understanding. She supported and comforted people in their hour of need. Organised things so people were fed and as comfortable as possible. Made arrangements when people and children passed on. This was a different problem that she was unable to cope with.

Thea stepped forward and said, 'I'm not going to die in here like this. We need to get out.'

Of course she knew she was being selfish. Of course she knew the risk of spreading the virus. Of course she was only concerned for herself and her kids. But that was what humans were all about when it came down to it.

'Yeh,' said someone shouting from the crowd. 'I don't want to be burnt to death.'

Everyone was looking at Thea now, Morag had willingly stepped aside.

Thea looked around the hanger for escape routes. Obviously there were none. It was then that she saw a masked figure appear at one of the upper windows, looking down menacingly at everyone. She spun around to see more masked faces appear at other windows all around the hanger. She instinctively picked up some nearby cutlery and flung it at one of them. Their heads twitched a little, but the plate failed to reach its target.

Everyone looked up to see what Thea was doing and did the same, the men had more luck and the masks eventually disappeared.

'They'll be back,' shouted Thea. 'Gather up everything you can throw and be ready.'

Everyone did as instructed and waited patiently with projectiles in hand and looking anxiously towards the windows. Silence fell as everyone awaited their fate. Thea guessed that everyone knew that this was a vain attempt to save their lives. She had to think of something else, but this wasn't her area of expertise. Why was everyone looking to her for leadership? Others must've been better qualified. The sense of responsibility lay heavy on her as she waited with the others.

Debris started being thrown through the windows. Thea suspected it was left by the army and the only common thing about it was that it was combustible. Wood. Clothing. Tyres, even old carpets. The onslaught went on and on and they couldn't do anything about it, apart from make a vain attempt to throw it back. It went on for what seemed like an eternity, then suddenly stopped and peace descended again.

'What're they going to do?' said someone from the crowd.

Thea felt she had to give the obvious answer and said, 'this stuff'll burn. We need to stop the fire. Everyone, gather as much water as you can. Use the buckets.'

Drinking water and food were delivered on a daily basis and stored in the kitchen area, but a day's rations wouldn't last that long. Buckets were used as toilets and there were quite a few dotted around.

She continued, 'don't throw the water until I tell you.'

Everyone did as instructed, but the barrel of water was soon emptied. There were about 20 full buckets, nowhere near enough, concluded Thea, but they had to try.

Thea looked up again. In the furore she hadn't noticed the pipes appear at some of the windows. They were about 10 centimetres in diameter and dangled menacingly, easily out of reach. Everyone stopped and looked up, waiting for what was going to happen next.

Suddenly fluid started spurting out. It was an acrid smell that Thea didn't recognise.

'It's petrol,' shouted one of the older residence. 'It's highly flammable.'

Of course Thea had heard of it, but it hadn't been used for a long time. Maybe the army had left it here and forgotten about it, she concluded.

'Quick. Get your buckets ready,' she shouted. 'But do nothing until I tell you.'

The deadly flames came flying through multiple windows, instantly setting light to the debris on the floor. The whole hanger was ablaze in seconds and the flames danced around as though looking for more food to eat. The smoke instantly made everyone cough and most doubled over to relieve the pain. Then as though through instinct, everyone moved to the centre of the hanger where none of the debris had reached. Someone moved to throw their water on the fire

'No,' shouted Thea.

The man instantly stopped. She looked back at the crowd to see her kids staring at her, the fear in their eyes sent shivers down her spine, but she had to ignore them. This wasn't the time to be a comforting mother. She looked up at the windows in the hope that something obvious would show itself and save them all. It did.

One of the pipes had dropped lower than they intended. It was within reach.

She turned around to the crowd behind her and shouted, 'throw all your water towards that pipe. Make a path so someone can get through.'

Everyone complied, sensing some hope, and started throwing on the fire.

Thea looked around and found the type of person she was looking for. A strong young man who had little sign of the virus.

She ran over to him and said, 'what's your name?'

'Will,' he replied coughing slightly.

'Can you climb that pipe,' she said turning around and nodding at it.

'Yes,' he said confidently.

He didn't wait for the confirmatory instruction and strode towards it.

Thea ran after him and said, 'you need to get that door open,' she said pointing towards the hanger door.

He nodded at her as though excited by the challenge and said, 'I'll go first. Get more blokes to follow me. I may need help.'

She was impressed by his leadership and turned to get volunteers, of which there were many. By now the water had done its job and Will had a path through to the dangling pipe. It wouldn't be long though before the heat of the fire evaporated the water and the flames took over again.

'Does anyone have any water left?' she shouted.

A few hands went up.

Thea continued, 'make sure this path stays clear as long as possible.'

Will looked back to see three willing volunteers behind him. He strode forward, covering his face from the heat before grabbing the pipe. He winced a little from the heat, then climbed up. His strength and agility made light work of it and it wasn't long before he reached the top. There was enough room for him to sit on the ledge and, looking down, he encouraged the next to follow him. He then turned his attention to outside.

It was daylight and he could clearly see everything. The calmness and serenity was in stark contrast to what was going on in the hanger. There was no one else around. Maybe they thought they'd done their job and it was safe to leave. Maybe they didn't want to hang around because of the virus. Their reasons were of no interest to him, all he was concerned about was that it gave him a clear run.

A tanker was parked immediately below the window. Various fuel pipes ran from it, including the one he'd climbed. He hadn't even thought about the drop on the other side, so seeing the tanker giving him an initial landing place was a bonus.

He steadied himself just as the next man reached the ledge. There was just enough room for both of them.

Will looked down into the hangar again. The next man was standing below and looking up. The flames were getting worse and he was instinctively bent over with arms raised to protect his face. He then started to move back up the slowly diminishing footpath towards the centre of the hanger.

'Is there any more water?' shouted Will.

Thea looked around then shouted, 'No.'

'Don't send anyone else. We'll manage.'

'Ok,' shout Thea.

By now the man was back with the rest and the path had almost disappeared.

Will looked across at the man and said, 'I'll go first Dan. Can you drive that thing?'

He nodded and said, 'only if they've left it activated. I've no chance if they haven't.'

Will decided not to question him and looked down at the tanker, waiting just a few seconds before lunging forward. He landed heavily, one leg taking most of the impact. He screamed out as he rolled a couple of times before coming to a stop. Luckily he hadn't fallen off the edge and continued his journey to the ground.

He grimaced as he looked down at his ankle, then he looked up at Dan and said, 'I'll get out the way. Then jump.'

Dan felt uneasy, but knew he'd no choice. The pathway behind him was totally engulfed in flames again and the tanker was the only way out.

Will steadily got to his feet and put some weight on his injured ankle. It was bearable for now, but would no doubt get worse as the endorphins wore off. He hobbled over to the ladders, which went up the side of the tanker, and climbed down, then looked up at Dan.

'Come on. Hurry,' he shouted.

Dan was a little concerned when he saw Will hobbling, but still flung himself forward, knowing he'd no choice. He jumped and landed heavily, but both legs hit the tanker at the same time so the force was equally distributed. He got up steadily, then hurried towards the ladders when he confirmed he was injury free.

By this time, Will was in the tanker cab looking around the unfamiliar controls.

He looked down when he saw Dan and said, 'I think it's working.'

'Let me in,' shouted Dan.

Will shuffled over to the passenger side and Dan climbed in, both put their seatbelts on and soon the tanker was slowly moving forward.

Will shouted, 'ram it into the front doors. We've no time to drop the petrol. We'll have to take a chance.'

Dan didn't hesitate, he guessed what was going to happen as soon as he reached the window ledge and saw the tanker.

The tanker gathered pace, going past the hangar and turning around so it was facing the large front doors. The tanker's electric motor fell silent, before it hummed loudly and shot forward as Dan pressed down hard on the accelerator. It crashed into the doors, but only succeeded in making a large dent. This was an ex-military establishment so Dan guessed the doors were resistant to such attacks. However, resistance didn't mean impenetrable, he concluded when looking at the damaged door.

He reversed so he was further back this time, then looked across at Will and said confidently, 'more speed'll crack it.'

Will nodded and Dan floored the accelerator again. This time the tanker was going significantly faster and it punctured a hole in the door, but the hinges stayed firm. The metal scraped across the tanker before it came to a stop and rolled back a few feet. Dan and Will looked into the cloud of dust they'd created. It soon cleared to reveal people desperately coughing and choking on the smoke. Some of the children were laid on the floor, obviously already overcome by the fumes from the fire.

Will saw Thea, but she wasn't staring at him. He looked in the rear view mirror to see fuel spurting from the tanker. The metal on the door must've split the tank when it rolled back, he concluded. His attention was then drawn to the flame creeping up the line of fuel spurting out, quickly entering the half full tank. He returned his attention to the crowd, but Thea was nowhere to be seen, others were also running away. That was the last thing he saw before the searing heat and light hit him, followed by darkness, followed by nothing.

CHAPTER 16 (BILL)

Additional struts had been put horizontally across the cage to strengthen it. As an additional measure, CCTV was in place to provide an early warning of escape and armed guards were outside and inside with enough weaponry to kill anything.

Despite these measures, Bill wasn't confident that the creature could be held in check. There was something about it. An aura that sucked people in, read their minds, influenced their thought processes. It wasn't enough to make them do things they didn't want to do, but scientists were baffled and it was the unknown that Bill feared. Would its powers increase as it got older?

It'd been a month since Bill's promise to let it go, but he was wavering. What was he letting go? Would it come back to haunt him? These questions needed answering and he'd got the scientists to devote all their attention to the creature, but answers weren't forthcoming. They'd created something new so didn't have a clue on how things would develop.

Of course the simple answer was to destroy it, but he just couldn't. Something inside his head was saying it wasn't a good idea. Something said the creature could be of use to him.

Bill looked at the creature on the CCTV. He hadn't been back in the room since the altercation, mainly because of the threat of harm, both physically and mentally. Did it really have that much power? If it did, why didn't it try and escape?

The questions and uncertainties whirred around in his head until he decided to dismiss them. He'd other more pressing concerns in the bunker. There seemed to be increasing un-rest, something he hadn't anticipated because everyone knew that life inside was more than tolerable and certainly better than outside. Despite this, dissenters felt that things could be better and secret groups had convened to air their grievances. Bill knew they were going on, but decided not to intervene, hoping that a good moan probably made them feel better, as long as it didn't go further. Well it had gone further and solutions to their grievances were now being discussed. They weren't some benign social events to raise moral, they were more around freedoms to do what they wanted. A change of leadership. More democracy around decision making.

These problems had only recently surfaced after the mass vaccination and increased freedom to move around and interact. It was the latter that Bill thought was the reason for the increased un-rest. People chat more and piss each other off. The solution? Lock them away again in small groups and don't let them talk to each other.

He broke his gaze from the CCTV and stood up, looking down at the screen one more time before turning around and exiting the room into the corridor. People were walking around in larger groups than normal and guards mingled amongst them, looking menacing, which was their main role.

He'd recently sent out instructions to increase their presence amongst communities to discourage mass gatherings, but this had only exacerbated the discontent and the way that people were looking at him suggested they were blaming him which wasn't surprising, he concluded. Stepping back now though wasn't the answer. He had to go further.

He put his head down, ignoring their stares and continued his journey, soon reaching the door where he and a few selected people could get in. He used his eyes, voice and finger prints to get in, the door closed soon after and he felt safe.

The cabinet room had changed and was in stark contrast to the other areas of the bunker which were now aesthetically pleasing. It was bland and various CCTV screens had been put in place to monitor people's movements.

Bill looked at the two people sat at the cabinet table. His head of security, Samantha White and Charles Orpington, who had no particular role and his only qualification for being at the top table was that Bill trusted him implicitly. The remaining cabinet members had left their posts or rather had been sacked, because Bill knew that a democracy simply didn't work in extreme circumstances where tough decisions had to be made that the populous would be against. This was one of those decisions.

He sat down with them, pausing a few seconds before saying, 'we need to come down hard on them. We can't introduce these measures steadily. It'll give them time to fight back. We all agreed?'

Bill spoke as though they were expected to simply rubber stamp his decision.

'They are the electorate,' said Charles. 'The future of humanity on our planet.'

One of Charles's many attributes was to stand up to Bill, make him think again. Draw him back from his extreme behaviour and make him change his mind. Bill appreciated it, but this wasn't the time for a change in direction.

'What d'you recommend then?' said Bill.

Bill wasn't interested in Charles's response, but he felt the question needed asking at least. It was Samantha he needed on board. She was his powerhouse. The muscle behind his decisions and her silence suggested she was happy to support him.

Charles looked at Bill and said, 'get the ring leaders.'

'Others'll come to the fore. It has to be all or nothing.'

Samantha leant forward, resting her weight on her elbows and said, 'we're ready to go now,'

The look on her face suggested she was bored with the discussions and hungry for action.

Bill turned his attention to her and said, 'do it.'

She got up and went through the security room door, leaving Bill and Charles alone.

'Charles said, 'there was a time when you'd listen to me and change your mind. Now you just listen.'

'And I'll continue to do that. I need your opinion Charles, but I've made up my mind on this one. And it's my decision to make.'

'Yours and Samantha's? You're nothing without her.'

'Every dictatorship needs an army and every army needs a leader.'

'Is that you or Samantha?'

'Me,' said Bill with venom.

'Only for as long as she wants you there Bill. She'll take over at some point and then you're a dead man.'

'Then I'll have to get to her first, won't I.'

'How? She's got an army behind her. You've got nothing.'

Bill sat back and stared at the table as though Charles was reminding him of what he already knew.

He raised his head defiantly and said, 'I need a contingency plan then. We need a contingency plan. There's an escape tunnel from my room. I'm the only one who knows about it. It goes to the mainland, but there's also a living area with all the provisions I need for survival. If I can't live in here or out there, then that will sustain me.'

'But what for? What sort of life will that be?'

It'll give me time to think. Anyway, we're a long way from that. We've got the "now" to think about,' said Bill trying to change the subject.

'And the "now" won't work. You can't lock everyone up,' said Charles.

'It worked before. People were locked up and didn't complain.'

'They knew it was in their interest. It controlled the virus. Now you're just locking them up to control them.'

'It'll work Charles. It has to. We've no alternatives. We have to control the mayhem.'

Charles sat back and breathed out as though frustrated. But he was resigned to the inevitable.

....

Two hours later the attack had begun. Samantha was nowhere to be seen. Bill and Charles looked at the unfolding horror on the screen. It wasn't going to plan. Security guards were out-numbered and some seemed to be reticent about using their weapons. Some were doing nothing. Some seemed to be on the side of the rebels.

They both looked at the screens unable to say anything, until Bill eventually said, 'what's going on?'

'Don't you know?' said Charles looking equally perplexed.

'No. I left it to Samantha. It's her area.'

'Then you better find out,' said Charles angrily.

Bill immediately got up and headed toward the door to security, but stopped when the door opened and Samantha lunged into the cabinet room.

'They attacked us first. We don't stand a chance. A lot of the guards are on their side. We don't stand a chance,' she repeated as though trying to hammer the point home.

Bill looked at her blankly as though not knowing what to do next. A feeling he'd seldom experienced in the past, but it was becoming more frequent lately.

'What d'you suggest?' said Bill sounding panic stricken.

'Abandon ship,' said Charles behind him with a "told you so" look on his face.

Samantha said, 'they'll get in here eventually.'

'But you told me this room was impenetrable.'

'Only in normal circumstances. If they've control out there, then they have the weapons to get in here eventually.'

The sound of fighting was getting closer. Samantha looked at the door to the corridor before returning her attention to Bill and continuing, 'they must've got to the guards. Most are on their side. Those that aren't are being slaughtered. We have to get out.'

Charles said, 'what the fuck are you talking about? Was all this behind your back? Didn't you know?'

Bill turned around to face Charles sitting by himself at the cabinet table and looking as though he was about to score political points.

'You did didn't you Charles?'

The smug looked disappeared from Charles's face and he said, 'what're talking about? Of course I didn't.'

'You've been against me all through this. But you haven't really been fighting my corner that much have you? Is that because you knew my plan was going to fail? Are you on their side? Did you foreworn them of my plan to lock them down? Is that why they hit us first? Because you told them what was about to happen.'

Like a typical politician, Charles said with confidence, 'don't be stupid. I'm on your side and will always support you.'

The words sounded sincere, but the loss of eye contact for a millisecond said a thousand unspoken words. Bill looked over at Samantha who'd noticed the same thing and gave her a look to confirm he thought Charles was to blame.

'What d'you want me to do with him?' she said in a monotone voice with no emotion.

Bill looked back at Charles who now looked terrified and said, 'it's too late. Maybe we can use him as a bargaining tool.'

'D'you think he's that important to them?' she said sounding doubtful.

'Who knows. It's worth a try. Can you lock that door so no one can get in here, said Bill nodding towards the security door.

'Yeh, but why? They're all on my side, otherwise they would've taken us by now.'

'Just do it,' said Bill sounding frustrated.

Samantha did as she was told and took a device out of her pocket before pressing a button, followed by a clicking sound on the door.

'No one can get in or out, she said. 'For now anyway,' she continued remembering that nothing would stop the rabble outside eventually getting inside anywhere they wanted

Bill looked across at Charles who seemed to have shrunk in size and looked terrified.

He said as though pleading, 'your plan wouldn't have worked. You can't impose your will on everyone. The people will always win in the end.'

Bill walked over to him. Putting his hands on the table he slowly moved his head towards him until he was inches from his face.

'But it was my decision to make. Not yours. You've created this mayhem Charles. There'll be power struggles now and many will die. This'll all be for nothing,' he said looking around.

Bill moved back and returned his attention to Samantha before saying, 'I've got a way out of here.

'There isn't a way out. Trust me.'

'There is. Follow me,' said Bill quickly moving towards the door to his room.

He opened it and entered, beckoning Samantha to follow him. She looked confused for a second, then followed suggesting there was some truth to what he was saying.

Charles didn't move from his seat and said, 'I'm staying here.'

'You don't have any choice. You've lost my trust,' said Bill.

Charles nodded as though there was no more to be said.

Bill continued, 'you may've helped them, but they won't forgive you for being part of the establishment.'

'They will,' said Charles sounding a little unsure.

Bill smirked a little before walking up to him and placing his hands around his throat. He flung him to the floor, using his body weight to stop him struggling whilst still holding his throat and tightening his grip.

Charles started to choke, desperately searching for the oxygen his lungs needed. His eyes bulged and mouth opened. His face turned a crimson red. He started to hack as though trying to say something, but Bill's strong grip prevented him. His arms started to flail around uncontrollably in a desperate attempt to free himself, but his strength slowly waned as death took over. Within a few minutes he lay lifeless on the floor.

Bill stayed on top of him for a few more seconds before putting his face against his nose to detect any form of life.

He then got up, turned towards Samantha and said, 'he would've told them we were here and about the escape route in my room. This gives us a bit more time. They would've killed him anyway.'

Bill was surprised by how he felt the need to justify himself, but the look on her face suggested she wasn't concerned and understood completely.

'We need to get out of here,' she said raising her head to the increasing noise coming from the door to the corridor.

'Follow me.'

They went into Bill's room, the door closed behind them. He got on all fours and ran his hand underneath the sofa. One side of the sofa raised up to reveal steps leading to an underground passageway.

'Impressive,' said Samantha. 'I didn't know it was here.'

'No one did. My insurance.'

'Mine as well?' asked Samantha.

'Yes.'

He started to tentatively walk down the steps. It'd been a long time since his first and last visit and he needed to familiarise himself with it. A light came on automatically to reveal a long narrow chamber.

'Follow me,' he said looking back towards the entrance where Samantha was stood, but she wasn't looking down at him in readiness for her decent.

He continued, 'what're you doing?'

She held up a small device and pressed a button before rapidly descending to join him. The hatch behind soon closed, leaving them both in complete silence.

'I opened the door to the security room. They're my best people so they'll put up a good fight. Give us a bit more time.'

Bill nodded, knowing she'd sent them to their death, but death was an inevitable outcome anyway, he concluded.

'It's sound proof and no detection device will find it. We'll be safe in here for a while. Follow me,' he said walking towards the corridor.

It looked solid, but very basic. Struts were in place to give support, but apart from that, it was bare rock. They continued for a hundred yards, descending sharply before it levelled out and they entered an underground cavern.

The temperature was pleasant and huge quantities of tinned food and bottled water were stacked against the rock walls in one corner. Several beds were placed around the outside and pointing inwards. A large table and chairs were in the middle of the cavern and was very much the centre piece. A very small stream came out from the base of the wall and trickled through the cavern, finally disappearing through the wall at the bottom end. The lights were dim, but they were able to see everything. Just.

Samantha felt an air of calm, in stark contrast the mayhem they'd just left. She exhaled slightly as a sign of her relief.

Bill said, 'we've enough food here for a very long time. I thought there'd be more people down here.' He looked up at the lights and continued, 'that comes from a solar panel on the surface and that battery over there,' he said nodding towards a box in the corner.

'Won't they find the panels?' said Samantha instinctively thinking of the security risks.

'Not a chance,' said Bill confidently. He looked at the beds and continued, 'you've got a choice of bed and the cuisine is um…… Plentiful, although not exciting.'

She nodded and looked at the stream.

'That's our toilet, washing facility and drinking water, should we need it.'

She had an army background so this would be considered luxury in the field of battle.

'You've thought of everything then,' she continued. 'But it's not somewhere we can live out the rest of our lives.'

'That tunnel goes to the mainland,' he said pointing to the other end of the cavern. He continued, 'this place'll give us time to think things through. For now, it'll be safer in here than out there.'

‘What about them?’ she said nodding towards the tunnel they’d entered through. ‘They could find this place.’

Doubtful, but if they do, several doors will automatically block their way. We’ll have plenty of time to escape. The exit at the other end is well hidden.’

‘And what are your plans?’

‘I’ve been stupid. I should never have relaxed the rules. I should’ve kept people apart in their small communities.’

‘Yea, but here we are,’ said Samantha sounding frustrated at Bill’s pointless assessment of historic mistakes.

‘Yes, here we are.’ There was silence for a while before Bill continued, ‘I’m not going to give up. There’ll be anarchy in there and they need order. It won’t be long before the virus sweeps through and kills everyone outside. Then they can go into the outside world again to start afresh. We or I just need to find a way of making sure they don’t kill themselves before that happens.’

‘A very grand plan. An impossible plan. You’ve no clout behind you now. You’re just one man. Like any other man.’

‘And one woman,’ he said as though looking for her support.

‘What choice do I have?’

CHAPTER 17 (HARVEY)

Harvey was woken the next morning by the heat of the sun penetrating the window shutters. The sun shone relentlessly during these hot spells and gave little respite from the heat. Temperatures didn't drop that much at night and he had been suffering, mainly because his male chivalry and guilt had forced him to give his cooling suit to Louise, who was still sleeping soundly. Also, he'd been used to the comfortable temperatures of the bunker and his body hadn't yet adjusted.

It was the first time he'd had a chance to look at her closely. She was very pretty with a slender, well-proportioned face and shoulder length auburn hair. There was a hint of freckles, which he suspected had been encouraged by the sun to show themselves, and her slender neck was still smooth and taught. A thin sheet hung limply over her body, showing her curves and he wondered if she was wearing any clothes, eventually concluding she must at least have the cooling suit on, otherwise she would be awake and suffering by now. As indeed he was.

He was sat naked on the bed apart from his underwear. He got up when he finally finished examining her, but quickly creased his face up when the movement released his trapped body odour. He sat down again, knowing there were no washing facilities in the room and the well was the only water source. Cleaning himself could wait. He and Louise needed to stay together for now, he concluded.

He continued to look at her, then a rush of adrenalin snapped him out of his day dream, quickly looking down at his hand. Relief swept over him as he saw the spot had gone overnight. The vaccine had worked and he was no longer infected, but his relief was short lived. The vaccine worked in two ways. It either stopped you getting the virus or would cure you quickly should you get it. Either way you would be ok. The problem is that, if it's the latter, there is a risk you could infect others between getting the virus and the vaccine doing its job.

He stared at his hand for a few more seconds before looking over at Louise again. In his panic he hadn't heard her stir. She was still laid out, but had a frown and her eyes were open and staring at nothing in particular as though trying to make sense of where she was and what had happened. She suddenly looked over at Harvey and her demeanour changed to anger at the realisation of her predicament.

'Sleep well?' said Harvey with a slight smile on his face, hoping to defuse her obvious anger.

'No,' she said abruptly.

She rose from her prone position and the sheet slipped off before she sat on the edge of the bed staring at the floor. She still wore the clothes from the day before, obviously the cooling suit underneath was still doing its job.

'I'll make things right Louise. Promise.'

About a minute passed before she slowly looked up and said, 'and what does that mean? Staying here until the virus gets me?'

'No. I'll get you back to the bunker where you'll be safe.'

'How do I know I haven't got the virus now?'

Harvey immediately looked away, unable to say anything, the look on his face betraying what he was thinking.

She continued, 'what?' What's wrong? D'you know something I don't?'

He looked across at her and his mouth opened a bit as though trying to say something, but no words came out.

She shouted, 'tell me.'

'Is everything ok?' said a woman's voice from outside.

'Yes,' she snapped. 'Go away.'

The silence outside suggested the woman had obeyed.

Louise returned her attention to Harvey again and said a little quieter, 'tell me.'

Harvey took a deep breath and said, 'I found a spot on my hand last night. I think it was the virus.'

Louise hurriedly looked at her hands, then her arms, lifting her sleeves up as far as she could.

'Like this?' she said pointing to a spot on her arm.

Harvey nodded and said, 'yes.'

He wasn't surprised. He suspected they'd contracted it at the same time, possibly from the man who'd been killed by the leader of the other gang. No matter the source, he had to do something.

'Listen. I can sort it Louise. I brought some of the vaccine when I escaped. It'll cure you, but we can't tell anyone.'

'Cure me. It hasn't helped you. You caught it.'

'Yes. The vaccine'll stop the virus or cure you if it gets through the first line of defence. It'll cure you Louise.'

She saw the hope in his eyes and calmed down a bit.

He held out his hands and turned them from side to side then said, 'looked the spot's gone. I'm cured.'

She looked at his hands for a long time as though searching for any signs of the virus.

Eventually she said hurriedly, 'Do it.'

He reached for his trousers on the floor next to his bed, opened a zipper and took out a small package.

'Lift up your sleeve,' he said opening the package and taking out a small capsule.

He attached a needle to the capsule and injected the life-saving fluid into her arm. She winced a little, then looked at him with a look of hope and scepticism.

'Are you sure this'll work?'

'Yes,' he said assertively. 'It worked when we tested it, so it'll work now. It's worked on me hasn't it.'

Louise knew that little testing had been done, but decided not to pursue her concerns. There was little point.

'Who knows you've got that?' she said nodding towards the package.

'Only Dave and now you. And we need to keep it that way. They seem like good people, but they'll want to get their hands on it if they know it's here. Life and death situations can bring out the worst in people.'

Louise nodded her approval then said, 'how many doses?'

'There're 40 in a package.'

'For your family?'

'Yes. And Dave's, but he won't need them anymore.'

'D'you think he's dead?'

Harvey shrugged and said, 'probably, but that's his lookout. He's a good man. Intelligent. But he gave you up to save himself and that's not right.'

'As you said, life and death situations can bring out the worst in people.'

'True. Still doesn't make it right,' he said moving away from her as though the conversation was over.

'What now?' she persisted. 'We can't just stay here. You need to get to your family and I. Well I can't stay here can I.'

Harvey was standing with his back to her and staring at the thin line of bright light penetrating through the gap in the window shutters. She was supposed to be a hostage. Someone who he could use to guarantee his escape from the bunker. She'd not been useful in that respect and was now just a problem. He cursed her. He cursed his conscience. He cursed his inability to come up with a solution. He turned his attention to the open packet containing the vaccine and slipped it back into his trouser pocket.

'Come with me,' he said tentatively as though regretting the offer immediately.

'No way,' she said. 'I need to get back in that bunker. Everyone has been vaccinated in there and it's safe. I don't want to live out here. You got me into this mess

Harvey,' said Louise hoping that he felt a sense of responsibility towards her.

'Ok. Ok,' he said grabbing the back of his neck and slowly moving his hand across it. He turned around to face her and continued, 'I'll get you back in there somehow.'

'How?' she said with a slightly raised voice.

'Look. We're safe from the virus, but they're not and we've probably given it to them. They'll rightly blame us and then who knows what they'll do. They're placid now, but that could easily change. One thing we have to do is get out of here and I reckon we've got maybe a day before they see the symptoms.'

'Then what? There're only two of us and we have to get past that fucking gang.'

'If I got the virus from them, then they're probably all infected by now and they'll know it. If we're lucky they'll start killing the infected ones one by one when the virus shows itself. Maybe there aren't many of them left by now.'

'And maybe there are,' said Louise.

'We've got to take a chance. Staying here isn't an option.'

Louise looked down at her arm and brushed away the blood from the injection before saying, 'then what? After we get out of here and get past the marauding gangs, how am I supposed to get back into the bunker? That place is guarded. It can repel armies. We don't stand a chance.'

'They know you Louise. You're the ace in the pack. Bill probably needs you, just like he needs everyone in the bunker so I don't think getting you inside'll be a problem. We just need to find a way of telling them who you are before they. Well.'

'Before they kill me?' she said.

'Yes. Before they kill you. And me.'

She took in a deep breath whilst staring at him and said, 'let's do it.'

CHAPTER 18 (THEA)

The fuel tanker explored, releasing its deadly contents into the hanger, killing those that couldn't get away fast enough. As nature dictates, the slow and the weak were the ones that perished and only the strong survived. That's how evolution works and this was a speeded up version of it.

The young and the old. Those in the latter stages of the virus. Those with injuries and unable to move quickly. Those desperately trying to save their children. All perished. But some survived. The fit and healthy and the ones further away from the blast site were able to run to safety, ignoring the plight of others around them. Even though they'd built up a community spirit in the hanger, the desire to survive superseded the needs of others.

Thea was one of the lucky ones. She was close to the blast site, but saw what was going to happen and those extra few seconds gave her a head start. Her kids were close by and on the route to safety so she didn't have to waste time looking for them. She grabbed them by the arms and dragged them along with all the strength of a desperate mother, barging past people who were still trying to make sense of what was happening. She was trying to warn them. Trying to get them to run, but her main focus was on saving herself and her kids.

She heard the blast and stumbled forward, falling on her face whilst still clinging to her kids. She was close to the kitchen area and heaved her kids to safety behind a cabinet before following them. Others had made the same journey and were huddled behind the same cabinet, covering their heads with their arms as though that would save them from the inferno.

Thea instinctively lay over her kids to protect them, just before flames roared overhead and to the side. They danced threateningly in an attempt to get behind the cabinet, but the force of the blast drove the flames on, keeping them safe. The noise and the heat were overpowering and an unfamiliar smell filled her nostrils. She suspected it was burning flesh.

The initial rush of the blast subsided, but not the danger. Everything was ablaze, including the far side of the cabinet they were still hiding behind. She stood up to see scorched lifeless bodies littering the hanger floor. They were all laying in the direction pointing away from the blast site and Thea's initial thought was relief for them as their hell had ended.

She started to cough un-controllably, before ducking back down behind the cabinet again for relief.

'We have to get out of here,' she said to the petrified faces looking at her. Her kids still lay on the floor and sat up when she spoke. She continued, 'the truck's left a hole in the wall. It's our only escape route. 'You've got to be brave and do as I tell you. Understand.'

They both nodded frantically. Her tone was authoritative. This wasn't the time for comforting words saying everything would be ok.

She stood up again whilst covering her nose and mouth with her arm to minimise exposure to the smoke.

A door led from the kitchen area to a cupboard where clean blankets were stored, one of the few luxuries given to them by the village. She opened it and flung the blankets into the kitchen area.

'Wet them under the tap,' she shouted in a muffled voice in between her coughing fits.

There were about five people crouched behind the cabinet and they all grabbed a blanket and stood up, making a beeline for the kitchen sink, but got in each other's way.

'One at a time,' shouted Thea whilst getting up and pushing through until she was at the sink. She looked back and continued, 'put the blankets in a pile behind me.'

She turned the tap on, praying that it still worked. The water came gushing out and she quickly put the plug in. She turned around again to see a pile of blankets sitting on the floor. She grabbed them and threw them into the water, thankful that the basin was big enough to accommodate them.

She waited impatiently as the water slowly seeped into the fabric, whilst continued to cover her nose and mouth to protect her lungs from the deadly smoke. She looked back briefly to see others doing the same. There were more people. Maybe another five.

'Get more blankets,' she said to the person nearest.

She got the wet blankets out of the sink and started handing them out, then put the new batch in the waiting water.

'Put the blankets over your heads,' she shouted in a muffled voice.

They all complied and Thea was a little disappointed that they were so reliant on her. The sense of responsibility lay heavy on her again, but her kids were the priority and she had to remember that.

She found a large blanket in the second batch and took it out of the sink, pushing through the crowd to see her kids cowering on the ground and coughing furiously. The guilt ate into her. Why hadn't she stayed at the bothy. She'd been so selfish. So desperate to find her husband and seek human company, ignoring the risks.

She got herself together and grabbed them both by the arms, yanking them up and putting the blanket over the three of them. She lifted one end up so she could see out and turned around to see the others who were by now all similarly covered by blankets.

'Follow me,' she said turning back round again and tentatively walking forward.

The fire had taken hold by now and the coughing reached a crescendo, but Thea focused on the journey to freedom. Thankfully the blanket was hiding some of the horrors around her.

The flames were feeding off the easily combustible materials which lay to the edge of the hanger, leaving the middle safe for now, but Thea knew it wouldn't be long before the deadly flames spread out and engulfed the whole hanger. She picked up her pace. The flames were getting closer.

'Help,' said some from behind followed by uncontrolled coughing again.

Thea looked back to see a blanket completely covering someone who'd collapsed on the floor. Some were trying to lift up the body, but the smoke had sapped their strength. She had to make an instant decision. An easy decision. They couldn't halt their progress and the majority had to survive. She looked around and found a large pan. Picking it up, she smashed it down hard onto the prone body until there was no movement, whilst her kids looked on in horror. Lance started to cry. But she felt no guilt. She was doing them a favour.

She grabbed him by the arm, shook him and yelled, 'shut up.'

The effort made her succumb to un-controlled coughing again. Lance looked at the pan as though he thought she was going to use it on him and stopped crying immediately. She dropped it and continued her journey, the others followed without questioning what she'd done.

The tanker had been blown apart. Most of the blast had gone into the hanger, but the hanger doors were now swinging loosely from their hinges, suggesting the blast had also gone the other way.

She made a beeline for the doors. A blast of fresh air from outside hit her arms which still held the blanket up. She looked to the side and the brightness filtering through the blanket was a lot more vivid, suggesting the flames were getting closer. The blanket hissed and a sharp pain hit her arm as some of the flames touched the blanket, but it did its job. She smelt the steam, knowing it wouldn't be long before the protective water would evaporate, leaving her and the kids to a certain and painful death. Would she witness them being burnt alive?

She expunged the thought from her head and looked straight ahead through the blanket still giving her tunnel vision towards the target. The inky blackness outside was starting to dominate her vision. She was getting closer. She was in sight of freedom. Any concern for those behind her had gone. The hope of escape was her priority now, even though that would only mean a prolonged death as the virus ate into her body tissues.

She tried to pick up the pace, but the kids made it difficult. Shadows appeared on either side of the blanket as those behind darted past her in their desire to reach freedom. She was soon at the back, unable to see past the crowd in front. She was close. So close. Then a blast of cool air hit her face. More fresh air from outside. She ran past what was left of the tanker and then the doors which hung precariously from the hinges.

Freedom. She was outside. She heard a crashing noise and a whoosh of hot air as the hanger doors finally collapsed and fell to the ground, giving her full sight of the inferno inside. A wall of bright light engulfed the hanger and the flames danced around, rising from the open doorway and reaching into the sky. The temperature rose significantly and she turned her back, grateful that the blanket still gave her some protection. She looked ahead to see the others continuing to run and followed, desperate to get as far away as possible. To safety.

The herd ahead suddenly stopped, allowing her to catch up. They all turned around and looked back in horror, apart from Thea whose was looking down at her kids. She threw the blanket away and they sucked in the fresh air, causing them to cough again as the smoke in their lungs finally cleared, replaced by fresh air.

The look on their faces haunted her. They looked petrified. Petrified of their mother and not what they'd just run from. Fearful of crying or showing any emotions that would prompt retribution from their mother. The guilt sapped her strength and her face crumpled as she tried to hold back the tears.

'Sorry,' she whispered.

The kids burst into tears and Thea soon followed.

....

They'd walked a few hundred yards down the wide tarmac track and were sitting on a grassy bank, looking at the fire slowly eat away the hanger. In the few minutes since their escape, calm had descended over the group and there was a feeling of relief, mixed with sadness for those who'd died. Death was a common occurrence in the hanger and they'd got used to it to a certain extent, but the loss of so many had hit them hard.

This was the first time Thea had had a chance to look at the survivors. She recognised all of them, but couldn't remember their names. Now wasn't the time to ask, she concluded. One person still had the blanket over their heads and seemed to be looking down at their feet. They eventually took the blanket off.

'Judy,' whispered Thea, respectful of those who wanted quiet reflection.

Judy looked up, smiled and nodded before putting her head back down.

Thea didn't pursue a conversation, but knew that decisions had to be made soon. It was then that she realised the numbers had shrunk. There should've been 13, including her and the kids. One had died during the escape. Murdered, thought Thea momentarily regretting what she'd done. She soon got herself together and quickly counted. There were only nine left and five of those were men, leaving her and Judy as the only surviving female adults. More must've died during the escape, she concluded.

The distant lights twinkled as they slowly moved along the road. Vehicle lights? Thea remained seated and stretched her back and neck to see, before standing up and squinting in a desperate attempt to make out what was happening. Her kids had fallen to sleep next to her and the disturbance didn't even affect their rhythmic breathing.

'What's that?' said, Judy following Thea's eye line.

'Trouble.'

'They're coming from the village,' said Judy.

Everyone was by now looking down the track at the approaching vehicles.

'We've got to get out of here,' said a man. 'They're here to finish us off.'

'No,' said Thea. 'They're too scared of the virus to come back. They must've assumed the fire's killed everyone.'

'So why're they coming back?' said the man.

Thea stood silently for a few seconds before saying, 'they must've heard the explosion. Maybe they weren't expecting it and are coming back check it out.'

'But they left the tanker next to the hanger and must've known it would go up at some point,' said Judy.

'Maybe they forgot they left it there,' said Thea. 'Anyway it doesn't matter. They're coming and you're right,' she said looking at the man, 'we've got to get out of here.'

She looked down the valley for an escape route. The road followed the contour of the hill and there was a shallow valley on one side with a river running through it, swollen from the frequent heavy showers. The hill rose sharply on the other side. There was no tree cover and the inky blackness had been replaced by light from the full moon which had emerged from the clearing clouds.

'The valley is the only way out and they'll see us,' said the man looking at Thea and noticing her bewildered look. He continued realising her awkwardness, 'my name's Devon Scuttlebuck.'

'So what d'we do?' said Thea sounding unsure for the first time.

Devon looked around and said, 'get off the road to start off with. That rock over there,' he said pointing further down the track. 'We can hide behind it.'

They all mustered their weary bodies and stood up, shuffling down the track towards the rock and squatting behind it, even though it was easily tall enough to hide them.

'Everyone keep quiet,' he said. 'When they've gone past, we can head down the valley.'

'And what do we do when we get to the village? How do we know they won't turn around straight away and see us walking along?' said another man.

'I don't know the answers,' said Devon. 'All I know is that we've no choice.'

No one spoke whilst they all thought about another way out. One by one their shoulders slumped as they realised there was no alternative. They all turned their attention to the approaching vehicles, listening for the sound of wheels on tarmac and the whirring of electric motors.

They were about a quarter of a mile away from the hanger, but the noise from the inferno still made it difficult to hear anything. Devon tentatively poked his head around the corner, then quickly recoiled.

Looking over at Thea he said, 'they've stopped?'

'Can we get away?'

'No. Not without being seen.'

Thea cursed her luck. Why'd they have to stop there? A hundred yards further on they would've turned a corner, letting them escape without being seen. She poked her head out and saw the rear of the vehicle, before slowly moving further around the rock until she saw everything.

There were two vehicles, but she couldn't see anyone inside. The light from the fire gave her good vision so she was confident there was no one inside. She slowly walked to the other side of the rock until she would've been in full view, should anyone still be in the vehicles. Nothing. She eventually stepped out to see five figures in the familiar masks walking towards the inferno. They were fanned out across the road and verges and their heads were moving around as though looking for something.

She looked back and said, 'they're walking towards the fire. This is our chance. Come on.'

Everyone rose from their squatted positions and followed Thea. A few yards from the rock, Devon stopped, looked across at the vehicles and then started walking quickly towards them.

'Come on. We can use them,' he said.

Everyone started to follow him, apart from Thea.

'Stop,' she said resisting the temptation to shout. 'We can't. We have to walk.'

'Why?' said Devon sounding perplexed.

'If we take it, they'll know we're alive. It's safer if they think we're dead.'

Devon immediately ceded, realising the logic of what she was saying.

'Let's get going,' said Thea, hoping to quell any further discussion. 'We need to get through the village.'

'Then what?' said Judy.

'Trust me. I know somewhere where we'll be safe.'

She quickly walked off, not wanting to say anymore. They followed in silence. Devon stayed at the rear constantly looking around at the vehicles until they went around the corner and out of sight. Thea cursed herself. What a stupid thing to say. They'd never be safe. Never be free from the virus until it took them.

CHAPTER 19 (BILL)

Two days had passed without incident. There was no sign that their hideout had been found and things had calmed down since the time of their escape. Sleep had been intermittent because of fears for their safety and they both had concerns on what'd happened in the bunker.

'I can't believe they haven't found this place,' said Samantha.

'They're probably still checking out the place. Anyway, we're no longer a threat so why should they bother.'

'Because we're lose ends and they won't stop until they find us.'

Bill shrugged and said, 'as I said, there's security here which'll give us plenty of time to escape,' he said nodding towards the exit tunnel.

An image of the creature flashed inside his head. He was standing and immediately slumped to the floor, finally sitting with his legs to the side and leaning on one arm. His mouth was slightly open and he was staring at the floor, but not really looking at it. The creature was too vivid.

'What's wrong?' said Samantha looking concerned as she walked the few steps towards him.

He didn't have the energy to respond and continued to stare at the ground. The creature dominated all his senses. It was inside him. No longer the benign experiment it once was. It had hold of his conscious, trying to tell him something. Trying to tell him what to do, but the message was blurred. Its mouth was moving in slow motion and the words came out like one unintelligible deep echo that fluctuated with the slow opening and closing of the creature's mouth.

The image eventually faded and disappeared, leaving him exhausted. He looked up to see Samantha with a concerned look on her face.

'What was that all about?' she said.

He shook his head without saying anything and slowly got up, whilst thinking about what he was going to say. How could he explain what he'd just experienced, so he decided not to.

'Just felt a bit wheezy, that's all.'

Her security training told her it was a lie, but she decided not to pursue it.

'We can't just stay here,' she said turning around instinctively towards the exit tunnel.

'And we can't go out there. It'll be mayhem. There'll be desperate people doing anything to avoid the virus. And you know about the weather. The climate's changing quicker than anyone thought so if the virus doesn't get them, the weather will. And it'll get us as well.'

She turned back to face him and said, 'so we can't go outside and we can't go back in?'

'You're not stupid. You know that and I know that. We just have to stick it out in here. It's not ideal, but we've no choice. We just have to see what happens.'

'We need to create our own destiny. Not wait for someone to make it for us.'

Bill stared at her for a short while, knowing how she felt then said, 'I agree. We need to do something, only if it's just for our morale.' He looked at the exit tunnel and continued, 'let's see if the exit tunnel's clear. If they do find us. we'll need a clear run to the outside world.'

She looked at the dark abyss and said, 'it'll be good for us. Anything's better than sitting here doing nothing. I assume there's lighting in there?'

'It's activated by movement and turns off when we've gone past.'

She nodded and said, 'right. How far is it? What d'we need to take?' she said looking around enthusiastically.

Bill looked at her. The sparkle was back in her eyes and her demeanour was totally different. For the first time he saw her as a woman and liked what he was seeing. The prolonged look betraying what he was feeling.

She held his stare, then looked away looking confused. Her job had turned her into a robot and she couldn't process or understand such emotions.

'It's about six miles. It'll take us to the mainland,' said Bill getting himself together.

'Great. At least we'll be able to check the exit's clear. Then we can decide what to do.'

'We're coming back here, that's what we're doing,' said Bill assertively.

She ignored him and said, 'let's get going.'

She picked up two large rucksacks and busily filled them with food, weapons and general kit for surviving on the mainland.

'We don't need all that for a day trip to the exit and back.'

'You never know,' she said eventually closing both rucksacks and standing to face him.

She'd already made plans, he thought. But Bill wasn't about to argue. If she wanted to go then she's welcome. He simply wasn't the survival type, preferring political battles, not physical battles. Samantha on the other hand would relish the challenge, her training would've prepared her, but not him.

'Come on then,' he said grabbing a rucksack and walking towards the tunnel.

Within a few yards a light came on showing some of the path ahead. They walked tentatively down the tunnel, looking ahead into the dark abyss, then another light came on.

'Was this tunnel just for you? Seems a bit elaborate just for one person,' said Samantha.

'I was the only one who knew about it.'

'What about those who built it?'

'A machine built it. That's why it looks like a cave. It just tunnelled its way through.'

'You sure no one else knows?'

'I'm sure. And yes, this tunnel is just for me and anyone else I deem important enough to use it. It's a contingency. I never expected to use it.'

'And I'm important enough?'

'You were in the right place at the right time. Look Samantha. This thing's not here to save my life. It's here to re-group should anything go wrong in the bunker and it has. I was expecting more than two people to use it.'

'Ok. Ok. I believe you.'

The next light came on lighting up the tunnel further ahead. They continued in silence for another five minutes before the next light that came on, then went off making them both spin around. They looked at each other briefly before carrying on.

....

An hour passed and they were over half way. Their keenness to get the job done and confirm the exit was clear made them quicken their pace.

They both turned around at the same time as though their instincts told them something was wrong. A light was shining dimly in the distance, way beyond the last one that'd turned off for them. In between, the inky blackness persisted.

'What's that?' said Bill.

Samantha said nothing, preferring to focus on the distant light.

Bill continued, 'maybe some animal.'

'I don't think so,' said Samantha in a monotone voice.

Another light came on, then another.

'It's coming for us and it's moving fast,' she said taking off her rucksack and searching desperately for a weapon.

Bill did the same, periodically looking up to see more lights coming on. It was getting closer. The light was flickering as images danced around. Both were holding their weapons in anticipation of an imminent attack.

Samantha turned to Bill and said, 'we need to run. We'll stand a better chance if we can get outside and pick them off as they come out.'

She turned and ran before Bill had a chance to respond. He followed. She ran purposely without looking behind, not wanting to do anything that would slow her progress. Bill wasn't as calm, frequently looking behind. She was getting further ahead. He had to run faster, but his fitness levels weren't good. His breathing was becoming laboured and the sweat stung his eyes. He wasn't going to make it. He looked behind yet again. There was hardly any darkness between the two sets of lights now and he braced himself for an attack from behind as he continued to stumble along. Samantha was by now a long way ahead, but seemed to have stopped. She'd reached the end, he concluded. The door to freedom. There were no sophisticated locks on the door, just a simple handle that needed to be pushed down. The security focused on stopping people coming in, not going out.

The outside light engulfed the tunnel, nullifying the artificial light. Bill was in sight of freedom. His eyes squinted as they adjusted to the brightness. The unfamiliar waft of hot air was a sign that he was almost there. He didn't have time to analyse what was happening. How had their pursuers got through the security measures he'd put in place? How were they catching up so fast? Why hadn't a shot been fired? His sole focus was on survival.

Samantha was outside and had quickly found a high point behind a rock a few yards from the door. Claiming the high ground was a sound tactic and gave her the advantage. She still had hold of her weapon and was crouched behind the rock, looking down at the door, hoping that Bill would be the first one to come out. Oh how she cursed him for being slower than her. Oh how she cursed her conscience and training for telling her not to continue running and save herself. It was her duty to protect others she reminded herself before remembering that she'd opened the door, condemning her security men and women to their deaths. They would've died anyway she placated herself with.

She squatted down behind the rock, her weapon pointing towards the open door. She was a long way ahead of Bill so expected to wait a few more seconds. The silence was deafening. Why was there no sound? Any noise in the tunnel was exaggerated, but there was nothing. Absolutely nothing. If Bill had been killed, she would've expected some noise. A squeal. Gunshots. If he'd escaped then he should've appeared by now. She should've just run. Given him up for dead, but the unanswered questions gnawed away at her.

CHAPTER 20 (HARVEY)

'Everything ok?' asked Maggie. 'Couldn't help hearing you.'

Harvey had forgotten that someone had overheard them arguing and feared they'd grasped what they were arguing about.

He smiled in an attempt to disguise his worries and said, 'lovers tiff. That's all. We've had a tough time lately and this is the first time we've had to. Well. Discuss things I suppose,' he said continuing to smile.

Maggie returned the smile and said, 'everything's pretty safe around here. We've got a good life and plenty of food. We grow most of it and the men go out hunting sometimes.'

'Yeh,' said Louise looking around. 'And a good source of water.'

They'd come out of the bedroom and were in a large communal area in the house. Maggie had been the first to greet them, the others were busying themselves getting food ready. The room was modern, but had none of the appliances most homes used to have. There was a large wooden table in the middle with chairs all around it and a kitchen area to one side, giving it a rustic, farmhouse like charm, despite the modern design of the house.

Maggie continued, 'I'm Maggie and they are, Grant, Teresa and Jack,' she said pointing them out as she introduced them.

They all smiled and nodded.

'Louise and Harvey,' said Louise smiling.

'Yes. Spencer told us your names. We didn't want to disturb you last night when we came back from the fields. Thought you'd probably be a bit tired.'

'Thanks,' said Louise. 'We were a bit. You've got everything sorted here,' she said looking around and hoping to divert attention away from them.

'Yes. We've got Spencer to thank for that. He's very practical and very fair. Things have got very bad in the past few years. What, with the weather and the virus. Others haven't been so lucky.'

'You've made your own luck,' said Harvey sounding impressed.

'I suppose so. We don't get much trouble at the moment, but some may want what we've got. Spencer thinks that the best way to defend yourself is to welcome newcomers, not fight them. It's worked so far and the more people we have, the more chance we have of defending ourselves if things get nasty'

'Makes sense,' said Louise nodding. 'What about the risk of infection?'

Louise immediately regretted her question, knowing that they'd probably given them the virus.

'This area's clear of infection. Most people went north so there aren't many left now. I don't think anyone'll come south again and bring the virus with them. Where're you from?'

Oh how wrong they are, thought Harvey. A strong northerly wind could easily transport the virus south.

They obviously didn't know about the dangers of the virus or how transmissible it was.

Harvey said, 'we're from the island.'

'What. The Isle of Wight?'

'Yes,' said Harvey regretting his admission and hoping for no further questions.

'That place is well guarded. I've heard that's where the government is.'

'It is,' said Louise not wanting to elaborate further.

Maggie looked at her suspiciously and said, 'you're that pretty one. The home secretary. Louise umm.'

'Gardiner,' said Louise concluding there was no point denying it.

'That's right. But what're you doing here? And who's he?'

'Harvey. Harvey Burton,' he said as though reluctantly admitting his name.

She stared at him for a while and said nothing as though she was trying to remember something.

'He came from the island as well,' said Louise.

'Yes. Yes I've heard that name before. And you look familiar.'

'He's our chief environmental scientist,' said Louise

'Yes. That's right,' said Maggie. 'You've been on TV a lot.'

'Not anymore,' said Harvey.

'No,' said Maggie. 'Everything's gone wrong. You didn't predict this did you,' she said as though blaming him for climate change.

'I did,' said Harvey defensively, 'but not this quickly. It'll take hundreds of years before things start calming down.'

Harvey cursed himself for being negative. These people had been through enough and the last thing they needed was more bad news.

Maggie shrugged and said, 'every day's a bonus then. Let's eat.'

Harvey was impressed by Maggie's attitude. Telling her about the virus would probably result in a different reaction.

Maggie beckoned them to sit down and the rest joined, bringing bowls of porridge. Louise skilfully steered the conversation to their hosts to understand how they lived. All lead normal lives in the old world with jobs that had a practical side to them, which was probably the reason why they were flourishing. They seemed quite happy with their lot, dismissing the luxuries of their previous lives as something that wasn't important anymore.

They had fears for the future, particularly the worsening weather and Harvey hadn't done much to allay their fears. But he did offer practical measures to counteract the effects of the weather and they all sat enthralled by his suggestions.

'You must stay,' said Teresa. 'You can help us and life here is good.'

She seemed to be making the offer to Harvey, making Louise feel a bit awkward.

‘I have family up North,’ said Harvey. ‘I need to find them.’

‘But the virus. We’ve heard the virus is rampant up there. Sorry, I didn’t mean to scare you. Your family I mean. I’m sure they’ll be all right,’ said Teresa awkwardly.

Harvey held his arms up and said, ‘I know the risks, but I have to know.’

‘Anyway,’ said Maggie changing the subject. ‘You’re welcome to stay as long as you want.’ She paused a bit before continuing. ‘Is that why you escaped from the island? To find your family. Is escape the right word?’ she quizzed.

Her tone had changed a little, sounding suspicious about why he was here.

Louise said, ‘look. It’s a government establishment where key people are held up.’

Maggie interrupted, ‘which key people?’

Louise looked across at Harvey, who nodded and said, ‘you may as well tell them everything. Go and get Spencer.’

Louise told them about the virus and the climate and that the bunker was there to save key people so they could re-populate when the virus had run its course and start again. She didn’t tell them about the vaccine, saying that the bunker alone would protect them.

‘So you chose to take a risk?’ asked Spencer looking at Harvey.

‘I can’t live without my family so this is no risk at all to me.’

‘And you Louise?’ said Spencer.

I'm not here by choice, she said looking over at Harvey. 'He used me as a hostage for his escape.'

'Not a hostage,' said Harvey. 'Insurance should anything go wrong.'

'But it didn't go wrong so I've been of no use to you. I'm here for no reason apart from your insurance,' she said angrily.

'Is that what you were arguing about? In the bedroom,' said Maggie.

Both tried to hide their relief, realising that Maggie hadn't heard what they were really talking about.

'Yes,' said Louise angrily.

Spencer glared at Maggie and said, 'you didn't tell me.'

Maggie's eyes danced around nervously as though looking for an excuse.

'I was going to tell you after breakfast,' she said nervously.

Spencer continued to glare before turning to Louise and saying with an alarmed look on his face, 'so what you're saying is this is all for nothing. The virus'll get us.'

Louise's diplomatic training was telling her what to say. Waffle. Avoid the question. Blame someone. But this wasn't the time or place.

'Yes.'

'But the bunker is a safe place?'

'Yes,' said Harvey. 'That's your only chance.'

Spencer looked at him suspiciously and said, 'but you prefer to die with your family.'

'It's not the life for me.'

Harvey instinctively touched the pocket with the life-saving vaccine and recoiled un-naturally, but Spencer didn't seem to notice.

'Haven't others in the bunker got family they need to find or are you just different,' said Spencer.

His tone was becoming more suspicious, totally different to his demeanour when they first arrived.

'They have their close family with them. Close family being spouses and children.'

'Grandchildren?'

'None are old enough for grandchildren.'

'So they just forgot your family did they?'

Harvey had to lie, it didn't come easily to him, but he had to be convincing.

'No. They just couldn't find them before the. Well. Lockdown I suppose.'

'What? You didn't know where they were?'

'No. Look it wasn't good back then. Things were breaking down and the weather. Well you know about the storms. For all I know they're dead, but I have to find out.'

'You wouldn't even know where to start looking.'

'I've got some ideas. They wouldn't let me look when I was in the bunker. They just battened down the hatches and that was it. This isn't important Spencer. You saved our lives and we owe you. It's your only chance. Their defences don't work that well in the storms and there's a good chance you can get through.'

'Through to what? We'll be out-numbered and I doubt they'll welcome us with open arms even if we get past their defences.'

Harvey was floundering. He was suggesting the impossible and Spencer knew it. He looked at Louise for inspiration.

'What else? What aren't you telling me?' said Spencer suspecting he wasn't being told everything.

Louise said, 'you're right Spencer. It is impossible. You won't get into the bunker, but I need you to get me inside.'

He stared into her eyes for any signs of a lie, but she was a politician and therefore well practiced at lying.

'So what's in it for us? Can't you get us inside? You're the home secretary.'

'No I can't. Not even with my help. The bunker is strictly reserved for people who will be of use and they can't risk the virus getting inside.'

'But they'll risk it with you will they? Are you that important?'

'It's no risk with me because I've had the vaccine.'

Spencer stared at her blankly for a few seconds before saying, 'what vaccine?'

Louise said nothing, hoping that Harvey would take up the reigns.

Harvey said, 'I've managed the development of a vaccine that gives 100% protection with no need for boosters. All those in the bunker have been vaccinated, including me and Louise. We're safe. You're not.'

'So why haven't they given it to us then?'

'There's not enough. It's only just been developed and there's no chance of producing enough before the virus wipes everyone out. Anyway, there's no infrastructure to distribute it.'

Spencer looked away whilst he digested the information.

'I don't believe you. We've had no cases here.'

'That's because it's sparsely populated in the south, but it'll get here eventually. That gang you saved us from. Someone had symptoms and there's a good chance they passed it on. Check for small blisters or mild cold symptoms. Coughs. That sort of thing.'

Spencer looked across at Maggie and she said, 'I know who picked them up. I'll check.'

Spencer returned his attention to Harvey and said, 'so we're dead if we have the virus. So I ask again. What's in it for us?'

'If you don't have it now, you will get it,' said Harvey. 'But the vaccine'll also cure anyone who's infected.'

'So that's the deal is it? We get Louise inside the bunker and those inside willingly give us the vaccine. Bollocks. That's not going to happen is it?'

'I took some with me when I escaped.'

Louise shouts, 'Harvey, don't tell them anymore. That's our.....'

'Of course I'm not going to tell them where I hid it for fuck's sake,' said Harvey interrupting to stop her saying any more.

He turned his attention to Spencer and continued, 'I stole some when I escaped, but hid it when that gang attacked us. Only I know where it's hidden and I'll show you when Louise is safely inside.'

'How do I know I can trust you?' said Spencer warily.

'How do I know I can trust you?' replied Harvey.

They stared at each other for what seemed like an eternity, whilst they thought about the situation and their options.

Harvey eventually said, 'look Spencer. If I'd any sense I would've easily slipped out last night, picked up the vaccine and gone looking for my family. As you may've guessed, the vaccine I stole is for them. I could've left Louise here with no chance of getting back into the bunker and left you to the mercy of the virus. But I didn't did I? Because I'm not that sort of bloke. I'm trying to help you and Louise.'

A few seconds passed before Spencer said tentatively, 'ok. Maybe you're right.'

I took 500 doses, more than enough for everyone here and my family.

Maggie burst through the door and said with tears in her eyes, 'they've got it Spencer. They've got the virus. Small blisters that they hadn't noticed.'

CHAPTER 21 (THEA)

They reached the village, looking down at the lights twinkling in the distance.

Thea turned around to the group following and said, 'does anyone know how we can get around without being seen?'

The village sat towards the bottom of the valley where the sides climbed steeply on both sides. There was one road out to civilisation and one road up to the hanger. The rest were dirt tracks. The tracks following the contour of the hills represented a huge risk of being seen as there were no trees or rocks to hide behind. Going over the top was a possibility, but some were fit enough to escape the inferno, but she doubted if they could cope with the rigours of the climb. Her instinct was to give it a go and leave anyone behind who couldn't make it. Her compassion said they needed a solution which kept them together, even if it represented a greater risk.

The moon was hidden behind the clouds again, although it still gave out some light, meaning it wasn't pitch black. They heard a noise behind.

Thea hurriedly looked around and said, 'quick. Get behind the bank.'

A bank had been built on one side to stop water cascading down the mountain and ruining the road. A military road was something worth saving, roads and tracks for civilian use were not.

They squatted behind the bank and watched the vehicles trudge by quietly. The fuel truck that rammed into the door would suggest that an attempt to escape had been made, but what were their conclusions? Did they assume that the subsequent blast killed everyone, or did they think some had escaped? Thea erred on the side of caution and assumed the latter, in which case measures would be taken.

When they'd passed and were out if sight, she got up and walked purposely down the road, ushering her kids to do the same. The others followed without question, suggesting they still trusted her leadership.

The road swung left and right as it followed the shape of the mountain. After about a quarter of a mile, Thea stopped as they rounded a corner and stepped back a little. Those behind almost ran into each other before they realised.

'What's going on?' said Devon.

'We're close enough to see what's going on.'

'Well. What's going on then?'

Thea slowly crept around the corner until she could clearly see what was happening, confident that the light from the village wasn't strong enough to reach them.

She turned around and whispered to Devon, 'they're stationery on the main street. They were up at the hanger a long time so they may've been looking for survivors.'

'They won't have found any,' said Morag.

'That doesn't mean they think no one's escaped. We've got to convince them we're all dead so they'll stop looking.'

'How d'we do that?' said Morag.

'By keeping hidden,' said Devon. 'It's the only way. They'll eventually give up and assume everyone's dead.'

But that may take days, even weeks before they stop looking. We've no food or anything,' said Morag.

'Listen,' said Thea. 'I know a place. We just need to get to it. Once we're there we'll be safe. There's no way they'll guess we'll be there. All we need to do is get past the village.'

'Where is it?' said Morag sounding frustrated.

Devon said, 'it doesn't matter. I trust Thea and if anyone doesn't. Well they may as well fuck off now.'

Silence descended. Devon went ahead of the group and looked around the corner. People had got out of the vehicles and were talking.

He looked back and said with his eyes wide open, 'there were more up at the hanger. Either they're still up there or they're walking back to see if any've escaped. Quick we need to hide.'

Everyone looked around for somewhere to hide.

'Climb. We need to climb up the mountain side,' said Thea.

'No they'll see us. There's no cover,' said Devon

'Then let's go back up the track so we can climb without being seen.'

'But we may meet them,' said Devon. 'Then we'll have no time to hide.'

'But they may've stayed at the hanger and not be walking back, said Thea'

'We can't take that risk.'

'What then?' said Thea raising her voice slightly I frustration.

'The only way is down and maybe now is the best time.' Devon looked down at the village again and continued, 'everyone's coming out of their houses. They'll be distracted. That's our best chance.'

Thea said, 'we don't want to give them the virus though.'

Devon looked at her with incredulously and said, 'they tried to burn us alive.'

'They're desperate. Whose to say any of us wouldn't have done the same.'

Devon looked at the group who looked blankly at him. There was no fight in them. They were simply tagging along without complaining or indeed saying anything at all. They looked dead already.

'Ok. Ok,' he said, Devon sounding resigned. He looked up into the sky and continued, 'there's a storm brewing. If we're lucky, it'll be here in the next few hours.'

'Lucky?' said Morag as though questioning him.

'Yes. Lucky. If it's bad enough, they'll stay inside, giving us a chance to get through without being seen. And I think it will be bad enough,' said Devon looking up to the sky again.

'What about those walking back down the track?' said Thea.

They'll see the storm coming so will be wanting to get back rather than looking for us. The cloud'll thicken, so there'll be no moonlight. We stand a good chance. Look, if we all lay flat behind the bank, the only way they'll see us is if they come looking and I don't think they will.' He looked over at one of the men and continued, you. 'Go back to the last corner and tell us if you see anything. It'll give us time to hide.'

'Terry's the name,' he said looking a little annoyed.

'Sorry. Yes sorry. Terry,' said Devon sounding a little impatient.

Terry, like the others, had been quiet and offered nothing since the escape from the hanger. Now was not the time for resistance.

Terry thought about saying something else, but soon chose not to and did as instructed.

Once Devon saw he was on his way, he returned his attention to the village. It looked like everyone was out on the street discussing something. Some were looking into the sky, probably thinking the same as him.

Devon turned to face them again and said, 'sit on the bank so you're ready to hide behind it if we need to.'

All did as instructed, apart from Thea who remained with Devon. She was glad someone had taken up the reigns and that the others seemed to be ok with it. She wasn't familiar with the village so was grateful that Devon seemed willing to take them through

'D'you think we stand a chance?' said Thea.

Devon looked up at the sky again and said, 'it's not them we have to worry about. It's the storm.'

'But we've no shelter anyway, so we may as well give it a go.'

Devon nodded and said, 'I know.'

....

The storm gathered pace and the meagre moonlight had long gone. As expected, the men had walked past, eager to get back to the village before the storm took hold, meaning they weren't searching for them. So good so far, thought Devon as he looked down at the deserted streets. They'd even moved their vehicles off the road and into garages or other buildings that gave them protection from the elements.

The winds had increased significantly in the last hour and it wouldn't be long before the rain followed. Daylight hadn't yet made an appearance and the grey clouds added to the gloom and the now familiar feeling of disaster and destruction.. The rain was still holding off, but the darkness intensified in the distance, meaning that darker clouds and rain would soon arrive. It was warm and humid and would not doubt stay that way until the storm had passed by, at which point they'd cool a little before heating up again ready for the next deluge.

Most were behind the bank in case more men were spotted coming back from the hanger and also to hide from the increasing winds. Terry was still on the lookout and had found a vantage point behind a rock that also gave him some shelter from the elements. Devon and Thea were looking down at the village.

'We have to make a move now before the weather gets too bad and we can't walk,' said Devon.

'What about when we get to the other side?' said Thea shouting so she could be heard above the noise of the increasing wind.

'There'll be more shelter from the wind there. Let's get back.'

They both made their way back to the bank where everyone was still huddled down. Lance was cradling his sister and they were both looking forlorn, but neither cried or moaned, knowing there was no point. Attention just wasn't on the cards. Thea felt a swathe of guilt, but grateful that they weren't causing problems.

Devon remained on top of the bank waiving furiously towards Terry who eventually saw him and started walking back unsteadily as the wind buffeted him.

When he eventually arrived and settled in Thea said, 'this is our chance now to get through the village. You know it's our best chance. But we've got to stick together. No one's going to be left behind. No one. Do you understand?

All nodded their agreement. She continued, 'Devon's going to take us through, so we all need to do as he says. Are you ok with that Devon?'

He nodded and smiled a little as though grateful that he'd been formally asked.

Devon said, 'the wind's coming from behind us so when we get down to the village, it'll be coming from the rear right. We'll go to the left so the wind takes the virus away from the village. We don't want to infect them.'

'Fuck them,' said Terry. 'They tried to burn us alive.'

Thea screamed at the top of her voice. 'Devon. Is. The. Boss.'

Terry immediately backed down.

'It's the best way around anyway,' continued Devon. 'Once we swing around the other side up the other valley, the hill should give us some shelter from the wind and rain.' He waited a few seconds to give them a chance to come up with a better plan. There were no dissenters, so he continued, 'we need to go now before it gets too bad. He looked over at one of the men and said, 'you carry Lance, I'll carry Nicola. Hand over to someone else if you get tired.'

The man nodded and with that Devon picked up Nicola and walked quickly and purposely down the track towards the village. The man picked up Lance and they all followed.

The wind battered them, but Devon didn't slow the pace, knowing it was critical that they got to the other side quickly. He looked behind occasionally to see that some, especially the women, were frequently being blown to one side as the gusts hit them, meaning their pace had slowed.

'Keep up,' he shouted. He waited for them to catch up before continuing, 'women walk on the sheltered side of the men and let's keep together.'

They continued, soon reaching the outskirts of the village. The only artificial light now was coming from the cracks in outside shutters which had been closed to prevent windows being smashed from flying debris. Devon felt the first splashes of rain hit his face.

He looked back and said, 'hurry. Follow me.'

They continued down the empty street until coming across the first house about 100 yards in front of them.

Devon shouted above the wind noise, 'follow me and stay together.'

He veered off to the left down a side street where the wind behind them was pushing them along, but it gave them some relief from the endless buffeting from the side. He held onto Nicola as she clung onto his neck, burying her head into his chest. The wind was ferocious, making the rain sting the parts of his body that weren't covered by clothes.

He turned right, following a path that went behind the houses, which meant they were buffeted by the wind again. The vegetable plants in the gardens were rocking in the wind, but were easily coping. He past his house, the outside shutters flapping around un-controllably and the darkness inside confirmed it was still empty. His wife and children had succumbed to the virus a few weeks ago, leaving him to mourn. His only hope was that he would soon join them.

'Stop,' said a voice from behind.

Devon stopped and looked around to see the man carrying Lance, hand him over to Terry, he obviously needed a rest He waited a few seconds before carrying on.

There was no light. The black clouds had engulfed the landscape with darkness and Devon was feeling his way down the path. But he was familiar with it and knew exactly where he was going. Knew where safety was. Knew it wouldn't take long.

The village was based around one main street with the odd side road to other properties. However, on this side of the main road, only the river ran behind the houses and the other side was flood plain, meaning no other houses could be built on it.

'Hold onto each other,' he shouted even though the houses were protecting them from some of the wind.

They continued, still crouched down, until they cleared the last house, turning right to join the main road again. The full force of the wind hit them again from the rear right, but it was stronger than before and they all stumbled sideways before regaining their balance.

'Keep going,' he shouted. 'Stay on the road.'

They went past him, whilst he stayed still for a few seconds, looking back to see if there was any sign of life. There was none. Debris was starting to fly around, confirming the wind had picked up, but they were clear now. Clear to make their escape. No one could catch them now. But had someone seen them and, if they had, would a search party be sent out once the weather had passed. He couldn't be sure, but the first hurdle had been cleared. He was sure of that.

The road swept right up the valley and turned into a seldom used dirt track. There was no need for anyone to go up there, the main road to civilisation was at the other end of the village.

After about a quarter of a mile, the wind started to ease and swirl around more as the hill protected them from its full ferocity. Then the road started to climb, following the river that was tumbling down from the valley. Devon was at the front again and stopped when the road started to go up hill.

He turned around and said, 'we need to find shelter.'

Thea was behind him and said, 'I can't see anything. There's nothing here.'

They were all drenched and the cold was starting to take hold, despite the warm temperature. Something that no one was familiar with.

Devon said, 'quick. Lay down on the bank. Hold onto each other to keep warm. Children in the middle.'

They looked a bit confused so Devon grabbed Thea and dragged her to the bank, laying down and beckoning her to do the same. She lay down facing him, with Nicola between them. He reached out his arms and she did the same, moving closer to each other and sandwiching Nicola in between.

'Hold on as tight as you can,' he said.

All three of them were huddled together, retaining the heat. The thick skin on their back more than capable of keeping out the cold. Devon looked up to see others doing the same. Morag took control of Lance, her motherly instincts coming to the fore, and quickly found someone else to make up the threesome. Within a few minutes they were all laid out on the bank, their heads buried into their chests so the breath added to the heat being generated by their bodies.

Devon said to Thea without moving his head, 'it's up to you after this.'

'I know.'

CHAPTER 22 (BILL)

Samantha remained still behind the rock, hardly breathing. It was hotter than inside the cave and she didn't have a cooling suit on, but she was hardy and could easily deal with the pain. Her training in the early days had taught her that.

The temptation to run was overwhelming, but she resisted, knowing that facts had to be gathered before her next move. Bill wasn't essential for her survival, indeed he could be a hindrance, but she had to know what or who was chasing them. She had to know whether it was safe to go back into the sanctuary of the cave.

She eventually rose from her prone position behind the rock, whilst keeping her weapon trained on the opening, ready to react should danger arise. Still no sign of life. She looked around for escape routes in case they were needed, before slowly creeping forward.

The last light automatically turned off as she strode towards the tunnel exit, a sure sign that no one was at the exit at least. She relaxed a little and continued purposely towards the now dark abyss.

She slowed when she got closer, then sprinted to the side of the opening, pressing her body against the rock face and listening intently for any sounds that hinted of what was happening inside. Still nothing. A feeling of impending doom washed over her and a thin film of sweat quickly followed, encouraged by the unfamiliar heat. Her breathing became laboured before she used her training and self-control to calm down and think logically. Now was not the time to freeze should she be confronted by someone.

Going into the tunnel wasn't an option. It was a confined space and the only place to run was the way she'd gone in. She'd be a sitting target. However, the darkness inside suggested there was no one there. But where was Bill?

She quickly looked around the corner, then immediately pulled her head back. There was a distant light, suggesting someone was still there. She took a deep breath a looked around the corner again, this time staying there for a better look. Silhouetted figures stood, hardly moving. She pulled back again, knowing that the outside light would make her head stick out like a sore thumb to anyone inside the tunnel.

The heat bore down on her and she squinted as the sun poked out from behind nearby trees that'd managed to survive the extreme weather. She quickly ignored the discomfort, focusing again on her next move. She had to play a waiting game. Maybe those who'd been chasing them thought they'd got their prey and were now returning to the den. Maybe they knew she was there, but didn't see the point of chasing her.

She looked at the open door on the other side of the tunnel exit. The rock camouflaging it on the outside matched the rock face she was leaning against exactly and she suspected, when closed, no one would know it was there. Then the realisation hit her. They wouldn't leave the door open. Someone would have to come and close it.

It was then that she noticed a dim light coming from the tunnel. How could they've reached the exit so quickly? How long had the light been on before she noticed it? She cursed herself for being distracted by the door, if only for a few seconds.

She heard noises from inside. Scampering. No, it was more than that. Something running at speed. The sound quickly got louder as it got closer.

She moved away from the door, looking back to the rock she was originally hiding behind, then at the other hiding places and escape routes she'd identified before she'd approached the tunnel.

It was too late.

CHAPTER 23 (HARVEY)

Spencer's eyes widened, then he looked across at Harvey and said, 'so we've all got it?'

Harvey nodded without saying anything.

Spencer continued, 'how long before….. Before it takes us?'

'One, maybe two months.'

'And the vaccine'll cure us?'

'Yes,' said Harvey assertively.

Spencer gazed out of the window before turning around and saying, 'I've no regrets. I'm glad we welcomed you and, if you're right, we would've got the virus anyway. But that vaccine gives us hope that we wouldn't have had before'

Harvey shouldn't have felt guilty, but he did. They'd saved him and Louise from the marauding gang and in return they'd brought them the virus. Now he was blackmailing them. Putting them in danger in return for the life-saving drug. They could've tortured him to reveal where the vaccine was, but they probably hadn't even thought about that, he concluded. And it was also his fault for Louise being here. He instinctively started to reach for his pocket again, then stopped himself.

'And we're grateful,' said Louise, realising Harvey was in deep thought.

'Yes. Yes,' said Harvey. 'Once Louise is back in the bunker, then I'll show you where the vaccine is. I promise,' said Harvey staring intently at Spencer to show he was sincere. He continued, 'it'll save your lives and immunity'll passed onto to your off-spring so you could build a good life for yourselves here.'

Spencer maintained the stare, but said nothing. He had so many questions. What about the others living in the area? Didn't they deserve a chance as well? What would happen to them when those in the bunker came into the outside world again? Would they be seen as a threat that needs to be dealt with?

He dismissed his anxieties, concluding that short term risks had to be dealt with first and that meant doing what was needed to get the vaccine.

'Ok. I trust you Harvey. And you Louise,' he said looking at them both. 'I hope you have a plan because I haven't.'

Louise said, 'they regularly patrol the mainland with drones.' Harvey looked at her suspiciously. She continued, 'I'm the home secretary Harvey. Security of the bunker is in my remit. Anyway, as I say, they patrol the mainland for threats. An invasion or anything like that. But they also patrol a pick up point if someone of importance goes missing.'

'And you're that someone'? said Harvey.

Yes I am. Like everyone in that bunker, I'm of use. Why else d'you think I was going there? I would've been the last one to get in. I'd just finalised the security measures,' she said coyly.

'You sound unsure?' said Harvey.

'Well. There're still risks of course. There're a lot of people left on the mainland.'

'Won't they think we're a threat?' said Spencer. 'There aren't that many of us, but we'd be a fairly large group heading towards the island.'

'No,' said Louise. 'I don't need to be taken all the way. Just to a certain point. After that, I can make my own way.'

Harvey looked at her suspiciously then said, 'you sure? Why can't they take you all the way?'

'Because there's no chance of a pick up if there's anyone else close by. I need to be by myself.'

Harvey decided not to pursue it. He turned to Spencer and said, 'and you'll still have me and, as I said. I'll deliver on my promise.'

Spencer turned around to see Maggie and Grant looking at the back of their hands for any signs of the virus, oblivious to the conversation. He did the same and saw a tiny white spot.

'Is this it? Is this the virus?' he said holding out his hand.

Harvey looked intently at his hand, then looked up and nodded.

Spencer continued, 'we'll do it. Thanks for giving us hope Harvey. I understand why you're doing this. You're a kind man and you'll be more than welcome should you decide to stay with us.'

'Thanks,' said Harvey. 'But I'll be on my way afterwards.'

CHAPTER 24 (THEA)

The ferocity of the storm was un-paralleled, but was now waning. They'd spent the whole day walking steadily up the valley, fighting against the wind and rain and grateful that the valley was still giving them some protection from the worst of it. Devon was constantly looking behind to see if they were being pursued. There was no sign, either because they'd managed to get through the village without being seen or the villagers were just happy to let them go.

The kids were exhausted which meant they had to be carried, slowing the group down considerably. The only saving grace was the temperature. Despite the wind and rain, daylight hours had brought warmth that energised them and kept them going. More importantly, there was now hope of escape which seemed a distant dream when they were incarcerated in the inferno. But their escape to freedom only delayed the inevitable, the virus would finally get them. That thought hadn't yet hit home as they battled against the elements.

All day they struggled. The lack of food was starting to take its effect and they had little fat to live off.

'There,' shouted Thea at the top of her voice.

She was holding Nicola who was sound asleep until her mother shouted. She instantly started to cry, annoyed at being woken before she was ready and realising she was hungry.

Thea dumped her on the ground and turned her attention to the group behind her, pointing ahead and saying, 'look. That old barn over there. That's where we need to be.'

Everyone looked unimpressed, but said nothing.

Thea continued, 'come on. It'll give us shelter.'

She strode forward, but stopped after a few steps, turned around and said, 'Terry. Pick up Nicola.'

Terry immediately did as instructed and Thea walked on. The others followed without complaining and they soon reached the run down barn. Thea went straight through the open doorway and was instantly protected from most of the wind, although some still swirled around a little. The others hesitated for a few seconds before following her in.

Devon looked around and said, 'is this it? Is this where we're supposed to live?'

'No,' said Thea. 'It's somewhere for us to rest. We'll carry on tomorrow.'

'What about food?' said Morag.

'There isn't any.'

'But we won't have the energy to walk tomorrow.'

'Listen,' said Thea. 'Everything'll be fine. You have to trust me.'

'Why all the secrets?' said Terry sounding suspicious.

'As I said, you'll have to trust me. I've got you this far. Well, me and Devon have. So we just need to wait for this storm to pass, then we can carry on. It's not far.'

She turned around to indicate that line of enquiry was at an end, then returned to face them again and said, 'it'll be dark soon and we've no chance of drying our clothes so it may be a bit cold tonight. Do whatever you need to keep warm.'

They all looked sceptically at her before looking around for somewhere to settle down.

Devon whispered, 'can I have a word?'

Thea knew what it was about and glad that he'd asked. She needed some support and she trusted Devon. She nodded her head slightly towards the open doorway and they both walked outside and around the corner.

Morag noticed and said to the others, 'she's not telling us something and whatever it is, she's telling Devon. If he's ok with it then I am.'

'Why the need for secrets though?' said Terry.

'I don't know,' said Morag.

Thea and Devon walked to the Lea side of the barn to get as much protection from the wind and rain as possible.

Devon said, 'what's going? Why all the secrets?'

'I don't know really. It's just. Well. We've got this far and I don't want anything to go wrong.'

Devon looked at her suspiciously and said, 'so you're keeping it secret because if we know, then someone could scupper your plans?'

'No. Yes. Oh I don't know. Listen Devon, I know I'm worrying about nothing, but there's no point taking a risk now. Not when we're so close.'

'Then why are we here?'

'I just need you on my side. To share the responsibility. You'll probably think it's not a big deal.'

'Tell me then.'

Thea told him about Harvey and the bothy he'd created for him and his family to survive in, as indeed she had for the last 18 months. She told him about security measures and that she was confident it could sustain them all for whatever lifespan they had left.

'So where is this sanctuary?' he said.

'It's still a long way from here and there's no way we can walk it,' she said without sounding concerned.

Devon decided not to challenge her, knowing she was about to tell all anyway.

She whispered and nodded towards the barn, 'in there. There's a drone. It got me and the kids here and it's still in there. Under the floor. It can get us all to the bothy. To safety.'

'So why did you leave the bothy in the first place?'

'To find my husband. Why d'you think?' she said sounding surprised he hadn't worked it out.

Devon looked at her for a few seconds, realising there was no point criticising her decision.

He said, 'so you think if they know there's a drone there, someone may take it for themselves and leave the rest behind.'

'Yes,' said Thea thankful that Devon was thinking the same as her.

'So how do we get to this drone?'

The panic spread across her face. Last time she'd done nothing, a face recognition beam had automatically scanned her and the drone had risen from the ground.

She looked up at Devon and said, 'I don't know.'

CHAPTER 25 (BILL)

It was her job to know everyone in the bunker, if not all by name, then certainly by sight. As head of security she needed to know where they worked and how important they were to the cause. This particular one was not only important, but also infamous for being one of the two who'd escaped from the bunker.

Samantha immediately recognised Dave, even though he was in amongst a crowd of maybe 10 men. He wore different clothes and had no beard. Why were they there? Was it just a coincidence or did they know where the exit door was and were hoping to get inside? She concluded it was the former. If she as head of security didn't know of its existence then surely Dave didn't know either.

They looked at her a little perplexed, before one of them shouted out. 'Who the fuck are you?'

'I need help,' she shouted hoping to appeal to their sensitive, caring side.

'Come here then,' said the man stepping forward a bit.

She looked hesitantly at them then stepped forward, concluding that if Dave was still alive, then she also had a chance. Her focus was completely on them. They were the immediate threat or salvation and she'd forgotten about the tunnel. She walked slowly towards them with her weapon on display.

The man who'd been speaking noticed it and said, 'put that down.'

His eyes widened. She wasn't sure whether it was fear or the excitement of potentially gaining a new weapon.

'No way,' she said holding the weapon up.

He instinctively shuffled back a few paces and held his hands up before saying, 'we're not going to hurt you.'

'I bet you're not since I've got this,' she said waving her weapon from side to side a bit.

'We don't want trouble,' he said backing away more, making those behind him do the same.

The hairs on the back of her neck prickled as fear took hold of her senses. There was no particular reason. She was in charge. She was calling the shots. Or was she?

She spun around to see the creature stood at the open doorway looking menacing. Of course she knew about it. It was an experiment. Something that the scientists had created and wasn't a security risk. At least it wasn't until now.

It had grown significantly since she last saw it. Its scaly skin glistened in the sunlight and the now muscular limbs twitched in anticipation. It's bulbous head had grown a large protruding snout with nostrils that dribbled snot. There were no ears, just large holes with hair partially covering them. Horns jutted out from its head similar to the screx it was partially related too.

And the eyes. The red eyes looked towards her, but were focused on the group behind. Its teeth were clenched and it was slightly hunched forward as though ready to pounce. Physically threatening, intelligently frightening. She was good at assessing people just by looking at them and the creature had an intelligence that was superior to anything she'd seen before.

It started running towards her.

....

Bill was back in the comfort of his room in the bunker, surrounded by the homely things that made him relaxed and comfortable. He looked out of the window onto the empty cabinet room, grateful that he was still alive, but fearful he was alone in many respects.

He was welcomed after returning to the bunker, as the creature had told him he would be. Although some looked as though they didn't mean it, but were fearful there would be consequences should they not welcome him with open arms.

Fatalities from the coup had been limited to those resisting, of which there were few. Most saw that there was no point fighting, especially as no one was particularly loyal to Bill. After all he was responsible for the restrictions they all hated.

But the creature quickly changed things when it descended on them. It had imposed its will on them and now, as the creature had told him in the tunnel, he was in charge again. Bill didn't know how the creature had done it and didn't care. He was in charge again and the creature was gone. That's all that mattered. Things couldn't have gone better. Still. What were its motives?

He quickly dismissed his concerns, before getting up a striding towards the door. This would be the start of his new regime. From now on he would rule with an iron fist and no one, absolutely no one would dare to complain. He had the creature on his side.

CHAPTER 26 (HARVEY)

'Here. It's here,' said Louise confidently.

She looked up pretending to look for drones, then turned to the group behind and said, 'this is where the drones'll be looking.'

'What? Why here?' said Harvey suspiciously. 'There's nothing to indicate this is a pick up point.'

'They're not going to advertise it are they,' said Louise as though mocking him. She continued, 'anyway. I've got this to show me the way,' she said, pulling back her sleeve and showing Harvey a tracking device on her wrist.

'I wondered was that was for. That's why you've been looking at it.'

'Everyone's got one. Well everyone who's important enough and not in the bunker.'

'So that's just you then.'

'I suppose so,' she said looking up in the air again.

'So what now,' said Harvey.

'Leave me here. I'll be ok. There's no way they'll pick me up if they see you lot.'

Harvey looked at her suspiciously. She seemed a little too relaxed for a woman who was about to be left alone. He quickly dismissed his concerns. He'd done his job and relieved his conscience in the process, now he had to focus on what to do next.

'As long as you're happy with that.'

'I can hide behind those rocks until the drone comes,' she said pointing to them.

'And you're sure they'll pick you up?'

'Absolutely. Now leave me here,' she said sounding exasperated.

'Ok,' said Harvey holding his hands up. He turned to Spencer and continued, 'let's get going.'

'What about your part of the bargain? We've got you here and….'

Harvey interrupted, 'and I need you to get me back. We'll pick up the vaccine on the way. Take me to where you first found us.'

Spencer looked at Louise and said, 'you ok?' She smiled and nodded. He continued, 'come on then. Let's get out of here.'

They walked away slowly, some were occasionally looking behind until Louise finally hid behind the rock. When they'd gone, she stood up and looked around. There would be no drone coming to pick her up. She had other plans.

CHAPTER 27 (THEA)

It was the next day and everyone had woken to sunshine. They were standing outside to let the heat dry off their clothes and a happy aura suggested they were glad to have got this far. Not everyone was happy though. Thea had had a sleepless night thinking about the drone. There was no way they could walk to the bothy, it was too far. The drone was their only chance.

'What're we going to do?' whispered Thea to Devon.

She'd told him about the face recognition beam before they went to bed and hoped he'd had a chance to think about it.

'It kept me awake till the early hours thinking about it. It came to me when I woke up after a couple of hours kip.'

'And?' said Thea sounding frustrated.

'It's simple. It's a security thing. If there're other people around, it won't activate. We need to get everyone as far away from here as possible, then you and the kids go in.'

'Brilliant. But if that doesn't work?'

Devon shrugged his shoulders and said, 'we haven't got the tools to break into it, anyway even if we had, nothing short of a bomb could get in, then we'd destroy the drone.'

'It's our only option then? Me and the kids going in alone?'

'Yes. Now come on. We've got to give it a go.' Devon looked up the track and continued, 'we'll walk about 30 minutes up the track in the direction of the bothy.'

'Why that far?'

'The sensors'll probably look for anyone in the immediate vicinity. Trouble is I don't know how far immediate is.'

'Ok. Ok,' said Thea impatiently. 'Let's do it.'

Devon turned to the others and said, 'listen to me everyone. We have to walk up the track a little and leave Thea and the kids here.'

They all looked confused for a short while, but said nothing. Devon took that as their agreement to what he was asking. Had they really become so tame and timid that they didn't challenge anything? thought Devon. Thankfully yes.

Devon continued, 'come on then,' before walking past them and up the track. They all dutifully followed.

Thea watched them go out of sight, waiting the full 30 minutes before making her move. She stared at the barn, praying to herself that it would work. Her kids stood by her side, not saying anything as though they'd also been beaten into submission and would do anything that was asked of them.

'Come with me,' she said.

All three slowly walked towards the barn. The tension was excruciating as they went through the open door. Thea felt the blood rush from her head, making her feel a little dizzy.

The beam danced across her face and she was greeted by the same words from Harvey as before. Then the floor rolled back and the drone rose up.

CHAPTER 28 (BILL)

The creature reached Samantha in a few seconds, giving her little time to raise her weapon, but she did. It was a few feet away when she had her finger on the trigger, but her finger refused to press down, despite her brain telling it to do so.

It stopped suddenly, but the look on its face suggested it wasn't through the fear of being shot. Was it taunting her? Daring her to shoot? Wanting to show her that no weapon could kill it?

No matter its reasons. Her overriding feeling was of safety. For some reason she was sure the creature was not a danger to her and that was why her sub-conscious was telling her not to pull the trigger.

She tentatively lowered her weapon, before the creature continued towards its prey. They were already running away as a group, instinctively keeping together, thinking it would give them greater protection against the approaching threat. They were wrong. It wasn't long before it caught them, despatching them to their deaths with ease.

Samantha looked on in horror.

....

Louise looked on in horror as the carnage unfolded, then towards Samantha who was routed to the spot.

Her route back to the bunker through the tunnel was barred by the carnage before her. Of course she knew about the escape tunnel Bill had created. She was the home secretary after all. She also knew how to get in the door from the outside. None of this could be shared with Harvey and the others. Secrecy was the only sure way of security, therefore as few people as possible should know. Which was her and Bill only.

But all the knowledge was pointless as she stared open mouthed at what was happening. Within a couple of minutes, silence engulfed her senses as lifeless bodies lay still on the ground and the creature towered over them as though relishing the kill before it moved on.

There was movement between her and the creature. Someone or something was running towards her. She realised she was out in the open and crouched down behind some withered foliage in an attempt to hide. She saw the creature look up at the running figure and moved towards it, slowly at first before picking up its pace.

She could see it was a man. He was running towards her. Bringing the creature with him. Should she run? She'd be out in the open and a sitting duck. She had to stay where she was and hope the man diverted in another direction, taking the creature with him. He didn't. He was suddenly upon her with the creature not far behind. Dave. It was Dave. He was still alive. How?

She instinctively got up, thankful to see a familiar face, even though he'd given her up to save his own skin. He stopped in his tracks and looked at her blankly. Why had she done that? She quickly crouched down again, but it was too late. The creature was upon them. Standing. Towering above them. A slimy brown substance dribbling from its mouth as its tongue danced across its lips.

Within an instant it was gone. Louise and Dave stared at each other without saying anything. Then towards Samantha who'd almost mysteriously survived. Louise and Dave instinctively knew what to do and ran towards the exit door. Samantha followed even though she'd spent months trying to escape. She didn't understand why. Maybe she saw it in the creature's eyes.

They reached the open door at the same time and stopped.

'Why've we been spared?' said Louise.

Samantha grabbed the door and closed it before saying, 'it needs us. I had a connection with it. I don't know why.' I don't understand.'

They didn't challenge her because they felt the same.

'Let's get back to the bunker,' said Louise.

CHAPTER 29 (HARVEY)

They arrived at the place where Harvey, Louise and Dave had been attacked by the marauding gang.

'It's around here,' said Harvey looking around.

'You sure?' said Spencer sounding worried.

The stakes were high and he didn't like relying on a stranger to save his life and the lives of his community.

Harvey ignored him and continued to look around before slowly walking off. The others followed close behind until Harvey broke out into a sprint. They were taken by surprise and took a few seconds to realise what was happening before also sprinting, fearful that Harvey had been lying and was attempting to escape.

They soon realised they were wrong when they caught up with Harvey, who was now bent down behind a rock.

He looked up when he saw them and said, 'it's here.'

Luckily the rock hadn't sunk into the ground so there a small cavity where it met the ground, ideal for hiding something. Harvey had time to take the vaccine from his trouser pocket and hide it in the cavity. Of course he could've just told them it was in his pocket all the time, but he didn't want to be caught lying.

They all looked down at the small package, eager to look at what was inside and hopeful that Harvey was telling the truth. It really was the life-saving vaccine.

'Open it up,' said Spencer, his normal calm and caring tone had disappeared.

Harvey opened the package and said, 'I'll do it now if you want, although waiting until we get back won't be a problem.'

'Do it now,' said Spencer holding out his arm. 'I assume it goes in the arm.'

'It does,' said Harvey as he looked down at the open package and attached a small syringe to one of the tiny capsules.

'Is that enough?' asked Devon sounding a little unsure.

'It is.'

Harvey injected Spencer as the others looked on as though expecting something to happen, good or bad.

'Is that it?' said Spencer as he looked at his arm.

'It'll start working straight away. It won't take long before you see the effects. Maybe a couple of hours.'

Harvey injected the others and then put the vaccine in his pocket. Spencer looked at him as though he thought he should be carrying it.

Harvey said, 'now let's get back to the village and vaccinate the rest. as I promised. You've kept your side of the bargain so I'll do the same. You lead the way Spencer. And afterwards I'll be on my way.'

'You sure?' said Spencer.

'Yes,' said Harvey walking off.

The others followed, but it wasn't long before they all stopped and stared in the same direction as something unfamiliar strode purposely towards them.

'What the fuck is that. Is it some sort of screx,' said someone.

There was no response as the creature continued towards them.

A few more seconds passed before Spencer said, 'no but it's coming for us. We need to get out of here.'

'No,' shouted Harvey.

He didn't know why, but his instincts told him not to run. Of course he recognised the creature. It was locked in a cage the last time he saw it when he escaped from the bunker and looked rather pathetic. Not now though. Its long strides ate up the ground and it had grown significantly, even from this distance its demeanour looked threatening.

'It's going to kill us,' said Spencer naturally assuming the worst when confronted with something unfamiliar.

'We've got nowhere to run and judging by the speed it's walking, it'll catch us anyway when it starts to run.'

'We have to try.'

'No, we need to stay here. See what it wants.'

'Are you fucking stupid or something? I'm off,' said someone in the group before turning and running.

It wasn't long before the rest did the same, including Spencer, leaving Harvey alone. The creature saw what was happening and began to run. He was right. There was no way they could outrun it and doubted that, even as a group, they could kill it. He stood his ground and awaited his fate.

The creature soon reached him and suddenly stopped about 20 yards away. The familiar eyes bore into him, the body looked tense as though it was ready to pounce and its breathing was slow and deliberate. Harvey looked defiantly at it, his intention was to go down fighting. He was a scientist and not used to these situations and was surprised at how brave and resourceful he was.

The creature's shoulders dropped. It stood upright, looking beyond Harvey to the fleeing group. It then looked at Harvey one more time before turning around and walking off. It never looked back.

Harvey sucked in the oxygen he desperately needed, after instinctively holding his breath. He then turned to see the others had stopped running and were looking towards him, although he suspected they were more interested in the creature heading away. Harvey walked towards them after a few more seconds when he was happy the creature wasn't going to return. They all did the same.

'What was that all about?' said Spencer nervously.

Harvey turned to see the creature still walking away in the distance, then he turned around again.

'I don't know and I'm not about to ask it,' he said with a grin on his face, trying to lighten the situation.

How had it escaped? Why had it come toward them if it didn't want kill them? It didn't look like the sociable type. What was it going to do next? The questions whirred around in Harvey's head, but the one thing he did know was that he felt an affinity for it and didn't know why. That was the question he knew he could never answer.

'We need to get back to the village,' said Spencer walking off.

The others followed and Harvey soon joined them.

....

The rising smoke could be seen from a distance and signified that something was wrong. Something bad had happened and whatever it was they were already too late. Spencer was the first to pick up his pace, after all they were his people and he was their leader, meaning he had a responsibility to protect them. Had he failed by leaving them to help Louise get back to the bunker? he thought as he ran along, soon putting his doubts to one side as he focused on getting to the village.

He stumbled frequently, knowing that slower would be faster, but unable to himself. He didn't look back, knowing that others would be following him. He didn't need to tell them that something was wrong.

He slowed down when the village came into view, realising the hopelessness of the situation. Buildings. Solid brick and stone buildings were razed to the ground. Fires burned everywhere. The heat scolded his face as the wind wafted the flames towards him.

He ignored the discomfort and continued slowly, then stopped in his tracks when he saw bodies strewn across the ground. Still. Lifeless. Nothing moved apart from the flames and the smoke, as though eager to eat everything before they eventually died.

Spencer turned around to see the rest approaching fast. He waited for them to arrive, but his focus was on Harvey. He had to blame someone for this because blaming himself would cripple him. The anger swept through him as the group got close.

Harvey quickly realised what Spencer was thinking and said, 'come on we need to look for survivors.'

He suspected it was pointless, but had to distract Spencer. He ran past him and started looking around, whilst trying to cover his face from the searing heat. The others followed, leaving Spencer alone, the anger still etched across his face.

It wasn't long before the flames intensified and they had to retreat back to where Spencer was still standing.

'This is your fault,' said Spencer very quietly.

Harvey didn't quite hear him, but guessed what he was saying. This certainly wasn't the time to ask him to say it again.

'This is nobody's fault,' said Harvey assertively. You. Me. None of us could've done anything about this. Look at it,' he said turning to face the burning village. 'Buildings've been destroyed. We couldn't have done anything to stop whoever's done this.'

'So who's done this?' said Spencer sounding desperate for answers.

Harvey looked around as though searching for inspiration then said, 'well, it's not that gang we came across and I doubt anyone else has the means to do this.'

'The bunker?' said Spencer, the anger in him starting to wane.

'I doubt it. I think their defences are focused on protecting the bunker, not going to the mainland and destroying us. Communities. Anyway, they don't want to antagonise people, they know that the bunker is at risk if there's a concerted, joined up attack.'

'So who?' said Spencer impatiently and staring intently at Harvey. He continued, 'that creature did this.'

'I don't know for sure, but it's the most likely reason. It was heading in this direction when it left us.'

'Then it'll be after us next,' said Spencer.

Maybe Spencer was right, but for some reason Harvey didn't think so.

CHAPTER 30

She waited anxiously holding the hammers and looking up through the open doorway at the debris being thrown around by the wind. Desperate for it to continue because of the horrors that waited when it subsided. Those remaining in the cellar were now by her side as though demonstrating solidarity and resistance in the face of overwhelming odds. They looked defiant, but they knew the game was up and most were happy with their fate. If they'd been sensible and brave, they would've taken the hammers to themselves weeks ago, but something inside them said no. That something had got them here and it wasn't going to let them give in now.

The wind reached into the cellar and swirled around, but not enough to cause problems. No, the wind was a blessing at the moment and long may it continue.

She looked around at the few remaining souls next to her. Half of them that had arrived here had died from the virus and those that were left looked wretched, including herself. They were covered in open wounds, the skin that was left looked stretched and lined as though it was struggling to hold the body together. Still they looked strong and determined to make a final stand.

She looked into the corner of the cellar. Two bodies wriggled under a blanket and her heart sank. She quickly returned her attention to the opening. The wind was dying down. She gripped the hammers.

'Look around for anything you can use as a weapon,' she said.

They instantly scurried away and she cursed for having to tell them to do something that should've been obvious. They returned soon after, all had small rocks. It was better than nothing, she concluded.

There were weapons hidden outside. Enough to defend this place, but they were outside, not in the cellar. In her haste to hide and escape the weather, she'd forgotten to take them. Now she cursed herself for being so stupid. Then she cursed them again for not thinking of it either. Why should she be responsible for thinking of everything?

The wind continued to wane and the skies brightened a little, before a shadow took some of the light away again, then a figure appeared at the doorway looking down on its prey. The figure was silhouetted by the brightness behind it, but she could make out it was a man, the thick beard gave it away. She stood looking up, determined, steadfast, scared. She tightened the grip on the hammers in her hands and held them up as a warning not to enter. A pathetic and ineffective gesture, but it was the only thing she could do. The man didn't move, but continued to look down as though trying to work out what or who he was looking at. Why hadn't he made his move?

She relaxed her grip on the hammers and lowered them. Her shoulders slumped and she breathed out, emptying her lungs of oxygen. Her eyes welled up a little, but crying wasn't an option until she was sure. The others noticed her demeanour and confusion spread, looking at each other for an answer, but none was forthcoming. They got themselves together and focused again until their leader told them otherwise.

'Harvey?' she said tentatively.

'Thea?' said Harvey.

His questioning manner suggested he wasn't sure. Did she really look so bad that he didn't recognise her? Her doubts were put to one side as emotions took hold. The moisture in her eyes turned to proper tears and she dropped the hammers, one hit her foot, but she didn't even notice the pain.

She held her arms up as though beckoning him towards her, her face was now contorted with the emotion and the tears rolled down her face. Harvey turned around and started to descend the ladder.

'No,' shouted Thea before stepping back. 'The virus. We've got it. Go. Please go. You can't come in.'

Harvey continued to descend the ladder and Thea stepped back further. The others did the same, the confusion was written across their faces, but they realised this wasn't the time to ask questions.

He eventually stepped off the bottom rung and turned around to face her. The happiness of seeing her husband again made her want to lunge forward and hold him, but the fear of giving him the virus was telling her to run away. The result was that she was rooted to the spot. Frozen and unable to do either.

A broad smile came across his face and his eyes moistened a little. It was a reassuring smile, not a look of happiness and relief that they were together again before they died. Then the smile instantly faded as his eyes quickly scanned around the basement.

'Nicola. Lance. Where are they?' he said, the terror now written across his face.

She turned around to see the others behind her and beckoned them to move to one side before turning around to Harvey again. There was no need for words as he stared at his two wretched children. Their faces staring at him from underneath the blanket that covered their bodies, wanting to call out to their daddy. Wanting to run towards him, but not having the strength to do either. Their faces were also ravaged, but Harvey showed no concern for them. He was here. He was with his wife. He was with his children. That's all he wanted for now.

A shadow came across the doorway again and Thea instantly looked alarmed again.

'Friends,' said Harvey.

She instantly relaxed as though trusting her husband implicitly, but tension rose again as he walked towards her, grabbing her hands he drew her towards him and wrapped his arms around her. She melted into him. The embrace lasted only a few seconds before he released her and walked towards his children. They looked forlorn and weak. He didn't embrace them or say any re-assuring words, that would come later. He reached into his pocket, attached a needle to the end of a tiny bottle and injected one, then did the same to the other. Thea looked on, not quite understanding what was happening, but trusting her husband to do the right thing. He got up straight away and turned to face his wife.

'It's a vaccine Thea. It's a cure.' He looked at the others and continued, 'a cure for everyone.'

He got out another dose and needle and injected her as well, before doing the same to others in the basement.

'Now everyone rest. The talking's for tomorrow.'

He went to sit next to his children, Thea followed, sat next to him and lay her head on his shoulder. Others in the basement did the same. There was no shouting with joy. No extreme gestures. No floods of emotion. Those sorts of responses had long gone been beaten out of them by circumstances.

'We'll stay out here,' said someone from outside. 'Look out for anyone.'

There was no answer and the figure standing at the doorway disappeared.

'You're never leaving us again,' she said lifting her head and staring at him.

He shook his head and she nestled back into him again. The weather had calmed down and dusk had started to descend.

Harvey thought, if death came tomorrow, he'd be a happy man.

....

Sunshine greeted them the next day. Stories had been told and introductions made. The survivors from Spencer's community had decided to go with Harvey on the promise of a better life, although they really had no choice. Their houses and way of life had been destroyed and, deep down, they knew that the deteriorating weather in the south would eventually drive them out. Looking at the bothy now though, they may think differently, thought Harvey. The part of the building over the basement had been destroyed by wind in the last few weeks, Thea had told him, but some of the bothy was still habitable.

Harvey surveyed the rubble strewn over the ground and what was left of the walls, which now only stood about six feet tall. The bothy was protected from the worst of the winds by the hills that reached up on either side, but a wind could be exaggerated if it was funnelled up the valley.

He cursed himself for not thinking of this when equipping the bothy, but soon came around to thinking of solutions. A protective wall on the valley side of the bothy? Re-build the bothy with walls shaped like the bow of a ship so that it didn't suffer the full force of the winds?

He wasn't a builder or architect so couldn't say whether these solutions would be effective, but looking around the group, he was confident that solutions could be found.

The other problem was food. The bothy was stocked with two years of food for him and his family, but there wasn't much left and it wouldn't last long with the extra mouths to feed. Thea had made a good job of growing crops, but still between the food that was left and the crops, there still wasn't enough to feed the enlarged group.

'Lost in thought?' said Thea coming up behind him.

He spun around with a huge smile came across his face and said, 'you look better already.'

'I feel better. Kids are sleeping in. They haven't slept well for ages. There skin's healing already.'

Thea's relief got the better of her and she lowered her head as though ashamed of showing her emotions. 12 hours ago she was desperate and her only hope was a painless death for her and her children. Now there was real hope for the future.

Harvey wrapped her in his arms and said, 'this virus is going to kill everyone. On the way here. Bodies everywhere. Those still alive look like zombies. I thought we were going to get trouble, but people are too sick to fight.'

'But we'll be alright Harvey,' said Thea looking up defiantly.

He looked down, then released her and pushed her back so she was at arm's length.

'We'll re-build this place Thea. Make it strong. Grow crops.'

Thea looked at him with a confused look on her face and said, 'Harvey. We don't have to. Don't you understand. Everyone's going to die. There'll be plenty of food and shelter for us.'

Harvey stared blankly at her, desperately searching for reasons for his stupidity. He soon gave.??

His blank expression turned to a smile before he said, 'common sense isn't my best quality.'

'But it is mine,' she said returning his smile.

‘Go and wake the kids up,’ he said. ‘We’ll have breakfast together.’

Thea turned and left, leaving Harvey with his thoughts. But they were only doubts. How bad would the weather get? No one had predicted this. Yes, there was plentiful food now, but all food was perishable and would eventually go off. What then. Could food be grown in the ever changing climate?

The creature suddenly dominated his thoughts!

20 YEARS LATER

CHAPTER 31 (THE BOTHY)

Global temperatures had risen sharply long ago causing tipping points to be reached and a rapid deterioration of the climate. Melting ice, destruction of the rain forest, the shifting of the monsoons was now irreversible and all life on earth was suffering. It was simply happening too quickly for life to evolve and cope with the new pressures.

The virus had long since killed off unvaccinated humans and the only ones surviving were imprisoned within the bunker with no hope of re-populating the world again within their life time or indeed the distant future, thanks to the inhospitable environment. Unbeknown to those in the bunker, there was a small cluster of humans that had adapted to the less extreme weather in the north, but only just.

The screx was the only animal to thrive. Its tough scales protected it from the extreme weather and the destruction of other wildlife removed the competition for what was left of the vegetation to feed off. They lived in herds where the food was most abundant, which was in the north, and they would only move around if they had exhausted the food source.

Their numbers had increased significantly, but not to the point where they exhausted the food. Their natural instinct was to limit reproduction so that numbers were manageable and therefore life was sustainable.

They lived on grass and anything else that was green. Unfortunately what was left of the vegetation wasn't fit for human consumption, meaning that Harvey and his clan had to grow their own.

Life had become harsh to say the least. The bothy had been reduced to rubble and they mainly lived underground and only ventured outside when necessary. They'd built a significant protective wall from some of the bothy rubble and it'd held firm, providing protection for the crops to grow, but food was becoming more and more scarce.

The men had attempted to hunt the screx, without success. Despite their size and power, the screx were scared of humans and would run away if felt threatened. Their speed across the ground was impressive and there was no way any human could catch them. They'd dug holes and chased the screx into them, catching some if they were lucky, only to find that their herd mentality made them protective towards any screx that was threatened and they'd turned aggressive, meaning the men folk couldn't kill their captured prey.

They soon found that hunting the screx was impossible and there was no other source of meat. Also the deteriorating crops caused by the weather was exacerbated by the screx, who'd recently found the crops and partially devoured them before being chased away by the men. Replacing the crops would take time, meaning there would be more food shortages. The fear was that the screx had found a food source and would no doubt return at some point.

Harvey and Thea were in their 60s?? and the harsh life they'd led over the last 20 years had taken its toll. Long life spans were a thing of the past and many of the group who'd entered the bothy were dead. But some were also young and new families had arrived.

The arrival of a new born was always greeted with joy as an addition to the community, but also despair that there was another mouth to feed.

Another problem in the beginning was the higher proportion of males in the group, mainly thanks to the all-male group Harvey had brought with him. This had led to tensions, with men frequently fighting for the attention of the women and, wrong as it may sound, the women eventually being shared around to lessen the tensions.

The community was now 20 strong and routines and hierarchies had been established. Thea and Harvey were part of the old brigade and had taken a back seat. Those in their forties were now taking the lead, having done their duty to produce children. Lance and Nicola had already had one child each and no doubt more would come, if the food shortage could be overcome. Thankfully the tendency to have female babies in the early days meant that numbers had evened up a little, but it meant that the younger men had the pick of the women and chose multiple partners.

To ensure the purity of the species and prevent in breeding, strict rules were introduced so that one man could only impregnate one woman. This meant the older men who already had families, had to do their bit with the younger girls. Again not ideal, but no one objected, realising the necessity of the situation.

Devon was one of those in his forties and had taken the lead in the group, simply because he was the most competent. He had assigned deputies to manage food production and the rule of law because starvation and anarchy were the biggest risks. He knew the former would lead to the latter.

'We can't survive here,' said Harvey to Devon. 'There's not enough food and the screx will be back. We can't keep them at bay forever.'

'I fucking know,' said Devon sounding angry and tense.

This was the first time he'd not known what to do and he wasn't dealing with it very well. The screx invasion had caused a problem that he didn't know how to resolve.

'The bunker Devon. I told you about the bunker. That's our only chance.'

The community was emaciated and the kids were suffering most, needing more calories for growth, but there was no point telling Devon the obvious, concluded Harvey.

'No one'll have the strength to get that far. It's at the other end of the country. You fucking know that so why the fuck're you talking about it. Anyway what about food. We can't carry it that far and there'll be nothing to scavenge on the way,' said Devon sounding irritated. Swearing was a sure sign that he was stressed.

'We can't stay here Devon. We need to find a better way of getting there than walking. Think.'

Devon immediately calmed down whilst his brain looked for solutions.

'There's the drone. But that won't take everyone. Six at the most. It also won't get all the way without a recharge. So that's not an option.'

They still had solar panels for the much needed electricity in the basement and had used it to keep the drone battery charged.

'Isn't it? asked Harvey.

'No,' said Devon assertively. 'I won't leave anyone behind. We live or die together.

'I know what you don't want to do. But what are your solutions. Look. Some of us are getting on a bit.....'

'The old ones stay behind? No way. Anyway, there're more than six youngsters. Would you want to choose? I wouldn't'

'Decisions have to be made Devon. The weather's only going to get worse so we can't stay here. It's your decision,' said Harvey walking away leaving Devon outside by himself.

'Stop,' said Devon. Harvey turned around to face him. 'You're right.'

Harvey walked back to face him and said, 'I know I am. There's something bigger than us. You know that don't you?'

Devon looked stunned for a short while before saying 'you feel it as well?

'Yes. And we need to go in search of that something.' Harvey looked passed Devon for a few seconds as though lost in his thoughts before continuing, 'I should've taken my family to the bunker and stayed there,' he said sounding regretful.

'Well, I'm glad you didn't. Otherwise none of us would be here.'

'But we can't stay here Devon.'

'I know. I know. Look. We've got the Drone. We just need to find the best way to use it that gets everyone out of here. Think.'

CHAPTER 32 (THE CREATURE)

The creature was weak. It was coping, almost relishing the pain, but its strength had slowly waned over the years and it was significantly smaller than when it left the bunker. It was still a child and knew it had many more growing years left, so why did it feel so weak?

It was living with a herd of screx and was happy to do so. It was after all partially built from their DNA. It was also relishing the freedom, now realising how much it hated being held captive inside the bunker, but it knew this couldn't last. It needed more than this. It needed to find an answer and fast.

A whirring sound distracted its thoughts and it looked up to see a drone hovering above. It quickly crouched behind a rock, whilst the screx carried on grazing, ignoring the intrusion. Their low intelligence failed to alert them to the potential danger.

CHAPTER 33 (THE BUNKER)

Bill had long since died, leaving Louise to take up the reins. She was in charge, with her power cemented by Samantha and her significant army of well-armed security staff. No one else possessed any weapons. It was a typical fascist dictatorship, with the figure head having complete control and power, even though Louise knew she was reliant on Samantha to keep her there. Nothing had changed since Bill was in charge.

Samantha was happy with this situation. Of course she had the potential to overthrow Louise and take power, but she'd little desire and knew that it could easily unsettle everything and lead to anarchy, meaning everyone would lose.

There had been few problems since she'd taken over from Bill. He'd reined with an iron fist, recognising the mistakes he'd made in the past, and she'd simply carried on in the same vein. Many had accepted their lives, knowing there were no other options. Living in the outside world just wasn't possible

Louise had selected appropriate men to impregnate her. Intelligence, ruthlessness and greed were key ingredients of those donating their sperm, although it was difficult to identify men with such qualities. Everyone had become fearful of demonstrating their gifts as it was likely to result in imprisonment.

Her offspring were coming to adulthood and she would soon step aside and let one of them take the lead, but that was for the future. For now, she had to manage the key problem which had crept up over the last couple of years. Food, or the lack of it.

The huge greenhouses used to grow crops were still working and had withstood the ferocious weather, as they had been designed to do. The solar panels were also working, for now, and they had plenty of power, including enough to manage temperatures within the greenhouses.

The water situation hadn't been a problem, until recently. The climate had become a lot more extreme than anyone had predicted and there were significant dry spells, meaning even the water beneath the surface dried up for long periods. Desalination plants removed salt from the sea water, so the lack of rain water wasn't a problem. Or it shouldn't have been. The maintenance of the desalination plants had become a problem, with frequent breakdowns caused by the weather and the lack of spare parts. They were originally built as a contingency in case there were occasional droughts and not the unexpected length and frequency of droughts they were experiencing.

The desalination plants just weren't built to be worked that hard. The upshot was that the crops went thirsty, which meant they died, which meant rations

The solar panels were still working, but they represented a risk. Latest predictions suggested the weather would get even worse and Louise knew that one really bad storm could demolish their energy supply overnight. They had emergency mechanical generators, but the fuel wouldn't last forever. That would be the final nail in the coffin

None of this would be a problem if original predictions had come true. The virus had done the planet a favour and wiped out most of humanity, which meant that carbon emissions disappeared overnight. But this hadn't halted the deteriorating weather, with the ice continuing to melt. Even when everything did eventually calm down, the climate would settle into something completely different to what they'd been used to. Predictions now suggested that it could take many more years for the weather to settle, by which time the bunker and all its inhabitants would be gone. The "garden of eden" they'd created to live in before emerging into the new promised land, would be their coffin.

Since the creature had left the bunker, all objections to authority had disintegrated and people had become compliant, encouraged by Bill's and Louise's heavy handed approach, but this wouldn't last if the food shortages continued. A mass migration north just wasn't an option. It would be almost impossible to move many thousands of people that far in the harsh weather conditions. Anyway, drones they'd sent up there suggested the weather wasn't much better and they would almost certainly starve to death before they managed to grow enough crops. They had to stay put, concluded Louise. Maybe something would happen.

Bills old residence had been joined with the old cabinet room to give Louise and her kids enough space. There was still a connecting door to security, should

Louise need their services quickly, but she was so well protected that the need had never arisen.

The new enlarged residence had a huge open plan living area with a kitchen dining room space and a lounge. The décor looked well used, an indication that such luxuries were in short supply now that the raw materials were no longer readily available.

It was bright and the walls were adorned with various paintings which hadn't succumbed to the ravages of time, simply because they were there to be looked at only. Doorways went through to bedrooms where her kids still slept. She doubted they would ever fly the nest, realising that they were in the safest place.

Their fathers were not proper fathers, having agreed that their only role was to impregnate Louise. They also knew that there would be consequences should they attempt to show their fatherly instincts.

Daily life had, inevitably, settled into routine and there was a formal hierarchical structure in place to ensure everyone knew their place and role as laid down by the all-powerful Louise. She no longer needed her political skills, there was no competition and no electorate to pander to. Consequently, she could devote all her attention to decision making and getting things done. The hierarchical structure made sure that she was fully informed of everything that was going on, although examples had to be made when she was mis-informed. She rarely left the sanctuary of her living area.

Her two eldest sons had recently become part of the hierarchical structure with responsibilities for food production. Although they had little experience, they had proved capable and Louise was proud of their performance, despite the problems. She doubted anyone else could've done any better. Their focus was on the desalination plants which had, yet again, broken down, leaving them to rely on the meagre underground stored water reserves, which wouldn't last long. It was never considered that the natural groundwater would run out, therefore the reserve tanks were only an afterthought when built and were nowhere near big enough.

Life for her two sons had become an endless fire-fighting job trying to keep the desalination plants going. There were further frustrations with the solar panels which were starting to show their age and frequent repairs were required, particularly after the heavy winds.

'This can't go on mother,' said Jed.

Jed Gardner was her eldest son and had responsibility for the food growing infrastructure, including the desalination plants and the solar panels. Her other son, Ben, managed the crops. Louise and her sons were sat around the dining table, the normal place for discussing matters of state. Louise said nothing, hoping her other son would pitch in before she said her piece. He duly obliged.

'He's right mother,' said Ben. This place wasn't designed to put up with this weather and we don't have the materials to repair anything. We just can't feed everyone.'

'I know all this. What d'you suggest then?' said Louise looking at Jed as he was responsible and feeling disappointed that neither of her sons ever came up with solutions.

It was a conversation they'd made many times recently. The same problem discussed in different ways.

Jed looked over to his brother as though he was going to say something they'd already agreed about.

'Well?' said Louise sounding impatient.

Jed leant forward and rested on his elbows before saying, 'we need to get out there. Scavenge for things. Anything that'll help us repair the desalination plants.'

'But there's nothing left out there. We've pilfered what's in easy reach and the weather's destroyed the rest.'

'There must be something left.'

'D'you know where to get these.... Things?'

'Well. No. Not exactly. But we've got to try. There'll be gaps in the weather when we can send drones out to look. I know we've done it before, but we may've missed something.'

'Yes. We have done it before,' said Louise sounding dismissive. 'And there's nothing left out there that's within reach of the drones.'

'Then we'll have to go further afield,' said Ben. 'Take a risk with the weather.'

'The weather only gives us a one day window at most,' said Louise.

'We don't have to use the drones though do we,' said Jed. 'Send a team of people.'

Louise sat back looking exasperated and said, 'they can't cover anywhere near as much ground as the drones in one day.'

'Who said anything about one day? I reckon a team could survive a few days out there with the right gear,' said Jed.

Louise continued to sit back in her chair whilst staring at her eldest son, before she eventually said, 'and who's going to volunteer for that? And, as I said before. You don't know where to send them to get what you need.'

'No. That's true,' said Ben. 'But if they die trying then. Well. It'll be less mouths to feed.'

Louise stood up abruptly and shouted, 'no one's going to die unnecessarily on my watch. I've done everything to keep people alive, even if that meant being heavy handed. I know they hate me for it, but I don't care.'

'And everybody'll die if we do nothing. They'll starve to death,' said Jed.

'If I send people to their certain death, then there'll be riots and more will die. No. I need other solutions. Solutions that don't mean people have to die. Now go and come back with something better.'

She walked off to indicate that the discussion was over, finally sitting on the ropey sofa and staring into her hand held screen.

Jed and Ben looked at each other, before Jed whispered, 'this place has got to last at least another 60 years. Any suggestions?'

Ben shrugged.

Louise was staring at her screen, but not looking at it. Her children were right. People were going to die one way or another. The only question was how they were going to die. She clenched her fist with frustration. It was her responsibility to come up with an answer.

She looked up at her kids who were still sat at the table whispering to each other and said, 'ok. I'll speak to Samantha. She'll give me some volunteers, but I want one of you two to lead it. I need to show them that I'm willing to sacrifice as well.

CHAPTER 34 (THE BOTHY)

'Down there,' shouted Devon. 'Land there.'

Plan A was simple. Take the drone south. Find a structure that'd managed to withstand the weather, drop four or five people off and return to the bothy to re-charge the batteries. Repeat the process until everyone was re-housed. Whilst doing this, transport supplies and some solar panels so the drone batteries could be re-charged in the new location. Then do the same again until they reached the bunker. After that there was no plan.

There were so many unknowns. Would they be able to find places to shelter all the way down? How much worse was the weather further south? Would there be enough days when the weather was good enough to travel, or would the storms last weeks? Was the bunker still there? How would they be greeted?

The burden of responsibility was wearing Devon down. The fate of the group was in his hands and so many unanswered questions meant the doubts were always at the fore front of his mind. He continually placated himself with the fact that there was no other choice. The food would run out or the weather would get them in the end. These two reasons alone meant that something had to be done.

Plan B was. Well. There wasn't a plan B. There was no way they could walk that far. It would take weeks and in that time there would be days when the weather could easily wipe them out. Using the drone was the only way,

Devon had concluded many times and Harvey's support gave him some hope that it could work.

The drone descended, ably guided by Harvey. Only he and Devon were in the drone. The rest of the space was taken up with the solar panels and food. It was felt that, should they find somewhere suitable, it was more important to set everything up first before transporting people.

The drone hovered over the building. It was a single story building made out of local stone, similar in some ways to the bothy. The roof looked intact, although the chimney had obviously seen better days, and doors and windows were still in place. The geography of the land around it may have contributed to its survival, concluded Harvey. Fallen rotting trees littered the countryside around it, a scene they'd become familiar with as they'd flown south.

'Looks ok,' said Devon.

Harvey took that as Devon's agreement to land, so he eased the drone down until it landed next to the building. There were still a few trees standing, but they were few and far between, and some low level shrubs seemed to have survived. There was also some grassland, but it looked parched and was nowhere near as lush as further north.

Devon looked around tentatively for any threats and, once satisfied there were none, he opened the hatch to the drone and climbed out. Harvey followed soon after and they tentatively walked towards the building, looking through the windows to see what it was like.

‘Looks ok,’ said Harvey.

Devon looked up to the sky and said, ‘the weather’ll turn tomorrow. Let’s get this place set up.’

Devon tried the front door, but it failed to budge until he put his shoulder against it.

‘Must be something behind it,’ he said continuing to push.

The door eventually opened wide enough so they could get in.

‘Shit,’ said Devon.

Both looked on in horror at the human bones piled up behind the door. They’d almost disintegrated, but they could just make out five skulls, two were adult size, the others were obviously children.

‘The virus probably took them,’ said Harvey sounding unconcerned. ‘The bones’ve lasted well.’

Devon was a little shocked by Harvey’s blasé attitude, but didn’t say anything.

‘Shouldn’t we, uh, bury them?’

Harvey said, ‘no. We haven’t got time. Let’s get the stuff off the drone, then you can set up the solar panels and get the food stored somewhere cool. I’ll fly back,’ said Harvey whilst walking back towards the drone. Devon followed.

Although Devon was the un-elected leader, he was happy for Harvey to take charge. He was still learning the job and didn’t have the same experience or intelligence and doubted he ever would.

They spent the next 30 minutes unloading the drone, careful not to damage the solar panels and equipment needed to re-charge the drone batteries. The food was more dispensable, if and it was a big if, the journey went smoothly and they were readily accepted into the bunker without delays.

Harvey was a little more hopeful of success in respect of the bunker. He suspected there would still be people there who knew him and therefore knew that he would be useful.

'Ok. That's it. All done. I'll set this lot up and you get back,' said Devon as though wanting to regain his authority.

'You sure you'll be ok?' said Harvey knowing it was a pointless question.

'I'll have to be,' said Devon. 'Now get going. Don't forget to shelter if you think the weather's going to turn. Remember that barn without the roof we saw. You could shelter in there.'

'It's only a couple of hours. This thing'll easily get there and I think the weather'll hold out that long.'

'Go on,' said Devon turning around to look at the food and equipment they'd brought.

'Ok. I'll see you the next time there's a gap in the weather. Hopefully in a few days time when the batteries have re-charged although it'll take longer cos you've got some of the solar panels.'

Harvey walked towards the drone, scanning the area as he did so. There wasn't that much around apart from a few demolished buildings. It may have been a small local community living in the countryside back in the day, but not now. The weather had done a good job of transforming the countryside into a barren landscape, with less vegetation than the bothy, even though it was only a couple of hours flying time away.

He reached the drone and took one more look around before climbing aboard. The drone rose into the air, hovering awhile so Harvey could make sure that Devon was ok. There was no sign of him, he assumed he was busying himself inside the building.

Something moved behind a rock. It was dark and stood out against the parched landscape. A screx? No, it stood upright, not on all fours. Was it a threat to the food and equipment they'd brought?

He eased the drone down to take a closer look. The dark shape began to run, then disappeared behind a hill. Harvey followed, but on reaching the other side of the hill, the dark shape was nowhere to be seen. He hovered for a few minutes looking intently for any signs of life, but there was nothing. He eventually turned the drone around and headed back to the building where he saw Devon stood outside. It was too far away to see the expression on his face, but Harvey suspected it was one of confusion. He returned his attention to the journey home and flew away after concluding that it was probably a baby screx, which sometimes stood on their hind legs.

The creature looked at the drone hovering above where it was hiding, realising it'd been found, but not running to start with as though defiant in the face of adversity. It eventually took flight and hid in a small cave it had created for itself.

The herd of screx it was part of had been in the area for a few months, but the depleting vegetation meant they would soon head north for pastures new, only to return south again when the rains put life back into the ground. It was a migratory journey the creature had tolerated, but it wanted more than this. It wanted to feel strong. Grow. Live. Feel. Not just exist.

It came out of its hiding place and walked slowly back around the hill, stopping to look at the building where it saw the humans busying themselves, before continuing the rock it was initially hiding behind and towards the building.

....

The flight had been trouble free, but the storm was gathering pace in the distance, encouraged by the rising early afternoon humidity. It would probably be a short, sharp one, concluded Harvey. The winds would be strong and there would be rain, no doubt their crops would suffer yet again. The weather further south had seemed more arid and drier, but the fallen trees and destroyed buildings suggested storms did occur, possibly less frequent, but more intense and with no rain, concluded Harvey.

Thea, along with the others were there to greet the drone as it landed. Harvey thought they looked a little tense, even though his return suggested the journey had been a success. He raised the hatch and got out of the drone, embracing Thea, then his children.

'Grandkids ok?' said Harvey to Lance and Nicole.

'They're fine dad,' said Nicole.

Harvey turned his attention to Thea and said, 'everything went well. Devon's setting things up so we can charge the drone batteries.' He looked towards the gathering storm and continued, 'we need to get the drone away.'

A few of the men instantly went to the drone and manoeuvred it to where they stored it in a small underground chamber they'd made so that it was safe from the storms. Harvey suddenly realised that he had to take the lead again now that Devon was gone.

He looked over to the others and said, 'have we got enough food in the basement?'

Lance said, 'of course there is dad. We're not stupid.'

Lance was still in his rebellious phase and often argued or over reacted when his dad said something. Harvey hoped he would've grown out of it at some point, but it was taking a long time.

He headed towards the hatch and opened it, letting the others descend into the basement before looking around one last time to make sure everything was in its proper place and secured. He then went down the steps, securing the re-enforced hatch door behind him.

Everyone was busying themselves in their own family units. Even those who had no blood family had been adopted by someone, meaning no one was alone. Thea was something of a matriarch in her old age and was arranging the food. Families didn't cook and eat separately, that was inefficient and increased the risk of wasted food. In these days of shortages, nothing was wasted, not even peelings.

The family units split up when the food was ready and everyone gathered together to eat. The familiar roar of the wind outside raised no concerns for anyone, they heard and seen it many times before. The hatch could now easily cope with whatever was thrown at it. That was Harvey's first priority when he arrived.

'Are we still going tomorrow?' whispered Thea thankful that the wind stopped others hearing.

Harvey didn't answer for a few seconds as though thinking, then said, 'Yes. Us and family that is. That's four and two little ones. We'll need to take some more gear so we can't fit anyone else in. That's what we'll tell them.'

'How'll everyone take it? I mean, the ex-bosses family going first.'

'They'll be fine. Some're a bit reticent about going anyway. We'll be setting an example. If we're not worried, why should they be.'

'Are you worried?'

Harvey thought back to the dark shape he'd seen behind the rock, before dismissing his concerns. Whatever it was it didn't look threatening and was probably only a baby screx as he originally concluded.

'Of course I'm worried, but not as much as I would be if we stayed here. Anyway. I don't think we'll be going tomorrow. The drone batteries need to charged first and there're fewer solar panels to do it. Plus there's been no sunshine so far. We'll have to cut back on electricity usage in here. Probably early the day after.'

Thea turned away as though happy with Harvey's re-assuring words and equally happy with his honest assessment of the situation. But her conscience was gnawing away at her. Telling her it wasn't right. Telling her that there were worse things than death. Living in hell for example. And hell is where they were probably going.

....

Nightfall had engulfed the countryside, but the darkness was invaded by the moonlight and the peace and quiet squashed by the ferocious winds. The rains still hadn't come to this part of the country, but when they did, torrents of water would cascade down the hills and into the valleys where the water would congregate and sweep towards the sea, destroying everything in its path.

Devon was sat in darkness., The moonlight penetrating the windows was barely making an impression and all he had for company were his thoughts. But he wasn't in control of those thoughts because they were nightmares. He was having nightmares whilst he was awake. Something had invaded his head. Feeding off him. Sucking the life out of him. Trying to control him.

He shook his head violently trying to get the thing out of his head, but it stayed there. Gnawing away. He eventually screamed until the power in his voice waned, exhausted and worn out by the effort. His head suddenly cleared and he was free again. It was only a nightmare, he concluded as his eyes darted around the room looking for anything that may have been a theat. A stupid nightmare he told himself again as tiredness descended, but his eyes wouldn't close tonight.

The creature was feeding off Devon and felt stronger. It wanted more.

CHAPTER 35 (THE BUNKER)

Of course Samantha knew what was going on. Louise wasn't stupid, she needed Samantha on her side and to do that she needed to give her access to everything. Not that Samantha needed Louise's authorisation, she would've done it anyway.

Recording devices adorned the whole bunker and she had a team analysing everything that was going on, particularly for any signs of rebellion. These particular recordings though were for her eyes only and this one was particularly interesting, not just for what was being said, but also the body language.

She'd heard these types of discussions between Louise and her kids many times before, but this one suggested action. Action that needed her, but she wasn't part of the decision making process and should've been.

She was seething by the time the recording had finished, initially determined to argue against such action out of principle alone, but eventually calming down in the hope that Louise would seek her advice. But it'd been two hours since their meeting and she'd heard nothing. Surely Louise must've realised she knew what they were talking about.

Her patience finally wore thin and she stormed into Louise room, determined to remain calm, only to fail.

'What the fuck was all that about?' said Samantha.

Louise was sat on her rickety old sofa staring down at a screen and didn't immediately look up when Samantha came bursting in, as though dismissing her.

'What're you talking about?' she said sounding surprised.

Don't bite. Don't bite. Calm down. You won't win with anger, thought Samantha.

Samantha held her hands up and said calmly, 'I know it's your decision, but it involves my team.'

'I can't involve you in all decisions Samantha. Don't want my sons to think you're part of it.'

'But I am and I need to be involved.'

'And I was going to tell you. Anyway, you know everything that goes on in here.'

Samantha considered carrying on the argument, but concluded it was pointless.

'So that's it is it? You're going to send a team out there to find spare parts for the desalination plants. What're the chances of that?' said Samantha not sounding confident

'You got another idea?'

'Thanks for asking,' she said sarcastically before continuing. 'You know it won't work. Even if you find the parts, those desalination plants won't last another 60 years.'

'Where else can we get water then?' said Louise

'We need to think of the short term first and find those parts. And quickly.'

'Then what?'

'We may need to get the numbers down if we can't get those plants working,' said Samantha

'What? Kill people?' said Louise.

'Yes. But only if the worst comes to the worst. A contingency.'

Louise initially dismissed the idea, but coming from Samantha it gave it some credence.

'And what about the next 60 years?'

'This'll give us time to think about that. All we need at the moment is time to think of a clear strategy.'

'So you've not really come up with anything new?' said Louise angrily.

'No. But now you know you've got my support. And you need it. There's plenty of fresh water around. We just need to find it and get it here. We need to increase our storage capacity as well.'

'I know what we need to do Samantha. I just don't know how.'

'Then let's work together on this. Your sons are plotting something. I know it.'

Ordinarily, Louise would've leapt up to defend them, but her silence spoke volumes.

Samantha continued, 'you know I'm right then. They're up to something. I'm on your side Louise.'

'I've brought them up to be ruthless. I think it's going to back fire.'

'Let's stand together on this. Side by side. I've got my team behind me. They've got nothing.'

'I've got nothing,' said Louise standing up to face her.

'Together we have.'

Louise looked at her suspiciously. Did Samantha really need her? Maybe she did. Samantha had all the power, but no public profile and the public needed to be brought along. Strong arm tactics were a last resort and Samantha knew that.

'Together indeed. Ok. I'll leave it with you to get the team together to look for the parts. I'll get our engineers to look at water storage options again, but creating underground capacity will need drilling equipment and we haven't got any.'

'Maybe the team could look for that as well,' said Samantha

'Good idea. Let's get going.' said Louise walking past Samantha towards her private room.

'Wait,' said Samantha. 'I think Ben and Jed should each manage a team. They can cover twice as much ground.'

'But you don't trust them remember.'

'Whatever they're plotting, they need to keep this place going so I trust them to do that.'

'Ok. I'll leave it with you,' said Louise without hesitation, accepting that putting both her kids at risk was a necessity.

....

The teams were assembled and ready to go. Samantha had taken personal responsibility for the two boats taking them to the mainland. The secret tunnel she and Bill had used was still a secret and she wanted to keep it that way.

The gap in the weather wouldn't last long and they'd decided to camp up soon after disembarking to test the equipment against the elements. It was a risky venture, but needed to be done. If they and the equipment survived then the first hurdle had been overcome. Locations for potential sites for the spare parts had been identified and the teams would fan out using old fashioned communication devices to keep in touch with each other and the bunker.

Louise was on the shore watching the boats being loaded and thankful that she was wearing her cooling suit. Rousing speeches and goodbyes had been done and their orders were implanted inside their heads.

The men eventually stopped moving when everything had been done, looking around one last time for anything they may have missed. Once satisfied, they looked across at Ben and Louise heard him telling them to get aboard the two boats, each captained by her sons.

She looked on with a heavy heart. Had she done the right thing putting her children at risk? Were they capable of leading the expedition? Yes was the immediate conclusion. They were both very capable. They were a mixture of intelligence, practical ability, common sense and leadership. She and their fathers had these qualities and their up-bringing and education developed their skills. Her sons were her best bet. Her sons were everybody's best bet, she thought looking back towards the bunker.

She turned her attention to the sky, the distant murkiness a sign of the next expected storm force winds. They'd easily have enough time to cross the water and camp up, she concluded.

She watched as the boat silently moved across the almost flat water. It would be another few hours before the winds would start to gather pace. The eerie calmness at the moment was a lie to what was about to hit them. The weather forecaster expected the normal high winds and no rain in the afternoon.

The boats were soon just a speck on the horizon, then they stopped having reached the mainland. It was only then that Louise turned to return to the bunker, only to be met by Samantha who was the only other person to stay with her.

'They'll be fine,' said Samantha with a reassuring smile.

'How d'you know? You're not a mother.'

Samantha said nothing, knowing that Louise was right. She'd no children and empathy wasn't part of her character. It was all a show.

Louise brushed past her towards the bunker. Samantha watched before eventually following her. Everything was going to plan, she thought.

....

They landed safely on the mainland. There was a strong breeze and it would be a few hours before the strong winds hit them, easily enough time to set up camp and test their equipment, concluded Ben as he surveyed the area.

It was barren, like the island, and there was no living thing above ground level, only debris from what was once there. The ground was arid and dry and there was no greenery, although a brief period of life always appeared when the rains came, only to be killed off again by the searing heat. The ferocious weather in this part of the country had razed all buildings to the ground, only the fortified bunker had the capability to survive the harsh conditions.

'Ok,' said Ben. 'Let's get digging.'

Everyone knew what to do. If nothing could survive above ground, then they had to dig down. A simple army tactic that'd proved effective for many years. Light machinery was brought out and within 30 minutes huge holes had been dug about quarter of a mile from the sea and the equipment placed safely in the hole, leaving enough room for the two teams of five.

Ben had returned the boats to the island where they would be moored in the bunker, safe from the weather. Ben was very much the leader of the two brothers, but he was confident that Jed could take up the reigns when the two groups split up.

Ben looked over in the direction the wind was coming from. Winds were expected to be normal for this time of year and brief testing on the island had proved the shelter could at least hold up to these winds. They didn't have time to wait for the heavier winds, but Ben was confident they would hold out.

Ben shouted above the increasing breeze, 'ok. Everyone get into the hole.'

Each group then lowered themselves into their small cave, eventually covering the holes with a specially re-enforced tarpaulin, which was anchored to the ground using spikes that were buried deep into the ground.

Ben said, 'you know your orders and where to search. We'll report back to each other at this time every day,' he said looking at his watch. Everyone else did the same.

Readymade cooked food was handed around and everyone dutifully ate, knowing that calories would be important to ensure success of the mission. But it wasn't a lack of food that would scupper everything.

CHAPTER 36 (THE BOTHY)

The adrenalin in his body refused to go. Devon sat upright looking towards door that stood defiantly intact after the latest storm, which it'd done many times before. It was dark and the quiet was deafening. He couldn't take his eyes off the door, praying for daylight as though that would provide safety from whatever was out there. The nightmare hadn't left him because it wasn't a nightmare. He'd been awake. Conscious. Aware that something had control of his thoughts. But who or what was out there. No human, that's for sure. The virus had seen to that.

The uncertainty made him alert to every sound. He was ready to react quickly to anything, but he wasn't quick enough. The door crashed down and he was faced by the silhouetted figure of the creature stood at the doorway.

....

The batteries had been charged and the drone was ready to go. Harvey and his immediate family were ready to go and the last of the equipment was on the drone. Everyone at the bothy were happy that Harvey's family should be the first to go, trusting him to make the right decisions, as they had trusted him for many years. Harvey suspected that some were still a bit apprehensive about going so were glad not to stay for now.

It was early morning. Harvey and his family were saying their goodbyes and, particularly Harvey, was giving assurances, the main one being they had no alternatives. A few tears were shed, particularly between Lance and Nicola and their respective partners. They climbed into the drone and strapped themselves in, looking very uncomfortable cocooned amongst the equipment that surrounded them.

'We'll be back later,' said Harvey looking at the crowd a few yards from the drone.

'Be safe and good luck' said someone before Harvey gave a weak smile and lowered the hatch on the drone.

'Will we be safe?' said Nicola holding onto her sleeping child.

Harvey turned around to face her and said, 'we'll never be safe. but this is our best chance.'

He turned around again, not waiting for a response and the drone lifted into the air. Its rotors disturbed the loose soil and made those on the ground step back a little.

Thea looked across at Harvey with a look of trepidation. He noticed her out the corner of his eye, but continued to look straight ahead, knowing that he could do nothing to placate her. Thea soon looked away, then down at the watching crowd below who were looking forlornly at the departing drone. Guilt ate into her.

After a two hour trouble free flight they were approaching the house.

'Is that it?' said Thea sounding surprised. 'It looks in pretty good shape.'

Lance and Nicola were dozing in the back and suddenly woke at the indication that they'd arrived.

'I think it's been protected by that hill,' said Harvey without looking over at her.

'Doesn't look like there's anyone around.'

Harvey didn't answer. He didn't want to betray his fears and it was awkward for a few seconds before crying babies broke the silence, followed by comforting words from the parents. Harvey hovered over the house looking for any signs of life, but there was none. Even with the electric motor, surely Devon would've heard them.

The drone slowly descended until it landed close to the house.

'Stay here,' said Harvey looking across at Thea. 'Get this thing out of here if there's any sign of danger. Understand?'

The tone of his voice suggested that discussion wasn't an option so Thea simply nodded. Harvey climbed out of the drone and stood next to it, looking around for any signs of life. Nothing. He slowly walked towards the house, stopping just short of the open door and wondering why it wasn't closed. He looked back nervously at the drone to see Thea and the kids looking at him apprehensively. He returned his attention to the house again and walked slowly towards the open doorway. Stopping at the entrance, he looked inside for any signs of life.

His peripheral vision picked up movement and his head spun to the side only to see a dark figure disappear behind the house. He couldn't make out what it was, but knew it was dangerous. He should've run back to the drone and flown away with his wife and family. He should've at least looked over to the drone and ushered them to fly away without him, but his reflex action was to find out more, a scientist's instinct. Gather the facts before making a decision. Don't rely on emotions. All very sensible in normal circumstances, but this wasn't normal.

He crept towards the corner of the house where the thing had disappeared, pressing himself against the wall so he wasn't as much of a target. He put his head around the corner. Nothing. Was it simply a shadow he'd seen? Was his imagination getting the better of him? But where was Devon? Something was wrong.

He walked around the corner, looking ahead whilst using his peripheral vision to look for any hidden dangers. He reached an open window and looked inside, only to be met by a darkness that shouldn't have been there with the light streaming in. His didn't wait for his eyes to adjust and continued along the wall. The heat from the sun was intensifying. It was much stronger than further north and he hadn't yet acclimatised, but he ignored his discomfort and carried on.

The only think he could hear was his heavy breathing, brought on by adrenalin rather than physical exertion, and the sound of his footsteps. A sudden scream changed that and he stopped in his tracks for a few seconds before hurtling forward, disregarding all caution. Disregarding his own safety.

He reached the corner of the house, stopped and looked across at the drone. His eyes widened. His throat became drier and he sucked in air that filled his lungs and made him a little dizzy. The creature was stood next to the drone as though relishing the fear from its prey before it finally went in for the kill. Thea was hurriedly getting out, along with Nicola and Lance who each had one arm occupied holding their children, hindering their escape. The creature could've easily thwarted their escape, but chose not to as though it knew it already had them. Wanting them to run so it could enjoy the thrill of the chase.

Harvey instinctively ran towards the drone, not knowing what he was going to do when he got there, only knowing he had to do something. The creature turned around, the look on its face showed no sign of concern about the potential threat. It was only when Harvey got closer that he realised the creature was smaller than when he last saw it in the cage outside the bunker. Could he take it? Its scaly, rough skin looked impenetrable and its muscles still looked pronounced, despite its smaller size. Its face was the same. Horrifying. Evil. It's orange and red eyes were still penetrating and the horns on its head looked more developed.

His family were out of the drone and running away. Had his feeble attack distracted the creature enough so they had time to make their escape? That alone gave him hope that his almost certain death would not have been in vain.

He reached the creature, then swerved around it at the last second, having decided to join his fleeing family. He soon reached them and they fled together, but they had no chance. The creature was smaller, but it was quick and caught them up in a few seconds. It ran behind them whilst switching from side to side as though it was herding them. It wasn't long before Harvey and his family were running back to the house. His head started to throb more. Something was in his head. He quickly looked around to see the creature close behind. It looked excited. It looked hungry. He had to save his family. Nothing else mattered.

He stopped suddenly and Thea ran past, but then slowed whilst the others continued.

'Go. Get to the house. Now,' shouted Harvey.

Thea didn't argue and picked up her pace again, soon catching up with her kids. The creature stopped in front of Harvey, looking beyond him to his fleeing family before turning his attention to Harvey.

'Come on then you fuckin ugly twat,' said Harvey as though he was already doomed and had nothing to lose.

The creature stood taller. Harvey did the same.

'What're you waiting for?' continued Harvey.

He looked back towards the house for one last time to see his family stood nervously at the doorway with Devon alongside them. He'd forgotten about Devon. He was still alive. Why? Why wasn't he helping him?

Harvey returned his attention to the creature. It slowly made a move towards him.

CHAPTER 37 (THE BUNKER)

Louise was in her private chambers looking anxiously at the monitor. Ben and Jed had just reported their positions and everything was going well. Their shelters had survived the storms and they were making some progress, although they'd been hampered by the weather in the afternoons, meaning that travelling was limited to mornings only.

Louise had made a significant effort to communicate progress to the bunker inhabitants. Morale was a key element of her plan and minimised the risk of dissention. It wasn't difficult to portray a positive spin because everything was going well at the moment, but she was prepared to lie should events take a turn for the worst.

She was feeling very alone in the bunker, having no one to share the burden of leadership. She was contemplating bringing Ben and Jed's fathers into her now inner circle of one, but dismissed the idea, concluding that they couldn't be trusted to keep secrets. She had to keep aloof from the masses to maintain her mystique. They should only know what she was like by her actions and that was a confident, ruthless leader who would do anything to ensure the survival of the bunker and its inhabitants.

Samantha on the other hand wasn't part of the masses and certainly wouldn't divulge any secrets. For that reason, Louise trusted her and had given her Ben and Jed's responsibilities until they returned. That meant she was amongst the bunker inhabitants more frequently, along with her lieutenants, managing the day to day problems. Even though it'd only been a few days since Ben and Jed had left, she'd shown great aptitude.

Samantha went into Louise's room unannounced and saw her staring at the screen.

'Everything still ok?' she said.

Louise jumped a little and turned around feeling a little angry that she'd been disturbed.

Soon realising it was Samantha, who else could it be, the look on her face softened and she said, 'yes, but this is just the start of it. They've got to find the parts, get back here and fix the desalination plants. We can't bodge anymore.'

Louise was simply reiterating what Samantha already knew, so she didn't respond.

Louise stood up, turned to face her, took in a deep breath and continued, 'anyway everything ok out there?'

Samantha shrugged her shoulders and said, 'sort of.'

'What d'you mean?'

'I mean sort of. What d'you expect?' There're food and water shortages,' she said raising her voice a little.

Louise glared at her and said, 'everything'll be fine.'

'Let's hope so for all our sakes. You know I don't trust them.'

'Neither do I,' said Louise lowering her voice a little.

A confused look came across Samantha's face before she said, 'so why'd you let them go out there? They're our only hope. Why not send someone you trust.'

'Like who?'

'Well. I don't know. Me. Why not me?'

'Because I need you here.'

'What's more important? They could've carried on here.'

'Yes. But with you gone, who knows what they would've done,' said Louise turning away so she could lose eye contact with Samantha.

Samantha suspected something straight away, thanks to her training.

'What're you up to,' said Samantha. 'And don't bullshit me.'

Louise had her back to Samantha and instinctively brushed her hand across her nose and sniffed a bit as though trying to stifle a cry.

'There's no other way. There needs to be stability. We can't have a power struggle. There're more important things.'

'What've you done?' said Samantha raising her voice.

Louise turned to face her, the tears in her eyes were obvious and she made no attempt to hide her feelings.

'Ben and Jed won't be coming back,' she said her voice wavering a bit as though it was painful to say their names

'What're you talking about? We need them to get back here. The parts. You're their mother.'

'And I'm in charge and it needs to stay that way,' she said defiantly.

'What. You think they're that much of a threat that you're prepared to kill them? What sort of mother are you?'

'I'm the leader first and nothing's going to jeopardise that.'

Samantha looked away flabbergasted. Of course Ben and Jed were a threat to Louise's leadership, but they had nothing behind them to mount a coup as far as she knew. They could have infiltrated her security services or got enough support amongst the population to start a revolution, but Samantha had no evidence of this. What concerned her most was Louise. She didn't expect her to be so ruthless. A mother sending her children to their certain death was unexpected. Did she really know Louise at all?

It took her a few seconds before she got herself together and return her attention to Louise.

'So what's going to happen? If they're not coming back, the desalination plants won't get going again,' said Samantha hiding her disgust.

'We've got enough water in the storage tanks for a few more weeks, if we're careful.'

'Then what?'

Louise hesitated then said, 'I didn't have a choice Samantha. I know they were against my leadership and they were getting support. People aren't happy. There would've been bloodshed.'

Samantha stared at her as though not believing what she'd heard, then said, 'people're unhappy because there's a shortage of food and water and that won't change because your children are dead.'

Louise's eyes flickered for a few seconds before she said, 'and their answer was to kill people. Reduce the population. Well that's not going to happen.'

'What's your answer then?'

'We need water and I know how to get it.'

'What're you talking about?' said Samantha sounding exasperated. 'The desalination plants are our only hope and you've destroyed that hope.'

'The tunnel. Bills escape tunnel. He thought the drill that made it'd been destroyed. But it hasn't. It's down there in the tunnel. We can use it to dig for water. The spring that's down there has dried up, but there'll still be water underground somewhere.'

Samantha's eyes had widened and her mouth was slightly open, betraying her feelings of surprise and disbelief.

'What're you talking about? There's no drill.'

'There is.'

'If there is, why've you left it until now? Why wait until we're desperate?'

'We needed to use the desalination plants for as long as possible. Make use of them. Wait until things got desperate and now is that moment.'

'So you're going to magically reveal the drill are you? People're going to ask questions.'

'No they're not. Don't you see? I'll be the brave mother who sent her sons out to save the bunker and they returned with the goods. The drill.'

'And they died doing their duty.'

'Yes. They were attacked and died, but we managed to recover the drill. Don't you see? 'They'll be held up as heroes and I'll be the grieving mother who's sacrificed her children to save the bunker. Order will be returned and my sons'll no longer be a threat.'

All emotion had drained out of Louise and, along with it, any concern for her sons impending deaths.

'And how're they actually going to meet their deaths?'

'The men I sent out may work for you, but they're loyal to me. They have their orders.'

The coldness of her words made Samantha weaken at the knees a little, but she soon recovered. She was more concerned about, yet again, not being part of the decision making, but decided not to tell Louise, fearful that she may be next. Had Louise infiltrated her department?

Samantha said, 'order'll only return if we find water and you don't even know if that drill still works. Even if it does, there's no guarantee we'll find water.'

'We'll find it,' said Louise.

CHAPTER 38 (THE BOTHY)

Spencer had been Harvey's trusted lieutenant at the bothy until Harvey stepped back and let Devon take over the reins. Since then he'd become just another part of the group, dealing with the day to day problems, as everyone else did. He and Harvey were of the same age, but Spencer had only delved into fatherhood when he became settled in the Bothy, so his kids were in their early teenage years. He'd never really taken to being a leader and it hadn't sat comfortably with him when he ran the community. But now was not the time to shirk, what he thought were his responsibilities. With Harvey, Thea and Devon gone, Harvey had asked, or rather told, him to take the leadership role. Only a small sacrifice since Harvey would be returning in a few days if everything went well.

He assumed that was the case as he watched, along with everyone else, the approaching drone. Even from this distance he could tell the drone was nimbler than when it left, suggesting it had dropped off its cargo. Everything was going well, he concluded, although there would be a nagging doubt in his mind until it had successfully landed and Harvey had given reassurances.

The drone got closer and hovered above the waiting crowd for a short while as though basking in the glory of its return, before slowly descending and landing.

Spencer was the first to react and walked quickly towards the drone feeling a little relieved that Harvey was back to take up the leadership role again. The hatch to the drone opened and Harvey got out to be met by unexpected spontaneous applause, suggesting there had been tensions within the camp.

He held out his hand towards Spencer and they briefly shook before it turned into a hug.

'Everything go ok?' said Spencer releasing Harvey and stepping back. 'Thought you might not be coming back,' he said with a slight smile on his face to indicate it was a joke.

Harvey knew otherwise. It wasn't a joke' His original plan was to dessert them, but circumstances had changed.

'Fine. Everything's fine.'

'Come on. You must be starving. We'll talk after. Get this thing on charge,' said Spencer to the man standing closest.

They walked towards the bothy and descended into the cellar where the women were busily preparing food. Harvey smiled to himself. Despite equal rights and every attempt to blur the lines between the roles of the sexes, when the going got tough they reverted to type and no one complained.

The portions were small and the food was bland, but they did their best. Everyone was losing weight and it gave Harvey justification for his actions. They had to get away. Everything was ok at the moment, but as the food shortages worsened there would be fights, survival is everything to desperate people. They would probably kill each other before they starved to death.

‘So. What happened? Any problems?’ said Spencer wiping his mouth with the back of his hand.

‘No. The house is still there and everything’s been set up. I think we can get all the way down to the bunker on the next trip.’

‘Then what?’ said Spencer sceptically.

‘They’re bound to have some sort of surveillance on the mainland. They know me remember. They know I’ll be useful to them.’

‘There’s still a lot of ifs and buts though. What if they don’t recognise you? It’s been a long time and you’ve changed. What if they want you, but not us? They don’t know we’ve been vaccinated.’

‘I didn’t say it was risk free,’ said Harvey sounding a bit frustrated. ‘It’s our only chance. You know that. Anyway they must know we’re immune to the virus, otherwise we’d be dead.’

Spencer looked around the cellar at the drawn faces and thin bodies before saying, ‘I know. I know it’s a long shot and our only shot.’

....

The first step had gone without a hitch and the whole community was now camped up in the house. The drone was safety housed in an out building close by. They’d been very lucky to find the house, other structures in the distance had been flattened.

The storm raged outside but, as normal, there was no rain, only wind. Night was starting to descend, but Harvey could see in the distance how much worse the storm was compared to where they were. The hills did indeed give them some protection and he wondered whether they could make this their permanent home, but soon dismissed the idea. The weather would only get worse and even this place would eventually give in to mother nature.

'So far so good,' said Spencer noticing Harvey staring out of the window.

Harvey jumped a bit, turned around and said, 'sorry. I was somewhere else. Day dreaming.'

'Devon's been doing the same. Doesn't seem himself.'

'The burden of responsibility I suppose. We've all got families, but I suppose he feels responsible for everyone.'

'What's happened? Have you taken over again? Devon seems a bit aloof as though he doesn't want to take charge anymore.'

'Devon's weak. He can't cope with pressure. He's only any use with normal day to day stuff,' said Harvey with a hint of viciousness.

Spencer looked at him with a mixture of confusion and worry. He'd never seen Harvey like this before. He'd always been so mild mannered and calm.

Harvey looked beyond Spencer to his family and continued, 'yes. I'm in charge. I've spoken to Devon and he's ok with it.'

Harvey turned around to look out of the window again and also to indicate that the conversation was over. Spencer continued to look at him. Something was wrong. Something spelled danger. There was something that

Harvey wasn't telling him and the fear of the unknown scared him, but he trusted Harvey. Trusted him to do the right thing.

'What was that?' shouted Spencer.

Twilight was descending, but darkness suddenly took over for a second as though something walking past the window had blocked out the light that was left. Spencer continued to look intently through the window, trying to make sense of what he'd just seen. Harvey hadn't moved and showed no signs of reacting to the shadow or Spencer's question. Had Harvey seen anything? thought Spencer. He was closer to the window so must've seen what caused the shadow.

Spencer turned around to see everyone staring at him, confusion and fear written across their faces. He then looked at Devon who was still staring out of the window, seemingly oblivious to his surroundings. What's going on? he thought. Something's happened that he didn't understand and he didn't like it. He walked quickly towards the front door and opened it, only to be met by the wind almost ripping the door from his hand, but he managed to hold on to it.

He stood at the doorway, not daring to go any further and desperately looked into the fading light for anything that could've caused the shadow. Fragments were being thrown around by the wind and trying to get into his eyes so he squinted, but didn't give up. He needed to know what was out there. Hiding from the unknown simply wasn't an option.

A gust of wind caught the door and he was pushed back into the house a little before regaining his footing and putting all his efforts into fighting the wind.

The shadow reappeared and Spencer look up before going back into the house and closing the door, making sure it was secure before he finally let go of it.

'What was that all about?' said Thea sounding a bit angry. 'That door could've been ripped off its hinges and you would've followed it.'

'Sorry. I thought I saw something,' said Spencer sounding apologetic.

Thea said, 'what could possibly be out there in this weather?'

Spencer looked at the concerned faces around him and said, 'nothing. It was nothing. It's just some debris flying around. That's all.'

'Well I hope it was worth it.'

Spencer skulked away like a child who'd just been told off, and sat with his family. It was then that he noticed his aching joints A man of his age shouldn't subject himself to such excitement, he concluded. Thea was still looking at him with a disapproving look on her face, the others went about their business again, some were smiling slightly at the rebuke Thea had just given him.

Thea eventually walked away to join her husband who was still staring out of the window, seemingly oblivious to everything that was going on around him. Devon was doing the same. His stress levels rose again. Something was going on and he needed to be on his guard.

....

The creature felt stronger and no longer had to hide from the ravages of the storm it was walking into. It'd fed on a screx before leaving, having no regrets about eating the flesh of an animal it'd been living with for many years. Feelings were something it didn't have.

The herd had served its purpose and now it needed one more favour. The meat tasted good. Gave it the energy it needed for the journey ahead, a journey it had to make. A journey that would see the start of the life it was destined for and it had one weapon that would conquer humans.

CHAPTER 39 (THE BUNKER)

It was a few days after Louise had confessed her plans to Samantha and there'd been no sign that Samantha had any objections. In some ways it would've been safer to keep it to herself, but Louise needed Samantha on her side and decided that honesty was the best policy. In hindsight she should've brought her on board much earlier and hoped she wouldn't live to regret it.

She wasn't surprised that Samantha had willingly accepted everything that'd happened recently. Louise was a good judge of character and knew that Samantha was tough and ruthless, but she'd been trained to accept orders from her superiors and that inbuilt sense of duty was unshakeable. Nevertheless she was concerned that Samantha had openly expressed her own misgivings. Should she be worried?

It was late at night and Louise was in her private quarters dreading the moment when she'd get told of the death of her children. Of course it wouldn't be a surprise, but she had to put on a show. Shock. Horror. Grief. Pride. But above all she had to show determination and hope for the future, citing the drill as the bunker's saviour. It'd all been planned out. No one could return. She couldn't trust the surviving members of the expedition to keep secrets, there was too much at risk. They'd be left on the mainland to fend for themselves and the weather or starvation would eventually get them. That particular fate would not befall her children.

There's would be a quick and painless death and that placated what conscience she had.

She had told Samantha of these plans and she seemed to be accepting of them, stating that disloyalty isn't welcomed by her anyway and knowing it was essential to minimise the risk of Louise's plans being exposed to the masses. That would create mistrust and a revolution.

Louise was sitting on the sofa staring ahead in her own little world. She suddenly jumped up, the sudden rush of blood to her head made her feel a little dizzy. After a minute or two she turned around to look at the sofa, bent down and pressed the switch. One side of the sofa raised to reveal the steps into the escape tunnel.

This had been a frequent journey over the years and hopefully her last one. The drill would be her saviour. Everyone's saviour and she had to make sure it continued to work properly. She simply couldn't reveal the drill, only for it to fail.

The doubts about her plans started to surface. Should she have revealed the drill's existence a long time ago to save the unnecessary anguish? Why had she let things get so desperate? Why hadn't she involved Samantha until now? The answer was simple. She needed to show herself as the one who saved what was left of humanity and only by doing this would she retain the power she so desperately craved for.

She dismissed her doubts and descended into the tunnel. The lights came on automatically and she proceeded towards the small living area that Bill and Samantha had occupied many years ago. On reaching it, she quickly scanned the area. As normal, nothing looked out of place. The small stream that once flowed through had long since dried up, leaving a deeply cut channel that exposed rocks smoothed off by the water.

She moved to the edge and stood looking up towards the roof. After about a minute, a laser scanned her whole body looking for various physical features that were unique to her. Reliance solely on the eyes wasn't good enough. After a few more seconds the laser disappeared and the drill rose from the rocky ground. It was relatively small, but cutting blades would unfold to the size of the tunnel it had dug out, showing it was more than capable of doing its job.

Louise took a few steps towards it and scanned it to make sure everything looked in order. She then searched for a plate door and opened it to reveal a small screen. She touched it and a familiar menu came up. She knew the workings of the machine inside out and quickly found the self-check function. On pressing it, the drill sprung into life. Lights came on and a gentle whirring noise came from its motors. She tentatively looked around for any signs of life, not something that she'd ever done before, but this was a key point in her plan and she was apprehensive.

Lights darted across the screen as the drill undertook a diagnosis of its operational ability and Louise looked at it intently, dreading that some sort of error message would come up. A long five minutes passed and an all clear message was displayed on the screen and the lights slowly faded away leaving the drill looking like a lifeless piece of metal, in stark contrast to a few minutes ago.

Louise took one last look at the drill before she returned to the cave wall where the laser scanned her again and the drill sank into the ground. She exhaled slowly and her shoulders slumped a little to reflect the relief that swept through her. This was the final check. The drill was working fine and she had no concerns about revealing it to the bunker, hailing her sons as the heroes and herself as the glorious leader who'd sacrificed everything.

....

Samantha had read about it before. People who'd been in power for a long time always ended up the same. Louise was a competent, nice and truly engaging person when she first met her all those years ago. She slowly changed over the years when she got to the bunker, knowing that she was next in line after Bill if she played her cards right. And she did. The transfer of power was seamless with no dissenting voices at all, meaning that Louise got an insight into her own self-importance and popularity.

The years past and the power became addictive, which meant she had to protect herself from any threats to her authority. She came down hard on the population and they'd buckled. The things Louise had done and was about to do was a sign of a leader who would do anything to keep hold of something she didn't want to lose, even though it threatened humanity.

Samantha knew that Louise was taking a gamble on telling her about her plans and she regretted showing her reservations, rather than dutifully agreeing. Was that a mistake? Maybe not. Maybe if she'd not questioned her, Louise would have concluded that she was holding something back. No. She'd done the right thing by challenging Louise and also done the right thing by not doing anything in the days that followed. But now was the time for action.

Without knowing it, Louise had slept a lot more deeply, thanks to a drug in her water. This enabled Samantha to inject a tiny, undetectable camera into her chin which would eventually work its way out after a few weeks and, looking like a black head, Louise would barely notice it. That camera had told her where the drill was and how to get to it. The problem was that Louise was the key to the lock. No matter, she concluded, at least she knew where it was. Information was at the heart of everything, especially security.

It was the following morning and Samantha was awake early to see the camera footage. She wondered if Louise would be sleeping in, having had a late night, but she couldn't be sure. Sleep deprivation had never stopped her before and maybe in this key part of her plan, she didn't need it or decided it was a luxury she could do without. No matter what Louise was doing, Samantha had decided to let things play out for a while. There was no point interfering at the moment. All she needed to do was show her support, not upset the apple cart and give Louise the impression she was fully behind her, but when the time was right, she would make her move.

CHAPTER 40 (BEN AND JED)

Many more nights had passed and Ben, Jed and their men had survived another night of relatively quiet weather. They'd made good progress towards their intended targets. Ben was seeking an old factory which contained spare parts for the desalination plants and Jed was looking for equipment and tools to build increased water storage at the bunker. There were also contingency sites, should they fail to find what they were looking for. The plan was to carry the kit back using special battery powered vehicles so that they could easily be carried and assembled when they needed to use them. They'd decided not to carry the kit back to a point within the range of the drones, as the equipment would be far too large for the drones to carry.

Ben had been in regular contact with Jed's team and the bunker, but failure of the communication equipment wouldn't be cause for concern. Each team was working independently and pre-determined pick up points would be regularly monitored by the bunker so communications were not essential.

Spirits were high, although there was an underlying feeling of responsibility within both teams. As far as they knew there was no contingency plan and the bunker was surely doomed should they fail.

It was the start of another day. Light was breaking through the darkness and Ben and his men were almost ready for another gruelling trek towards their target. Their only obstacles were the tumbled down building and roadways which needed to be navigated around. Their cooling suits were giving them some comfort, kept their energy levels up and improved their morale.

'Let's go,' said Ben.

He wasn't a military man, but his manner was authoritative and he thought the men seemed to respond to him. He was open about his lack of experience and this seemed to be acknowledged by the team who regularly volunteered advice, which Ben readily accepted.

The men rose from their prone positions, hauled up their kit backs and equipment and slowly followed Ben who was already on his way and was about 10 yards in front of them.

In true military style and in line with highly trained and competent soldiers, timing and execution were impeccable. The knife slid into Ben's back and he collapsed to the ground before looking up at his executioner staring down at him with little emotion on his face. He felt the warmth of his blood on his skin and heard a hissing noise from his cooling suite as it also started to die. His vision started to fade and darkness descended as his life ebbed away. His twitching body eventually lay still and lifeless.

'He was useless anyway. No reason to let him live any longer,' said Ben's killer.

Geoff was a seasoned professional in his mid-fifties, having spent all of his working life in the military before ending up as one of Samantha's key enforcers in the bunker for the past 20 years. He was loyal to Samantha, but Louise was the commander in chief and he didn't hesitate when she asked him to do the barbaric act, citing Ben and Jed's disloyalty as a risk to the bunker. He also relished the thought of making the kill, something he was trained to do, but had never had the opportunity.

Geoff was second in command of the group, although in reality, he'd been making all the calls, so Ben's death wouldn't cause any problems. He continued looking at Ben's body for a few seconds after it had stopped twitching, then turned around to face the onlookers.

'Yeh,' said one of the men. 'Traitor. Like his brother. Leave him here. Let's get going.'

'I'm calling the shots now and I say when we go,' said Geoff angrily.

The man immediately backed down and said nothing, recognising the chain of command.

Geoff continued, 'strip search him. See if he's got anything useful we can take.'

The men immediately did as instructed, eventually finishing empty handed.

'Ok. Let's carry on. We should get to the factory by the end of today if the weather holds out. Then it's back to the bunker and away from this hell hole.'

The men wiped their blood stained hands on the ground, then stood up and walked off in the same direction, whilst Geoff took one last look around before joining them.

....

Jed and his men were staring into the distance. They shouldn't have been scared. It was five against one after all, but the distant figure looked threatening even though it was difficult to make out what it was. It suddenly disappeared as though it realised it'd been seen, but Jed and his men continued to stare.

'What the fuck was that?' said Jed looking across at his men.

'A screx?' said one of them.

'It was standing up,' said Jed dismissively. 'We need to carry on, the weather'll be coming in soon. We can't do anything about it now.'

'Something's not right. That thing didn't look human,' said Luke.

Luke was young and new to security, but had risen quickly through the ranks, having been identified by Samantha as a potential leader in the future.

'Of course it wasn't human you idiot. There's no one left. The virus got everyone, remember,' said Jed angrily as though panic was setting in.

The men exchanged glances with each other, some shook their heads a little before turning around and walking off, apart from Luke.

'We need to find out what it is,' said Luke. 'Maybe it's coming for us. We need to get to it first.'

'And maybe it's just some timid creature that's scared of us and has just run off.'

'Did you see the size of it?' There's no way it'd be scared of us.'

'The screx are bigger than us and they're scared.'

Luke looked at him whilst deciding his next move then said, 'well I'm not just going to wait around to find out.'

He turned around to see the other men stood staring at them.

'Well,' said Luke. 'Let's do it now and get rid of this worthless piece of shit.'

'What're you talking about?' said Jed. 'Do what?'

Those were the last words he said. The bullet hit him in the head and he was dead before he hit the ground.

Luke turned to face the men again and said, 'he was getting on my nerves anyway. You knew this was coming, so the sooner the better.'

Everyone was looking at the still body laid on the floor before one raised his head and said, 'what now?'

Luke looked back towards the place where they saw the figure and said, 'we'll carry on. There's no point trying to chase something we can't see. It'll come to us if it wants anything. Keep your eyes peeled.'

'But that's what Jed was going to do,' said one of the men.

'He was a dead man anyway. Now come on.'

Luke walked off, soon followed by his men, but it wasn't long before movement ahead stopped them in their tracks. It couldn't have got here that quickly, concluded Luke. Was there more than one? Were they hunting in packs?

'Spread out. Don't make yourself a target,' he said without looking at his men.

They instantly did as instructed, fanning out in a semicircle as though setting a trap for the potential victim, but were they the victim, thought Luke.

'Stand your ground. Did anyone make out what it was?'

There was no response so Luke continued, 'if they'd weapons and wanted to kill us, we'd be dead already, so wait for them to make the first move. Then shoot on sight.'

They stood motionless, weapons held up and fingers placed softly on the triggers, waiting for any signs that would prompt them to twitch. Their breathing was a little laboured, but it didn't hamper their focus. They'd been trained for such situations, but never before had they been required to use it. The mere suggestion of force and violence in the bunker was usually enough to quell any dissent.

The creature slowly stood up from the low wall it was crouching behind and stood defiantly as though it had nothing to fear. A volley of shots rang out and it stumbled backwards from the impact, soon regaining its composure and standing upright again.

'Stop firing,' shouted Luke.

They had already lowered their weapons before the order and were staring at the creature as though mesmerised. No one made a sound as they all seemed totally spell bound and unable to move. Luke moved his mouth in an attempt to speak, but the creature immediately focused on him, making him back down and join the others in silence and awe.

The creature slowly moved forward. The drool dribbling out of its mouth suggested it was excited by the situation. The men stood still. One hurriedly looked around as though searching for an escape route, then fled. He didn't get far. The creature ran towards him, running past the others, who remained still, and within a few strides it grabbed the fleeing man. He writhed around in a desperate attempt to escape, all to no avail. The creature drew the man towards him until he was inches away from its mouth, then sniffed.

'You're not like the rest,' it said squeezing the man until breathing became difficult for him.

The creature turned to look at the onlookers, who showed no emotions on their faces and said, 'he's all yours.'

The creature threw the man towards them and he fell unceremoniously in front of them. They all looked down on the crumpled heap in front of them, the confusion was etched across their faces before everything became clear. He hadn't had the vaccine.

CHAPTER 41 (THE BOTHY)

It had taken two days to recharge the drone batteries in which time tension amongst the group had risen. They were in unfamiliar territory and it felt like the house was their prison against the dangers that lay outside. They were also surprised by how much warmer and drier the weather was, even though it was only a two hour trip from the bothy. This led to concerns about how much worse it would be further south and some even suggested going back to the bothy.

'There's no food left up there. It's all here. And there's not much in the fields. Remember. That's why we're here. Because we'll starve to death if we stay at the bothy.

Devon had a strained and frustrated tone to his voice as he explained why they were where they were. And yet again it was Spencer who was raising his concerns.

'Well I'd rather die up there than in this hell hole. And where we're going'll only be worse,' said Spencer.

'It's our only chance Spencer. You know that.'

'A slim chance.'

'A chance all the same.'

Spencer turned away as though dismissing Devon's reassurances and walked off before spinning around and saying, 'and what was that thing I saw out there the other night?'

Devon said, 'it was nothing. Debris remember. You said it yourself.'

Spencer turned around again and skulked off.

Harvey walked up to Devon and said, 'don't let him change our plans. You know it's our only chance. We have to get there.'

Devon nodded and said, 'over my dead body, or his if needed.'

'Nothing. Nothing'll get in our way. Understand,' said Harvey assertively.

'You don't need to convince me. But they might need a bit more convincing,' said Devon nodding towards the others in the house. 'Spencer's getting to them with his constant questioning. And things could get worse when we make the next trip in the drone. He'll be here alone with them and we won't be able to control him.'

Harvey took a deep breath and looked past Devon to the group sat on the floor before saying, 'I'll deal with Spencer.'

'How?'

'I said I'll deal with him.'

....

It was early morning the following day and the drone was being loaded up with equipment and food for the final leg of the journey. As before, Devon and Harvey were to go first and look for a suitable place where people could stay. What was different this time was that Harvey would attempt to make contact with the bunker and if everything went well, then Devon would return to the house and bring more people down. If it didn't go well, then. Well. They'd have to return to the bothy and die.

This was the riskier part of the journey, but they were both a lot more confident than before. They had an ace up their sleeve that wouldn't guarantee success, but would greatly improve their chances even if they weren't welcomed.

Harvey was with Thea and his children and grandkids, away from the group and was saying his goodbyes.

'Everything'll be fine,' said Harvey with a reassuring grin on his face.

'I know it will be. But they don't know that do they,' said Thea.

'Including Spencer,' said Nicola. 'He's going to be trouble.'

'He'll be ok in the end,' said Thea.

'I don't think he'll get to the end and he won't believe us if we tell him now. It's too far-fetched,' said Lance.

Harvey said, 'then you'll have to deal with him. Do whatever you have to do, but don't kill him. We need him alive.'

They all nodded, then Thea said, 'we just need a reason to keep him away from the rest. Leave it to me.'

Harvey embraced his wife, then encouraged his kids to do the same, leaving the grandkids happily wriggling around on the floor.

They eventually parted and Harvey looked at his kids and said, 'this is for you and them. Not us. The creature will look after us, so there's no need to worry.'

They both gave their dad a quick smile and he turned to go, soon reaching the others who were already gathered around the drone to give them a farewell wave.

Harvey made his way through the crowd, accepting the good luck gestures and reached the drone to be met by Devon.

'Everything ok?' whispered Devon.

Harvey nodded, turned around and said to the crowd, 'we'll be back in a few days like before. They'll have us in the bunker once they've scanned us to confirm we've been vaccinated. I know I've told you this before, but I need you to believe everything'll be ok. Doubt is our only threat,' said Harvey looking towards Spencer who instantly looked away.

Devon said, 'listen to Harvey and to me. This is the only way. There's no going back.'

Devon was a little more forceful than Harvey which, going by the body language of the crowd, seemed to have driven the point home. They both gave a final wave before climbing into the drone, doing their final checks before looking one last time at the expectant crowd and climbing into the sky.

Looking down, Devon said, 'I know this wasn't part of your plan.'

'What're you talking about?'

'You and your family. You just wanted to take them didn't you?'

'Yes. Well. Things've changed haven't they. This is better. Anyway, I don't have a choice do I.

'No.'

Thea looked up at the departing drone, watching it until it went out of sight. She then looked across to the others who were doing the same. She walked across to

Spencer, grabbed him by the arm and dragged him away. He was a little surprised and didn't resist, thinking only that Thea wanted to talk about what they were going to do for the next few days.

'Everything ok Thea?' he said looking unconcerned.

'About your outbursts Spencer. They're distracting. Putting doubts in people's minds and we can't have that,' said Thea sounding authoritative.

'Well it's got to be said. I'm not convinced by this and people need to know.'

'They need to know that this is the only way.'

'Well I don't think it is. You're giving up on the bothy and I think you're wrong.'

Thea stared at him, desperately looking for any sign that she may be able to convince him that the bunker was their only option.

'Well we can't get back without the drone can we?' said Thea.

'What? You agree with me?'

'No. Why did you bother coming Spencer if you don't agree?'

'I'd no choice. I wasn't going to stay there alone. Anyway, I can see it in their eyes now. Everyone's having doubts. Can't you see it?'

'Only because you're putting the doubts in their heads and that can't go on.'

'So. What're you going to do about it?' he said defiantly. 'Kill me?'

'No. That's not our way. You know that. But I can keep you out of the way.'

The veiled threat immediately put Spencer on edge, but it was too late. He slumped to the floor lifeless and Thea was faced by Lance with a brick in his hand.

'He's not dead. I didn't hit him hard enough.'

'How long will he be out? said Thea looking down at Spencer.

'I don't know. This is a first for me. Not long,' said Lance shrugging his shoulders. He continued, 'quick. Whilst everyone's together talking about the drone.'

Lance picked up the lifeless body and dragged him to the barn where the drone was stored.

He propped him up against the wall and said, 'is Nicola out there keeping them away?'

Thea nodded and said, 'yes. Now come on, let's do this.'

Lance grabbed a small box from the back of the barn and dropped it into a pre-dug hole.

'Now you stand guard and let me know when,' said Thea before starting to walk back to the crowd leaving Lance with Spencer, who was starting to groan a little.

'Hurry,' said Lance. 'He's waking up.'

She picked up her pace to join Nicola who was talking to a group in an attempt to keep them all together.

'Everything ok?' said Thea as calmly as she could.

Nicola nodded and looked around before saying, 'yeh. Looks like they got away ok.'

Thea looked back at the barn. Lance was nowhere to be seen.

Thea said, 'has anyone seen Spencer? He seems to have disappeared.'

‘I saw him go into the barn,’ said Nicola sounding unconcerned. ‘I think I saw him carrying some food. Is he responsible for that?’

‘No,’ said Morag sharply. ‘That’s my job and no one else’s.’

Morag’s tone caused an awkward quietness so she continued, ‘I think some food’s been taken. I’m not sure.’

‘Why aren’t you sure if it’s your job?’ said Thea as though accusing her of incompetence.

Morag instantly looked defensive, but couldn’t find the words. She instinctively looked towards the barn and Thea followed her eyes.

Thea said, ‘let’s have a look. I can’t believe that Spencer’s been steeling food. Probably a big mistake.’

Thea, Morag and Nicola walked towards the barn, watched by those who’d been listening. Thea tentatively opened the barn door to see Spencer rising from his prone position, holding his head. Perfect timing, she thought.

She flung the door open as though she’d discovered something extraordinary and had to show everyone.

‘What’re you doing Spencer?’ she shouted.

He looked across at her, but was distracted by the light and didn’t say anything.

Thea continued, ‘what’s in that box?’

He looked down and confusion spread across his face, then fear at realisation of what he was looking at.

‘That’s got nothing to do with me. Someone planted it,’ he said trying to stay calm.

Thea realised that she needed to strike whilst the iron was hot and avoid discussion.

She turned to Morag and said, 'get some of the men. He needs to be locked away.' Morag looked hesitant so Thea continued, 'this is your fault Morag.'

'This is nothing to do with me,' said Spencer.

'Go,' shouted Thea.

Morag disappeared.

'You won't get away with this,' said Spencer.

'It's your own fault and it's better than dying,' said Thea staring intently at him.

'It's her,' said Spencer to the returning group. 'She's done this.'

Thea ignored the accusations and said, 'take him. Tie him up and gag him.'

The men hesitated, unsure of what was going on.

'Do it,' said Morag.

The men instantly moved forward and Spencer made a vain attempt to escape, but they restrained him and then looked up for further instructions.

'Gag him,' shouted Thea knowing that the priority was to shut him up.

Morag looked around, found a piece of old cloth and handed it to one of the men who quickly tied it around Spencer's mouth.

'Tie him against that post,' she said pointing to one of stone columns that held up the barn.

Morag went out of the barn, soon returning with ropes. The men tied him up and then stepped back as though admiring their handy work.

'What's this all about?' said one of them.

'He's been stealing food,' said Morag pointing towards the open box.

They both looked incensed, before one of them made a move towards Spencer.

Thea grabbed him and said, 'no. No one gets hurt. Just leave him here.' She turned to Morag and continued, 'I'll look after him. Make sure he's got enough food and water. No one else is to come in here. I'll tell everyone what's happened. Now everyone leave. Morag take the food back.'

They all did as instructed, leaving Thea alone with Spencer who looked resigned to his fate.

'It's your own fault Spencer. You should've kept your mouth shut.'

She walked away, shutting the barn door as she left.

Spencer slumped a little before getting lost in his thoughts. She was right. He didn't know why, but she was definitely right.

CHAPTER 42 (EVERYONE)

The report of Ben and Jed's deaths was greeted with shock and upset by Louise, despite her knowing all along that it was coming. Both teams could now proceed unhindered by inexperienced commanders, she concluded trying to placate herself. The parts they were striving to get were not as important as they thought, now that she'd confirmed the drill was working perfectly, but they would be useful as a backup should something go wrong. The parts for increased water storage would be particularly useful.

She'd decided to hold back on delivering the bad news to the bunker, fearful that this may dampen spirits. Morale was an important part of her plan. When the teams returned with the parts she would release the news that they'd all perished from something or other just over the water on the mainland. She could make up any number of stories. Of course the bonus news would be that they'd miraculously discovered the drill that was sitting below ground in the cavern. An easy lie for her

But she needed Samantha on her side so had decided to tell her of Ben and Jed's deaths, particularly because she probably knew anyway and her openness would create trust.

Her tears flowed freely for a few minutes, not only for the loss of her sons, but also for the loss of her dynasty. It was a sacrifice she was willing to make. Any threat to her power and authority had to be quashed.

The tears dried up and she immediately looked up at the screen in front of her, hesitating for a short while before saying, 'Samantha.'

Ten seconds later, Samantha appeared on the screen.

'They're dead,' said Louise.

'You mean they've been killed,' said Samantha looking solemn and a little angry at the same time.

'It had to be done.'

'And you're sticking with your plan. You know finding the parts'll be a long shot.'

'The parts are a bonus. They'll definitely be coming back with the drill. You know that.'

'Yeh. Held up as heroes, the lot of um. Martyrs to the cause. And martyrs can't talk. Are you just going to let them all slowly starve to death on the mainland?'

'I've no choice. I can't send a team out to kill them. No one else can know what's going on. There rations'll be depleted by the time they get back. It won't take long. I can say we lost radio contact so didn't know they'd returned.'

'You've thought of everything haven't you?'

'It's my job to think of everything and if something goes wrong then you're in it as deep as me.'

The veiled threat angered Samantha a little, but she hid her feelings with a deft smile before saying, 'I know. But I'm behind you Louise. Behind you all the way.'

'Then let's get this done.'

....

Several days had passed and Jed's team had found the site they were looking for. Luke was now the leader and had guided them with all the expertise of a seasoned army man, something that Jed couldn't have done.

Luke had no regrets about killing his colleague who'd somehow avoided vaccination. The disease disappeared some time ago because it no longer had humans to feed off, but they couldn't take the risk. For no other reason, he had to go because he failed in his duty to protect himself and others.

'Ok. Search the place. You know what we need,' said Luke moving towards the demolished building..

The others followed, disregarding the bones that lay around the building. It was obviously a well populated area at one time. In all likelihood they probably thought a substantial building like this could protect them from the weather. And it probably could for a while, but it couldn't protect them from the virus.

On reaching the building, Luke turned around and said, 'right spread out. Look for anything that may be of use. And I mean anything. We can sort out the crap afterwards. Give it an hour, then we'll set up camp before the storms come.'

They all spread out and disappeared into the building, whilst Luke looked on for a few moments, lost in his thoughts. The creature was never far from his thoughts. It ate away into his conscious. Made him feel reliant on it, but was it a source of security and safety or was it a threat. He didn't know and now wasn't the time to make decisions. Now was the time to get the job done and get back to the bunker.

....

Geoff was reporting his position to Louise, having just spoken to Luke. Everything was going to plan and they would soon reach their destination. It'd taken longer than they thought and rations were getting low, but they would make it, Geoff was confident of that.

Their general direction was north and Geoff was surprised at how the climate had changed. It was more humid and there was more vegetation, suggesting there was more rainfall. This ultimately meant that there were more screx, but they were vegetarian so weren't a threat.

'What the fuck's happened here?' said one of his men before turning around to look at Geoff.

The man was about ten yards ahead and Geoff quickly caught him up. A dead screx lay in front of them, which wasn't unusual in itself. What was unusual was its condition. There was no sign of natural decay. What lay before them was a carcass that looked like it'd been devoured by something else. Fresh flesh hung from its bones and the earth around it was sodden with blood.

'Something's done this,' said Geoff.

'But what?' said the soldier. 'There's nothing alive that could've done this.'

The others had caught up by now and everyone was looking at the carcass, muttering their concerns to each other.

'We need to get going,' said Geoff. 'I don't know what's been going on here and I don't want to find out. Let's just get this done and get back to the bunker. We'll be there in a few hours if we get a move on. We'll set up camp and search for the equipment tomorrow.'

Geoff marched off and they all instinctively followed, grimacing at the screx as they passed it. None had experienced such carnage in their lifetimes. Circumstances dictated that they were all vegetarians and lived in a sanitised environment where the only deaths were natural and bloodless.

The vegetation was at a low level, although some was a little taller than them, meaning their visibility was a little restricted, but their hearing wasn't.

It was midday and, as usual at this time of day, there was no wind and the heat was unbearable without a cooling suit. It was the "quiet before the storm." The weather at this time of year was still ferocious, but it was predictable to a certain extent, unlike other times of the year when storms would come from nowhere, making forecasting almost impossible.

Geoff stopped when he heard the noise, looking around hurriedly to make sense of what he was hearing. Others did the same. The noise sounded distant, but loud and was in the direction they were heading. It was also getting louder, suggesting that whatever was causing it was heading towards them. Geoff quickly walked forward into a clearing where he could get a better view.

'You,' he said. 'Come here.'

The soldier approached Geoff and stood waiting for his next order.

'Lift me up on your shoulders so I can see.'

The man dutifully bent down and Geoff climbed on before being hoisted up.

'Hand me those binoculars,' he said to another soldier.

He scanned the area and it wasn't long before he saw the reason for the noise. The vegetation was swaying around violently in the distance and a grey mass of stampeding screx was causing it. They were moving fast and it wouldn't be long before they reached them. Something had spooked them, but what?

'Get me down,' shouted Geoff. He was lowered to the ground and continued, 'give me the radio and run in that direction,' he said pointing.

Without hesitation, one of the men gave him the radio and they fled leaving Geoff alone. He soon started to follow them whilst trying to contact the bunker.

'We're in trouble. There's a herd of stampeding screx.'

Those were the only words he could muster as the fast moving screx suddenly appeared from nowhere. The herd was probably about a hundred, thought Geoff when he looked through the binoculars, but counting wasn't his priority. His men ahead of him had a better chance. Or that's what he thought as he saw them mowed down and trampled into the dirt. The collision didn't even slow the screx down as they continued on their journey of fear. His last thoughts were of his family. The mission had failed. He'd failed and he'd failed his family. His death would be quick, theirs would be a slow starvation or death through anarchy caused by desperate people trying to survive. He was suddenly knocked to the ground and the last thing he saw was a large hoof coming towards his face. The last thing he heard was his screaming voice.

The creature was faster than the screx and soon caught its prey, sinking its teeth deep into the head and crushing the skull. Death was instantaneous, although its quivering body took a few minutes before it calmed. The creature was about to feast but was distracted by the scream. A human scream.

It strode purposefully towards the noise as though it was at the top of the food chain and had nothing to fear. The fleeing screx had provided a clear path through the sparse vegetation, making its progress a little easier. It soon reached the dead lifeless bodies scattered over the ground. Their squashed and contorted bodies clearly showed how they met their deaths and the creature immediately knew it was responsible for the carnage

It tentatively approached the bodies, sniffing each one like a wild animal, but its only motivation was to confirm they were dead. The creature looked solemn, hunched over as though weighed down with grief. It suddenly stood up straight, looked to the sky and howled as though it was releasing pent up tension and giving a final salute to the dead. These were the men it was searching for and it had killed them.

The howling stopped and it returned to staring at the lifeless bodies. It needed them. They were part of it. It needed their loyalty. It needed their fear. It needed to be strong. It needed to survive and live the life it wanted.

The creature stood staring, but it wasn't grief. It was more disappointment that something useful had been lost which threatened its plans. Reality soon took hold and it returned to the kill to feed off the flesh. It'd grown fond of the meat since it tasted it a few weeks ago.

After the feed, it would make its final journey. It suddenly looked up to see the drone passing overhead towards the south coast. It crouched down, making its natural colouring blend in with the dirt it was standing on. Its spirits suddenly lifted.

....

The final stage of their trip was, so far, without incident. The drone had performed admirably, indeed the increased sunlight further south meant that the batteries could be fed as they flew, meaning less time would be required for recharging when they eventually landed.

The drone was travelling slowly. High enough to see into the distance, but low enough so they could make out structures on the ground. They were getting close to the island now and needed to find somewhere safe to stay on the mainland, but all the buildings seemed to have been flattened. There was nothing that was habitable.

Devon had considered flying directly to the island, but Harvey had convinced him that it wasn't a good idea. A UFO suddenly appearing on the bunker's doorstep would surely result in them being blown out of the sky.

Treading carefully by first presenting themselves on the mainland stood a greater chance of their acceptance.

'There's nothing,' said Devon straining his eyes.

'We've got plenty of time before the weather turns,' said Harvey reassuringly, although inside the doubts were eating away at him.

'That's crap Harvey and you know it.'

'Have we got enough charge to get back?'

'Maybe. I'm not sure.'

'Well we have to decide now. Go on or turn back now. You're the boss so you decide.'

Devon went silent then said, 'there's no point going back is there?' he said as though wanting Harvey to agree.

Harvey said nothing so Devon continued, 'we'll go on. There may be something close to the coast. That's where most people used to live so there's a greater chance that some buildings have held up.'

'Ok. For the record, I agree.'

They both turned their attention to the ground below and it wasn't long before the coastline came into view in the distance.

'There's no turning back now,' said Devon. We don't have enough charge.'

'What's that?' said Harvey suddenly.

'Where?'

'Over there to the right. It looks like some sort of hole in the ground, but it's not a quarry. Looks fairly new.'

'Right I see it. I'll take us down.'

The drone descended slowly until it was about a hundred feet from the ground.

‘That looks like somewhere we could hold out in,’ said Harvey. ‘There’s probably enough room for the drone as well.’

‘It’s been used recently. Maybe it’s still being used.’

‘It’s the best thing we’ve seen since we started out. It’s our only chance.’

‘Let’s give it a go,’ said Devon before easing the drone down until it came to rest next to the cavern.

They got out and the heat hit them straight away.

‘Shit, it’s hot,’ said Devon looking around at the barren landscape.

‘No wonder there’s no life here. I bet there’s not even any screx.’

Devon decided this wasn’t the time for further discussion on the climate and climbed down onto the ground, soon reaching the huge hole that’d obviously been dug out by something or someone.

‘It’s deep,’ said Devon. ‘D’you think it’ll protect us?’

‘I hope so,’ said Harvey. ‘We don’t know what the storms are like down here. All we can say is that it doesn’t rain much at this time of year, so that’s a bonus.’

They descended down the steep bank, slipping frequently before reaching the bottom.

‘It’s cooler down here,’ said Devon.

Harvey looked up and said, ‘the sun probably doesn’t get in here through the day. It’s bound to be cooler.’

Devon looked around and said, ‘I think someone’s been here recently.’

‘Well we can’t do anything about that can we. If they come back, all we can hope for is that they’re friendly.’

'Why would they be out here in the first place? They can only be from the bunker. Everyone else has died from the virus.'

'You know I can't answer those questions Devon. All I know is that we'll be staying here and taking our chances. If they're from the bunker and friendly, then that'll be good news for us.'

'Ok then. You're right. Let's get the drone in here and get those batteries on charge.'

They climbed out and moments later the drone was in the trench. Harvey unpacked the equipment and food, whilst Devon put the batteries on charge at ground level where the sun was. When finished, they ate and settled down, both physically and particularly mentally exhausted.

'What now?' said Devon.

Harvey looked at him as though a little disappointed that he wasn't taking the lead before saying, 'we won't have a roof over our heads when the next storm comes, so we may as well get some sleep now whilst we can.'

'I think someone needs to stand guard. I'll do the first hour,' said Devon.

'Ok. Wake me up if you hear anything.'

'Obviously,' said Devon sounding a little annoyed.

Harvey made himself comfortable and began thinking about how lucky they'd been. He'd always been "a glass half full" type of man and finding the ready-made trench was definitely a plus. Others may have thought that they were unlucky not to have found another house.

He was looking up into the sky at the full moon. It was suddenly eclipsed as the creature jumped down, landing so hard next to him that the ground shook. He immediately leapt up in a vain attempt to protect himself. The creature stood staring as though trying to get inside his head. Its head slowly moved closer.

He could feel the hot moist breath against his face and recoiled a little, but didn't attempt to run, knowing it was pointless. He lowered his head and closed his eyes, hoping that this sign of surrender would increase his chances of survival. He then crouched down and covered his head with his arms, awaiting his fate, but nothing happened. It was inside his head. Searching for his inner thoughts. Looking to control him.

The creature let out an almighty roar and Harvey instantly woke up and bolted upright. His eyes darted around in search of the creature, but there was nothing. A dream. It was only a dream, he concluded. His body relaxed as the adrenalin seeped away, leaving him to shiver a bit from the thin layer of sweat that covered his body.

He looked up again to see Devon looking down at him from above.

'Everything ok up there?' said Harvey sounding a bit shaken.

Other men appeared next to Devon and also looked down on him. Harvey knew straight away that they were in trouble.

....

The drone was hovering overhead, warning those below of its intended descent. Everyone in the house was outside looking up as though it was their saviour, as indeed it was. The drone descended, landing close to the waiting crowd and Harvey got out. The look of hope was etched across his face.

He looked around hurriedly for his wife and ran towards her, grasping her by the shoulders at arms length at first and looking into her expectant eyes before dragging her towards him and holding her tight. Thea melted into him.

'Everything's going to be fine,' said Harvey. 'We've found somewhere and made contact with the bunker.'

Thea dragged herself away and said, 'what? So we can go straight to the bunker then?'

'No. It's complicated.'

'Don't treat me like a fool Harvey.'

'We need to get everyone down there first, then we go in as one.'

'Who've you met from the bunker?'

'Some soldiers. They were patrolling. They're on our side Thea. Our side.'

'That means they're not part of the bunker.'

'Listen don't worry. Everything'll be fine. We've got somewhere to stay and make proper plans before we try and get into the bunker. I didn't think we'd get this far to be honest. Did you?'

Thea stared at him, shook her head and said, 'no. Don't suppose so. I trust you Harvey.'

She stepped back and turned her face the onlooking expectant crowd before returning to look at Harvey and saying, ‘they’ll be on board as well. I’ve dealt with Spencer.’

CHAPTER 43 (THE BUNKER)

Louise listened to Geoff's screams and the sound of stampeding screx before the radio broke and silence descended. She looked away from the screen, lost in her thoughts. There would be no parts for the desalination plants and no returning soldiers from Ben's group. The latter was a problem solved. The former meant that the drill had to work. There was no longer a contingency plan.

She breathed in and took in the news before turning her attention to Jed's team. They'd been successful and were now on the mainland close to the bunker with the parts for increasing water storage capacity. This was more important than the desalination plants as water from the drilling would need to be stored before use and the more storage they had the less often they'd have to open the taps on the drill site. Everything was going well, she concluded.

Leaving Jed's team on the mainland was a necessary evil, but she was fearful that they may destroy the water storage equipment as revenge and she couldn't risk that. Bringing them back also wasn't an option so she'd decided that they had to be killed quickly and ruthlessly on the mainland. Samantha had a select group of soldiers she could rely on to do anything she wanted and to keep quiet about it.

Louise had long since resigned herself to the fact that she had to give up the location of the escape tunnel. The drill was in there and someone had to recover and relocate it to the drill site which was in another part of the tunnel.

'Samantha,' she said.

She appeared on the screen.

'Come here,' she said as though speaking to a servant.

It wasn't deliberate, but years of leading a dictatorship had made her that way. Within a few minutes, Samantha was by her side, seemingly like a dog looking for treats from its master.

'I want to make an announcement.'

'Really? Now?'

'Yes. Now. Face to face. I need a crowd for this one.'

'So you're going to announce the drill are you? Their saviour and you'll be the hero and Jed's team will be the martyrs who've delivered it.'

'Yes Samantha,' said Louise assertively. 'You know what my plan is. I'll need a couple of your trusted men to recover the drill so that I can show it to them. And I'll need those men to report to me only.'

Samantha glared at her for a few seconds before saying, 'I'll sort it out.'

Samantha switched off her screen and sat back in her chair. After a couple of minutes she got the ball rolling and within an hour the stage was set for the grand announcement. The thought of Louise basking in her own glory sickened her, but she only had to tolerate it for one last time. Until then she had to keep up the pretence.

Louise was faced by two tall upright men dressed in white boiler suites and white helmets with dark sunglasses. They looked immaculate and the colour had been chosen by Samantha so that any sign of dirt would be clearly visible, rather than hidden behind a dark colour. It was pointless in many respects, but getting soldiers to do pointless exercises was a good way to improve discipline.

'What I'm about to show you will soon be shown to everyone,' she said getting up from the sofa.

The sofa lifted up and the tunnel entrance was revealed. Their heads moved slightly, but they showed no emotion at all, standing perfectly still whilst they awaited Louise's final instructions.

'You know what to do. I've told Jed's team where the tunnel entrance is and that you'll be there to help them. Make sure that all the equipment is there before you kill them. They'll be taken by surprise so there shouldn't be a problem. Understand?'

'Yes ma'am,' they said together.

'Now go. Send me a message when it's done.'

The men descended into the tunnel and Louise saw the tunnel lights go on before she lowered the sofa and sat back down. The only thing to do now was wait, but it wasn't long before she heard a knock at the door.

'Come.'

Samantha entered with a sense of urgency and stood in front of Louise.

'It's all ready. I think we should go together with an armed guard. They haven't seen you in the flesh for a long time and we can't take chances. It'll show them that we stand together on this.'

'Why would they want to harm me? I've led them well.'

'There's no food and they need someone to blame.'

'But that's not my fault. Anyway, I'm the one that's going to solve that particular problem.'

'But they don't know it yet do they. And until then we need to keep you safe. That's my job.'

Louise admired her sense of loyalty and was grateful to Samantha's dedication.

'Ok. But after the announcement I'm on my own. I need to show them I'm one of them and not an aloof, protected figure head.'

'Ok,' said Samantha. 'Let's go.'

Louise got up and they went through to the main room to be greeted by several armed guards also dressed in white boiler suits. Neither broke stride as they passed them and exited into the white corridor where the guards caught up and surrounded the two women whilst looking nervously around for any threats.

The entourage walked purposely towards the conference room. Louise noticed that the plants that once adorned the corridors to make the place look homely had disappeared. Not surprising considering the water shortages, she concluded. The plants were replaced by more paintings on the walls, mainly of earth as it used to look, green and fertile. She briefly considered if this was a good idea. Would it remind people of what they were missing or would it give them hope of what the future could hold?

She quickly dismissed her thoughts and focused on the job in hand. People were milling around and instantly moved to one side when they saw the group coming towards them. Louise made eye contact with some of them and was a little shocked by how gaunt they looked. A sure sign of the food shortages, she concluded. Some started whispering to each other or stretching their necks so they could get a closer look, but none were shocked by her public appearance. This wasn't surprising since they'd all been told that she was to make an announcement.

They reached the door where she was to make her speech and Louise suddenly picked up her pace and swept into the room ahead of the others. Being hidden behind a group of security men wasn't a good look. The podium was ahead of her and she immediately strode towards it and climbed three steps before taking a deep breath and looking out onto the assembled crowd.

It'd been a long time since she'd addressed a crowd of people in the flesh and a surge of adrenalin made her shiver a bit, but like a seasoned politician she quickly got a grip and stood straight and tall to hide her nerves.

The crowd had been instructed by Samantha to enthusiastically show their support for what Louise was about to announce and she was confident that they would comply, knowing that a failure to do so would result in consequences for them and their families. A common ploy for any dictatorship.

Louise looked around the room with a slight grin on her face. Screens had been erected so that those in the room could see her close up. It was important that everyone could see the hope in her facial expressions and body language. Screens around the whole bunker would also be tuned up, meaning that nobody would be missing the announcement.

Samantha came up and stood alongside her on the podium. Louise turned to face her, the grin broadened a little before she returned her attention to the crowd.

She took a deep breath and said, 'I have some good news for you.' She waited a few seconds before continuing. 'The brave men I sent from here have surpassed all expectations. She waited again so she could gauge the reaction of the crowd in front of her. They were hanging on her every word, staring with mouths slightly open as though in anticipation of the winning goal. She continued, 'they have found a drill. A drill that can dig for water. Water that will give us food. Water that will save our community.'

There was silence as though they didn't quite believe her. She looked across at one of the screens to see the confusion on her? face, then spontaneous polite applause broke out as though they'd just remembered the script that Samantha had given them, quickly followed by jubilant shouting.

Louise held her arms out and moved them up and down, gesturing them to calm down.

'But every silver lining has a cloud, I'm afraid. The gallant young men have paid with their lives. Including my sons,' she said wiping a tear from her eyes and slumping as though weighed down with grief.

Samantha immediately went to support her, whilst impressed by her performance.

Louise eventually gathered herself and said, 'they have died to save us and we must survive. We will survive,' she said shouting out the words and holding her arms out again.

The crowd went hysterical, but it was genuine and not scripted. A broad grin spread across Louise's face and she nodded slowly in appreciation of the adulation she was getting.

She noticed a flicker out of the corner of her eye and looked across to see her face disappear from the screen, replaced by a film of her and Samantha discussing her plans. She turned to look at Samantha, but she was gone and two guards were making their way up to the podium. Louise was soon in their grasp and being dragged off the podium. She was held and made to look at the screen whilst Samantha took her place on the podium.

The film finished, then another came on showing Louise with the drill in the tunnel. Samantha decided this was the time for her to speak.

'This is your leader ladies and gentlemen. A conniving, manipulative woman who knew all along about the drill. It's always been here in a secret underground cavern. She lied to you and you've been made to suffer because she wanted to control you. Not look after you. Not provide for you. None of this needed to happen. We could've tapped into the underground water resources years ago. You don't deserve her and she doesn't deserve you.'

The crowd went silent as they digested what was happening. Louise started to struggle and made a vain attempt to say something, but a hand across her mouth prevented her.

Samantha looked at her with a look of disgust, then turned to the crowd and continued, 'Louise Gardener is no longer in charge and I will be taking over for now. The priority is to get that drill working and I need everyone's help to do it. Are you behind me?'

The crowd were still in shock and there was silence for a few seconds before someone shouted out, 'yes.' Another said, 'she doesn't deserve to live.'

The discontent started to spread so Samantha shouted out, 'and she will be dealt with, but later. I want everyone with an engineering background to come to the cabinet room. There're still problems to solve and we need to start now.'

Samantha looked at Louise again who still had a hand firmly placed across her mouth, but she could see the look of betrayal.

'And she lied to you about those brave men out there,' she said returning her attention to the crowd. 'Some died in an accident, but the others are still alive. Out there on the mainland. We'll bring our boys back and together we can do this.'

The anger in the crowd was replaced by clapping and cheering. Louise was dragged off.

'Treat her roughly,' said Samantha to the nearest guard.

They bent her arm up behind her back, making her squeal.

'You won't get away with this,' Louise said defiantly.

Samantha just grinned and said nothing, watching her disappear out of the room, shouting obscenities like a crazed woman.

'Let's do this,' said Samantha returning her attention to the crowd.

CHAPTER 44 (THE BOTHY)

'They're coming to get us,' said Luke.

'What? Who?' said Harvey sounding alarmed.

Everyone had been transported down in the drone and they were held up with Luke and his team in the cavern which had been enlarged so that it could hold all the people and equipment. It had proved more than able to cope with the weather over the last few nights, but it was never meant to be a permanent residence.

'I've had a message from my boss. A couple of guys are coming to get us. They need this equipment,' he said looking over at the haul they'd amassed.

'Will they take us?'

'I haven't told them about you.'

'That didn't answer my question.'

Luke broke eye contact with Harvey for a few seconds whilst he thought.

'We'll go first. I don't want to give them any surprises.'

'I'll ask again. What about us?'

Luke got out a screen and after a few seconds a map appeared

'Here. This is where we're meeting them. You could follow here.'

'Then what?' said Harvey looking at the screen. He continued, 'I know this area. There's a secret tunnel to the bunker.'

Luke looked confused and said, 'how d'you know?'

'Never mind that. It can only be opened from the inside. It must be the way you're getting into the bunker. You need to find some way of keeping it open so we can get in after you've gone.'

'And without them knowing?' said Luke.

'That's right. Once you get to the bunker you'll have to convince them to let us in.'

'No I won't,' said Luke.

Harvey looked at him and said, 'you're probably right. How long before you have to meet up?'

Luke looked at his watch, then up at the sky and said, 'in a couple of hours. Before the next storm.'

'Ok. I'll follow you to make sure I'm right and you're using the tunnel. Then it's up to you to make sure that door stays open.'

'And if it doesn't?'

'Then you'll have to come back later and open it for us.'

'Ok. You know you can trust me,' said Luke.

'And you can trust me.'

....

They were ready to go. Harvey had told Devon about the plan and he'd not openly objected, saying that he'd stay with the group to arrange things so that they could move quickly if necessary.

'I'll hang back so there'll be no chance of them seeing me,' said Harvey. 'I know where you're going anyway.'

'Good. If they see you then all hell'll break loose.'

'Then let's make sure it doesn't. Now let's get going,' said Harvey standing up and walking towards Devon, leaving Luke to make final preparations.

'If I'm not back before the storm, then assume I'm dead,' said Harvey to Devon.

'Then what?'

'Go to these co-ordinates and see how the land lies. You may be able to get in.'

'And if not?'

'You'll be alright. You know that don't you?'

'Yes,' said Devon straight away realising what Harvey was intimating.

Harvey said his final goodbyes to his family and went back to see Luke and his men climbing out of the cavern. Harvey followed them and confirmed plans with Luke for one last time before they walked off leaving Harvey to watch them disappear. He then looked down into cavern to see expectant faces looking up at him.

'We've done well to get this far. We will make it,' said Harvey confidently.

There was no response and they all dispersed, leaving Harvey standing alone. Things were looking up. It was a miracle they'd got this far, but now they had an insurance policy in the short term. As regards the medium to long term, that was less clear but they always had death as an option, concluded Harvey. The thought gave him some comfort, but until that time he was going to try his hardest to survive and have a decent life for him and his family.

He gave it ten minutes before heading out. The tunnel was about an hour away and it wouldn't be hard following the soldier's tracks on the barren earth, not that he needed to. He knew where the tunnel was. His plans at the bothy when arriving on the south coast were vague and the tunnel was a long shot. However, circumstances had been on their side and luck was one of many things they'd been short of lately.

The sun was beating down, as it normally did at this time of day, and the small mammals that were scavenging early on in the day had retired for a siesta, leaving an eerie silence. The heat was more intense than at the bothy, but Harvey took on plenty of water and this, coupled with his high spirits, kept him going.

He took one last look at the paper map to confirm he was getting close to the tunnel before looking around to see if he recognised the geography. In the distance he saw a cliff face and knew straight away it was the tunnel. He moved off again, but his pace was slower as he looked for potential hiding places ahead, should he need them.

The cliff face was now close and he was crouching as he carefully moved from one hiding place to another, finally getting as close as he dare.

He could see what was going on. Luke's team were stood outside the tunnel entrance, but they didn't know it, a testament to the skills of its makers. They were busily looking down at their maps and scanning the rock face for any signs of an entrance. Then, exactly at the agreed meeting time, a section of the rock face opened invitingly and Luke and his men picked up the equipment before walking inside.

The door was tantalisingly open and Harvey had a sudden desire to join them, but thoughts of his family and the others stopped him. The door started to close. Slowly at first then it picked up pace. Harvey looked at it with expectation and trepidation at the same time. It was like the final door closing to the rest of your life. We've been lucky to get this far, he reminded himself, but like all humans he wanted more.

The door finally closed leaving Harvey dumbfounded. What was Luke doing? Did he know the consequences of betrayal? He and his team would be shown no mercy and Luke knew that, so why?

He sprung from his hiding place and sprinted towards the rock face, soon reaching it and scraping his hands across the surface in a desperate attempt to find the opening. There wasn't even a crack to get his fingers in. He stood back scared and confused as he looked disbelievingly at the rock face. It moved a little and a weak light shone through the crack before it disappeared leaving a thing strip of inky blackness.

He thrust his fingers into the crack and pulled back. The door swung back easily and Harvey was looking down the tunnel at a distant light. He sprung back behind the rock face, fearful of being seen, then looked back into the tunnel again to see that the distant light had also been replaced by darkness.

He hurriedly looked around and found a boulder close by. He rolled it up to the open door and jammed it in the gap to stop it closing. He stepped back to admire his handy work, but a huge gust of wind swept him off his feet. He gathered himself and looked up at the darkening skies. It was going to be a bad one, most likely with rain which was a rare occurrence considering the parched landscape, he concluded. Did he have time to get back? It'd take an hour at most. 45 minutes if he ran some of the way. But he wasn't a young man and fitness training wasn't high on his list of priorities.

He started to run, but the wind hampered his progress when he moved away from the shelter of the rock face, meaning it was difficult to run in a straight line. 45 minutes, he thought. And he was running away from the storm. He could make it.

The first splash of rain hit him on the back of the head and the tension built inside. He ran faster, despite him knowing that slow and steady would mean he'd get there quicker. His lungs started to complain and his throat swelled as his stomach contents tried to escape. He could hear his heart thumping above the noise of the wind and, gasping for air. He realised it was impossible to keep up this pace.

He stopped and briefly looked up at the sky only to confirm his fears. It wouldn't be long. He looked around hurriedly for any signs of shelter, soon realising there was none. He ran again, but this time at a steadier pace. His body had now adjusted to the exercise and the second wind had improved his spirits. He could make it. Concentrate. All he had to do was concentrate. One step at a time. Keep a level head, like the scientist he is he reminded himself. He's still alive.

20 minutes later and he could feel the weight of his clothes as the rain came down heavier. Much heavier. The ground darkened and small puddles formed on the harder, less permeable ground. The cooling sensation from the rain was little consolation for his predicament and he cursed the weather for coming a lot earlier than usual. He cursed it for being worse than normal. He cursed it for the infrequent rain. He cursed his luck which had eventually run out.

He soldiered on, but the increasing wind slowed him down. Was he going in the right direction? Even if he was, the poor visibility meant he could pass within a few yards of the cavern and still not see it. Don't give up. Think positive, he thought.

A gust of wind picked him up and threw him sideways making him fall to the ground, dazed and in pain. He stayed still for a minute whilst his head came round and he was able confirm that his limbs still worked. He tried to get up, but the wind made it difficult. He finally stood upright, but another gust of wind threw him to the floor again and he lay helpless before thoughts of his family invaded his head. They would survive, but would he be part of their lives?

The skies grew even darker as something blocked out what little light there was. Harvey passed out having given in to the battering his body was getting.

He didn't know how long he'd been out. Maybe a couple of minutes, he thought. The wind and rain was as intense as before, but he felt less threatened by it. Something nestled in the base of his back had lifted him off the ground and he was slowly and rhythmically bouncing up and down. He looked to the side to see the ground moving rapidly which was in stark contrast to the slow movement he was experiencing.

He tried to look up towards the sky, but the rain stung his eyes, making him look to the side. He made a veiled attempt to break free, knowing there was no chance, but felt he had to try. He soon gave up and relaxed, but not for long. He wasn't moving forward anymore. He looked around trying to make sense of what was happening, then he felt himself being slowly and gently laid on the ground. There was no rain or wind anymore and the wetness of his clothes made him feel cold. He started to shiver, but soon stopped when familiar faces appeared and stared down at him. He was back at the cavern. Of course he was. How could he ever have doubted it. The creature had disappeared.

CHAPTER 45 (THE BUNKER)

Luke's team slowly walked down the long well-lit tunnel. He looked back to see the lights go off, lunging it into darkness, apart from a thin shaft of light from the open door. The lights around them came on as they moved forward and he was confident that everything would go to plan.

After an hour walking at a steady pace they reached the large area which was still equipped with all the home comforts to sustain life.

'Stop,' said Luke holding his hand up before entering

The group obeyed and he edged forward into the space, looking around for any signs of life.

'We'll camp up here for now.'

The group followed Luke in and quickly made themselves comfortable.

'This is the rendezvous point. Now we just wait. Eat whilst you can.'

There was a sudden rush of movement as kitbags were opened and food consumed. Luke did the same, whilst keeping a watchful eye on the exit tunnel towards the bunker.

'Stay.' he said putting the food back in his kit bag after a couple of bites. 'I'm going ahead.'

'But we're rendezvousing here,' said one of the men.

'There's no harm seeing how the land lies. I won't be long.'

Luke didn't wait for an answer and picked up his weapon before entering the tunnel. The lights came on as normal and he slowly walked on, only to stop after a few minutes when lights appeared in the distance.

He stopped and waited for a few seconds before shouting back, 'they're here. Get your stuff together and follow me.'

Within what seemed like seconds, the group were by his side.

'We'll wait for them to come to us. Keep your wits about you. Samantha's given us assurances, but I don't trust her.'

The men instinctively touched their weapons, but didn't draw them, knowing that a show of force could antagonise the situation. A firefight was a last resort.

They agonisingly watched the lights come on as Samantha and her entourage approached. She was leading from the front, suggesting she had no intention of reneging on her promise to welcome them back into the bunker. She finally reached them, a broad smile stretched across her face as she approached.

'I'm so glad you're safe.'

'Thanks to you,' said Luke appreciatively. 'Where is she now?'

'If you mean Louise. Locked away. I'll decide later what to do with her.'

'So you're in charge now?'

'Yes, for now. Until things've calmed down a bit. Have you got the gear? We need those storage tanks,' she said looking past Luke.

'Yes we've got them, but what's the point. There's no water to store.'

'I'll explain later. Let's get out of here. You can debrief me in the bunker.'

She turned to go and Luke and his men followed. She was accompanied by four security guards and a number of plain clothed people who continued in the same direction towards the living area.

'Where're they going?' said Luke inquisitively. They look like civilians. Why aren't you bringing the equipment we brought back?'

'I'll explain later.'

They walked on without engaging in further conversation and reached the hatch into Louise's quarters.

'Has this been here all the time?' said Luke looking back at the hole in the floor.

Samantha looked at the guards and said, 'take them with you. You stay her Luke. Sit down.'

Luke quickly searched out a chair and sat down. He didn't want to sit on the worn out sofa just in case Samantha decided to sit next to him. He needed to look into her eyes from a distance.

She remained stood and said, 'Louise is in custody. She ordered the death of her own children.'

'I know. I carried out the order.'

'Yes you did. Didn't you.'

'She's the commander in chief, but now I realise it was a mistake,' said Luke trying to show regret.

'Well she's not anymore. She'll be dealt with in the proper way through a trial. Of course the verdict is obvious, but we have to be seen to follow due process.'

'Yes, well that's for you lot to sort out.'

Samantha updated Luke on everything that had happened, then Luke did the same leaving Harvey and his group out, at least for now.

Luke said, 'so there is hope then? We've got water.'

'Not yet, but we will have. And the equipment you've brought back will give us more storage capacity.'

'So that's why those civilians stayed behind. They're getting the drill going.'

'Yes. And the drill is located in the very place where we think we'll find water.'

'So the tunnel will be off limits whilst the drilling's going on.'

'It'll be off limits to everyone apart from those who need to be there. It's too important for the bunker. We need to protect it and once the drill has done its job, we need to protect the water source. It's raining hard at the moment so the storage we have will be filled and the desalination plants are just about working so we have some time to get the job done.'

'There's something I haven't told you,' said Luke sheepishly.

'Go on.'

'We found a community out there. They've been living up north, but the weather's got the better of them. They want to come into the bunker.'

Samantha was stunned into silence for a few seconds, then said, 'what? No way. Why hasn't the virus got them? I don't understand.'

'They had some vaccine.'

How the hell did they get hold of that.

'Their leader. Harvey Burton. He escaped from here and took some vaccine with him. Vaccinated himself and a load of others.'

Samantha stayed silent for a while staring at the wall then said, 'I know him. A scientist. The head scientist. Louise said he saved her life and she mentioned that he had the vaccine. But after all these years. How the hell did he survive?'

'Well he did and they're here. On the mainland. They want to come back. They can't survive out there.'

'How many?'

'About 40 I'd say.'

'Too many. We don't need more mouths to feed. I'm not prepared to take a risk. They could have other diseases.'

'They're fine and healthy and they can give us a good insight into what's going on out there. Harvey knows his stuff. He's a scientist.'

'No. I've made my mind up. I'm not having them near this place. They can stay out there and take their chances.'

Luke sat back and said nothing as though readily accepting her decision. Samantha continued, 'now I need to show you and your men off. You're heroes and important to the moral of this place.'

Luke exhaled slightly and said, 'so we'll be propaganda will we?'

'I'm your commanding officer and you'll do as I say without question. Understand?'

'Yes ma'am, said Luke sheepishly.'

....

It was the following day and the storm had given way to a bright sunny day. The shelter had survived the onslaught, but only just and the wet, soggy inhabitants were busy getting ready for the final push. The look of anticipation was soured by fear and hunger, feelings they'd become familiar with recently. Harvey had taken control of the community again without it being formally discussed and sanctioned. This reflected their confidence in Harvey's leadership in times of crisis and Devon had willingly stepped back.

'Ok. Let's get going. Leave everything behind. We need to travel light. There's no point taking things we don't need today. If things don't work out, we're dead.'

Harvey's frank assessment stunned the community into silence, but he was only telling them what they already knew. They quickly got themselves together and climbed out of the cavern using the rope ladders.

'Follow me,' said Harvey before taking one last look into the cavern and walking off. The rest followed.

Although it was a bright sunny day, the rain gave a damp and cool feel to it. Small seedlings were making an effort to break through into the sunlight and Harvey suspected a carpet of green would soon cover the ground and produce the next generation of seeds before being scorched to death by the sun.

They walked in single file with their heads bowed as though they were going to the gallows, only what would happen in the next 24 hours could be their salvation.

It took an hour and a half to reach the tunnel door and Harvey was relieved to see the rock was still holding the door open, although it seemed to have moved a little, he thought before dismissing his concerns. His hope was that Luke had managed to convince Samantha to let them enter the bunker. Only time would tell, but the absence of anyone to greet them wasn't a good sign.

They tentatively walked through the tunnel in complete silence, eventually reaching the living area. There was no one around, but signs of recent activity was obvious. Some sort of machine was protruding into the cavern, leaving a hole behind it in the rock face, Harvey suspected it was some sort of drill, but wasn't sure. Equipment almost covered the available floor space, which didn't sit comfortably with the homely features which seemed to have been cast aside.

'Something's not right,' said Harvey. 'Keep your wits about you.'

They continued and it wasn't long before four shapes ahead lay still on the floor. They stopped and it didn't take Harvey long to work out they were bodies.

'Stay here,' he said before inching forward.

He soon reached the bodies and tested their pulses.

'They're still alive.'

'What're we going to do?' said Devon.

Harvey looked ahead to see a light shining through an open hatch. He looked back and said, 'the exit's ahead. We'll have to leave them here.'

They soon reached the hatch and climbed up into lounge area. The room was big enough to hold all of them, but only just. The cramped area made Harvey feel like they were sitting ducks. He pushed through the crowd to the door and opened it into the old cabinet office, a room he knew well. The door opposite into the corridor was open.

'Stay here,' he whispered. 'I'll check it out.'

He tentatively walked towards the door and poked his head out into the corridor. There was no one around. Had the bunker population decreased that much in the last 20 years or was there something else going on? It was then that he noticed the screen on the wall behind him. What looked like the whole bunker population was jammed into a room. They were looking around expectantly as though waiting for some event.

'Devon, come here. What d'you think's going on?'

Devon came into the room, looked up at the screen and said, 'looks like some sort of rally. Look. There's a podium. Isn't that Luke and his men stood next to it?'

....

Samantha stood next to the podium, hidden behind the men she was about to present to her people. Waiting for the moment when she would triumphantly climb the steps to be cheered by the expectant crowd. She wasn't a politician and never used to relish the limelight, preferring to run things from behind the scenes. The adoration she was about to received was spine tingling. Addictive. Exciting beyond her wildest dreams and it was only now that she realised how wrong she'd been. She'd never tried this so how could she possibly know she didn't like it. Well, she did like it.

She slowly climbed the three steps onto the podium. The buzz from the crowd increased until she reached the top when polite applause broke out. She looked out feeling a little disappointed with the reaction, but the feeling didn't last long. The applause got louder. A few started to shout out, then others joined in until a wail of appreciation filled the auditorium.

Samantha took in a deep breath, followed by a broad smile as she soaked up the adulation. It seemed to go on for an eternity, but she didn't want it to stop. Didn't want the feeling to go away, but it couldn't go on forever. She raised her arms up in front of her and moved them up and down to quieten them. The noise slowly waned until it was a low hum.

'Ladies and gentlemen. In the short time since I removed Louise Gardner from power, we have recovered the drill and it's working perfectly.'

A few yelps came from the crowd, so she put her arms up to quieten them again.

She continued, 'we also know where the underground water lies, but it'll take some time for the drill to get to it. But I can assure you that we will find it.'

Samantha waited for noises of approval from the crowd, but this time they seemed eager to listen rather than shout.

'Until that time, the desalination plants can provide us with enough water. And we have these gentlemen to thank for giving us the tools to increase our water storage capacity,' she said holding one arm out towards Luke and his men.

The crowd were in raptures again and Samantha decided this was best time to welcome them onto the podium. She beckoned them to join her, but they looked reluctant, looking at each other to see who would make the first move.

'We need to go up,' said one of the men to Luke. 'We need to distract them.'

Luke nodded and climbed the podium, soon followed by his men. The noise grew to a crescendo with no sign of abating, so they waved their appreciation to the adoring crowd. Samantha saw the doors to the auditorium swing open out of the corner of her eye. A minor distraction, but it made her look around. As far as she could see no one had come in, but her momentary confusion was superseded by the roar of the crowd. She turned to face them, only to be distracted again when armed security men stood across the doorway. She looked around the room to see other doorways to the auditorium similarly patrolled..

She maintained the smile on her face as she eased herself past Luke and his men and climbed down from the podium, making her way to the open doorway.

'What's this all about? I didn't order this.'

They all looked straight ahead without responding.

'Let me through,' she said trying to barge through, but they remained steadfast. 'I'm warning you. Let me past.'

She eventually gave up and stood back, then noticed that the crowd noise had subsided. She turned around to see everyone looking at her with confused looks on their face, apart from Luke and his men who had sickly grins.

She turned to face the security guards again only to be met by the creature standing behind them. She felt the blood drain from her face as the adrenalin surged through her body. Its hunched shoulders made it look as though it was going to pounce and Samantha instinctively stepped back until she was met by a wall of bodies.

The security men parted and the creature slowly walked into the auditorium to be met by squeals of fear. It stopped and took in a deep breath causing its shoulders and back to straighten to reveal its full size.

The creature felt stronger than it had ever done. It fed off the fear. Fed off the weakness. Fed off the power it had over these people and it needed to be fed so it could rule over them. This was its destiny. This was their destiny. They needed each other, but they would only get what they wanted by ceding to its greater power.

It strode towards the podium. The crowd parted, some made a run for the exit, but were thwarted by the security men who were out-numbered but had the weapons. It eventually stood by the podium.

Harvey and the rest quickly followed the creature into the auditorium, hoping that everybody would be distracted by the creature. He and Luke had done their duty and got the creature inside the bunker. It had a hold over him that he couldn't explain and the creature had spared them, despite having numerous opportunities to kill him. Why was that? Even the security guards in the tunnel had been spared. Why did he feel loyalty towards it?

The creature looked at the distraught crowd, most had given up trying to escape and were looking anxiously in anticipation of its next move. The creature stood motionless, knowing that its inaction encouraged jeopardy. A fear that made it strong.

It eventually boomed out in perfect English, 'I am now in control and you will obey me. Otherwise your lives will be hell. Death will be a mercy I will not afford you.'

The crowd looked perplexed that the creature could talk, rather than the words it was speaking.

It continued, 'you've condemned yourselves to this. You created me. You made me into what I am. You messed with nature and made something you couldn't control. But your biggest mistake was the vaccine.'

The creature stopped talking as it fed off the power it was exerting over them. It eventually continued, 'you made a vaccine out of my blood and now it's inside you. You all have some of me inside you and that makes you mine. You belong to me. You can feel it inside yourselves. You feel part of me. You feel beholden to me and I will use you.'

Harvey and Devon instinctively walked towards the podium and stood next to the creature, despite the fear ravaging their senses.

Samantha was still stood amongst the crowd by the door where the creature had entered. She was in control a few minutes ago, now she was a nobody. Cast to one side by this thing. It all felt so surreal, but it was real.

She looked back at the security guards who were still blocking the door and said, 'you answer to me. Only me. Now you do as I say and kill that thing.'

They remained motionless and ignored her instruction. The rage inside her intensified and she leapt at them in a vain attempt to hurt them, only to be grabbed and held. She struggled for a short while before realising it was hopeless.

'I order you to let me go.'

Still no response.

She raised her voice, 'let me go.'

It was then that she realised everyone was looking and their demeanour suggested they had no intention of helping her. She was stunned into silence and anger was replaced by fear as she was marched off towards the podium.

'Please. Please let me go,' she pleaded.

The blow to her head caused the top half her body to arch backwards making her spine crack, such was the force of the impact. The sickening noise echoed around the auditorium, but there was no sign of horror and disgust, only fear.

The creature swung its arm out again and Harvey and Devon slumped to the floor, dead before they hit the ground. The horror and shock hit Thea hard, making her run towards her husband, disregarding any potential danger. She could taste the vomit in her mouth. She could feel her legs giving way, but still she ran, pushing aside anyone who got in her way.

She eventually reached her dead husband and desperately searched for any signs of life, only to find there was none. She flung her arms around the dead body and wept uncontrollably. Her children weren't far behind.

The creature looked down at the pathetic sight of a grieving family and felt no empathy at all. It returned its attention to the crowd who had frozen with fear.

'I am your leader now. Your only leader,' it said looking down at the bodies. 'Does anyone want to challenge me?'

Predictably there was no response. The creature walked towards the exit, pushing aside those who didn't move straight away. It stopped at the doorway, turned and said, 'get that drill working.'

CHAPTER 46 (THE BEGINNING)

Greed was the reason. Pure and utter greed. It had ruled supreme over them for the last 50 years, but it wanted more than humans could give it.

They were still encased in the bunker. The weather had got worse and humans never ventured outside. The creature often roamed the land, seeking screx to feed off, sometimes bringing some meat back for the humans, but screx numbers had depleted as they moved further north in search of food. That left the local landscape completely lifeless and barren, only occasionally turning green when the ferocious rainstorms came.

Life in the bunker was comfortable, for those who obeyed. There was a hierarchy of sorts and the creature ruled supreme with the help of a team of enforcers. Any descent or signs of rebellion was instantly stamped on without mercy. Torture was regularly inflicted, but not death unless absolutely necessary because it needed live adults to feed off their fear. Of course dead people could be replaced, but it would take years before a replacement, that is a child, could give it the fear it needed.

The drill had done its job and a steady flow of water was available for food production and drinking. The population size had been stable because the bunker couldn't support greater numbers, despite an attempted breeding programme, and it was this that frustrated the creature. It wanted to build a civilisation to rule over.

The physical and mental control it had over humans was complete, but it had more than that. It used its intellect to learn the vast amounts of information collected by humans and had used to it to improve life in the bunker and for its own ends. And that end was to seek out another planet where it could grow a civilisation.

Humans had previously identified habitable planets in other solar systems and the enormity of the climate crisis had prompted them to design a spaceship to reach them. They had completed the plans, but the virus took hold and other priorities came along so no progress had been made on building it. Until now.

The drill had been improved by the creature and used to create a web of underground caverns to build the spaceship. The shortage of raw materials had significantly hampered progress and years of scavenging by the creature had kept things going. It had developed and improved the original design, including the means of propulsion and it was now complete.

The creature was confident it would work. The spaceship, travelling close to the speed of light, would take many years to reach the far off solar system it had identified as being very similar to earth's. The creature had longevity to easily last the journey, unlike humans who were burdened with a short lifespan. Their bodies would be cryogenically preserved so they were protected from the ravages of time. The added benefit was that they wouldn't need food or water. Only the creature needed sustenance and that could easily be stored on the spaceship. Everything was in place, but there was one problem that was causing un-rest.

'They know,' said 16.

Names were banned in the bunker as they personalised people. Made them individuals with their own thoughts and personalities and the creature didn't want that. It only wanted them to do its bidding.

'Know what?' said the creature angrily.

'They know some will be left behind.'

The enforcer was sparsely dressed in ragged clothes, as were the rest of the bunker inhabitants. Clothing was difficult to come by and the creature didn't see it as a priority. 16 was adorned with an array of weapons for use if necessary, but they were mainly a deterrent to anyone having ideas of going against the creature's will.

How? How do they know there is a spaceship? I am the only one whose been working down there.

16 said nothing. His head was bowed, eye contact was forbidden.

The creature continued, 'but you and the other enforcers know. Was it you?'

16's head sunk lower as though wilting under the pressure of interrogation and said, 'no. It wasn't me.'

'Then who?' shouted the creature.

'I don't know. Does it matter? They know. That's all that matters.'

16 instantly knew his mistake, causing a short surge of adrenalin before retribution was inflicted. His head snapped to one side and he slumped to the floor a little dazed, but still conscious.

'Sorry. Sorry,' said 16 shakily.

His arms were held over his head to soften the blow of a potential further attack. The creature stepped away, knowing that finding the culprit at this late stage was pointless, but also knowing that admitting 16 was right would be a sign of weakness.

'What are they doing about it?

16 slowly rose to his feet and said, 'my sources say they think they'll die without you.'

'They are right. They cannot think for themselves and the weather will eventually destroy the bunker.'

'Can I come?' said 16 sheepishly.

'Yes,' said the creature immediately. 'You are good for breeding and have proved loyal.'

Relief swept through 16. He decided to stay silent, fearful he may say something that would cause the creature to change its mind.

'I want you to bring these to me,' said the creature handing him a piece of paper containing a list of numbers. 'The rest I want in the auditorium. Make sure there are enough security guards to control them.'

He took the paper, turned and left the room, knowing that questioning the creature's motives would be fruitless and painful. He was just grateful to be one of the chosen.

The creature stared at an array of screens showing every part of the bunker. The feeling of anticipation was growing inside. Everything was set. The spaceship was stocked with enough food and water and it was confident that the radioisotope power system would work. It was crude, but the creature would develop it when it reached planets where it could plunder resources and develop something that was more effective.

It saw 16 walking down the corridor. Other guards soon joined him before they paired up and went their separate ways in search of those on the list. One by one it saw people taken and either marched into the auditorium or the cabinet room where the creature was waiting. They all immediately bowed their heads when seeing the creature, so as to avoid eye contact. No one questioned its motives. 16 and the other guards who were also on the list eventually joined them when the task was complete.

'Stay here,' said the creature walking towards the door, careful not to injure anyone.

Walking through the doorway, it bent down and stepped into the corridor. It had grown significantly since it first entered the bunker and was now well over 12 feet tall and still growing. Its physical and mental maturity had not yet been reached.

Its long strides saw it reach the auditorium quickly, ducking again as it entered and rising up to show its full power. Those inside looked across then lowered their heads, even the children knew the rules.

It strode across the room, looking down at the bowed heads then, without warning, struck out. Bodies flew across the room, smashing against the walls. Death was instantaneous. The creature continued to thrash out.

Some realised what was happening and ran for the door, but it didn't open. The guards looked confused and didn't know what to do. One desperately tried to override the locking mechanism, all to no avail. Only the creature could open it. Screams filled the room. Children cried as mothers and fathers grabbed them, but they had nowhere to run. The creature carried on relentlessly. Many started stumbling as blood oozed across the floor making it slippery. Some tried to attack the creature, but didn't stand a chance. It only hastened their deaths. The guards could only stand looking confused. The creature killed one of them, it was then that they realised they were also in danger. One fired at the creature, others soon followed, but the creature hardly noticed. Its scaly body was effective armour against such meagre weapons.

The mayhem continued until an eerie silence indicated that the creature had done its job and everyone was dead. It looked down at its handy work for any signs of life. A child whimpered underneath its mother's protective body. The creature strode across and silence descended again.

The killing had been satisfying and necessary for the creature. The people meant nothing to it, they only lived to satisfy its desire for fear and they could no longer do that. These were the ones to be left behind. The ones who fell short of the criteria for survival. The ones that no longer served a purpose, but their deaths would. Food. Meat. Sustenance for the short term, but first it wanted to feed.

It picked up the nearest body and sunk its teeth in. Blood squirted out and bones crushed before it swallowed the body almost whole. Blood covered almost every part of its body, making it glisten and twinkle under the lights.

It continued to gorge until it was full, the rest would be butchered and stored on the spaceship for the creature to eat before the preserved food. That job would be done by those in the cabinet room so they could see its strength. See its lack of mercy. See its hold over them.

It strode out of the auditorium and back to the cabinet room. Those inside cowed at the blood drenched creature when it entered, but the gruesome sight still didn't prompt questions, only fear.

The creature looked across at 16 and said, 'I've killed them all. It then turned its attention back to the others and said, but you will live. You will join me to find a better life.'

Confusion spread amongst everyone. Was the creature doing a motivational speech?

'Up there. A new home is waiting for us. A new life.'

'It's right,' said 16 sounding excited. 'We'll all die if we stay here.'

The creature looked across at him appreciatively and said, 'you will do as 16 says. There are many things to do, but tomorrow we will leave here. Come with me 16.'

They both left the cabinet room, leaving bewildered people behind trying to understand what was happening.

....

The creature was at the helm, looking up into the sky. The humans had been cryogenically preserved and the human meat stored. The last two jobs before the spaceship started its journey. Taking them to a place where the creature could grow a civilisation. There would be risks along the way, but remaining on earth would be certain death for humans.

Living with the screx just wasn't an option anymore, now that it had experienced a better life. And it had to preserve that life and make it better. Pure and utter greed, something it had inherited from humans when it was created. Something that humans had, but it had more.

CHAPTER 47 (THE BEGINNING OF THE END)

They found a new planet and the creature grew a civilisation, destroying any indigenous life forms that got in the way. The planet's resources were plundered with no consideration for sustainability, similar to how humans lived on earth, but the creature's greed hastened the process and they soon had to seek out other planets.

Over millions of years they would move from planet to planet leaving a barren waste in their wake until they met their match. A highly evolved and peaceful people, seemingly at the mercy of Idriss, as the creature was now called, but Idriss didn't stand a chance.

Earth had easily survived a small blip in its history. The environmental catastrophe was nothing to what that planet had previously been through during its lifetime and the climate soon settled to something more predictable. The screx would be the dominant species on the planet, with mammals taking a back seat for now. Over the next 200 million years the screx would evolve into the most successful species ever. Dinosaurs would rule the earth more successfully than humans ever did, until an asteroid wiped them out. Then by a twist of fate Idriss and humans would return to earth and rule again.

THE END

Leave a review and I'll send you a free copy of one of my other books.
My email address is dmb08@hotmail.co.uk.

"For God's Sake."

"Lovereading" review. This is a battle between good and evil that you've never seen before. The unique storyline kept me intrigued until the end.

Len Strickland is a successful ex-banker who sold his business to promote the environment. Seems like a nice guy, so why is someone making him suffer? If they hate him so much, why not just kill him? Len needs to find out who's responsible, but he's by himself. Or is he? Something is keeping him alive. Giving him the strength to carry on, but why? Len ends up losing everything including his reason to live. Then things get really bad.

Joyce is a confident and innocent 16 year old living with her devoutly Christian parents in the 1960s. She falls for the new young reverend, but his increasingly extreme views make her doubt their relationship. Is he mad? Does he really love her? Is he using her? She doesn't know what to do until something happens that shows her the way. Or does it?

Heviant is a truly peaceful planet where the inhabitants live together in pure bliss. Saul is their leader but has never had to lead before, until now. Idriss and his people plunder planets and Heviant will be easy pickings. They don't stand a chance.

The three separate stories come together and the final race to save humanity begins. For God's sake let's hope it all works out.

"To Hell With It." (follow up to "For God's Sake.") Idriss (Satan) is gone, but Len's job isn't done yet. He gets things going and the community lifestyle is welcomed by most, but not all. Some still want a life of greed and hatred. Some are resisting. Some are challenging him and they're winning. Len has to go into hiding and is gladly welcomed by Mary, a self-made gang leader. What's in it for her? Why's she helping him? Len has to use all his guile to thwart the enemy. He's losing. He's desperate. Worst of all, the power has gone to his head.

Harriet is a young girl who was dumped by her mum in the early noughties and doesn't know who her dad is. Numerous foster parents have failed to change her vicious behaviour until Annabel and Dan take on the task. They're devout Christians and simply tolerate her, hoping that God will save her. Father Jacob solves the problem. He shows Harriet how the Christian faith can be a family for her, a family she's always wanted. More important to Harriet, God will always forgive her. She can do anything she wants.

Idriss is dead and in Heaven along with everyone else who's ever lived and died. Saul (God) doesn't understand humans so takes him to Earth in the hope that Idriss can tell Saul what to do about the problems. Did Saul make a mistake? Idriss grabs onto something that gives him some power and he's going to use it to get what he wants.

Who's ging to win. Or will they all lose?

"Consequential Murder."

Ted Mason is highly intelligent man, but has opted for the simple life as a poorly paid farm hand. His wife Cathy is happy to begin with, but becomes increasingly frustrated with her life. She wants more money to fund a better lifestyle and that leads to friction. Cathy reacts in the only way she knows and makes Ted's life unbearable in an attempt to make him earn more. He eventually relents a little, but now hates his life. It can't go on. Something's got to give and it does. Regardless of the consequences.

Bernard Doddington is not a very nice man. Spoilt by his parents. A hater of women. Can't hold a job down. Loud and bombastic. His circle of friends tolerate him, only because he's a bit of a "cash cow," funded by his willing parents. Then things start to happen that make him suspect someone's out to get him. But why? Everybody likes him. Don't they? With the help of his only loyal friend, he gets his life back. Regardless of the consequences.

Harry Saunders is a copper who hates the bureaucracy imposed on him by modern policing, but he's coming to the end of his career so decides to tolerate it. Then something happens that gives him a renewed sense of purpose and he decides to make the most of his final days. Regardless of the consequences.

The three linked stories show what people will do to get what they want, but will they get away with it. Will justice be served? You decide.

Printed in Great Britain
by Amazon

56746898R00209